MADE TO CONQUER

ISBN: (Paperback) 979-8-9856434-1-1

Edited by: Paige Lawson

Cover Design: Cassidy Townsend

MADE TO CONQUER

MARIANNE A. SCOTT

For Rachel
You are a champion, and a scholar...and you have great boobs.

CONTENT WARNING

Your mental health is important! Please beware of the following while reading this book:

Anxiety

Depression

PTSD/Survivors Guilt

Sexually Explicit Scenes (MF) that include praise kink and anal play

Violence, War and Death

Chapter One

"MY MAGIC IS GONE," I repeat.

Adriana stares at me with hopelessness in her gray eyes, her Dark Magic flaring around her like a protective exoskeleton. She paces the length of the room she designed for me here in the Highland Coven. The room could be a carbon copy of the room I had in our home in Salem, minus the lack of windows since the coven's hideout is underneath the hills. She even painted the rock walls the same shade of blue as my childhood bedroom and scavenged a white vanity with the same chip in the mirror.

"What do you mean your magic is gone?" Edina demands, pulling my attention from my half-sister's pacing. My best friend runs her hands through her long blonde hair, tucking loose strands behind her pointed ears. I know it hasn't even been twenty-four hours since she emerged but seeing her with Fae ears and wings is still unsettling.

"I can't feel it," I say, reaching again into the pit of my stomach to see if I can locate my raw magic. I come up empty.

"It can't be gone," Adriana laments.

"No, she's right," Edina says, pushing the white comforter off her lap and standing up from her spot beside me on the bed. She walks to the wall of bookshelves, filled with everything from textbooks to my favorite fantasy books written by mortals.

Edina stops by the largest bookcase next to the door. Her fingers trail a line of frost across the tomes, showing her inner nerves even as her face remains impassive. She shakes her hands, releasing a giant icicle that sticks in the fuzzy gray carpet, and then goes back to her search, her fingers thawed and her magic under control. She plucks a large medical book from the shelf and starts flipping through it with purpose.

"Here," she says, walking back and sitting beside me again. She reads, *"Magic is tied to a witch's life force. While magic can be weakened from disuse, illness, or malicious magical intent, it can never be removed without killing the witch in question."*

"OH!" Adriana exclaims, her gray eyes clouded in a vision. "Try this." She plucks her wand from within her black robes and hands it to me.

"I've never had to use a wand before," I remind her, and she makes a motion urging me on. I sigh heavily, frowning at the unfamiliar weight of the wood. I give it a flick and feel magic spark through the end as the book in Edina's hand rises into the air and zooms back to its place on the bookshelf. Adriana releases a breath, her shoulders sinking from her ears, and she plops her thin frame into an armchair.

"So, Archer just fucked up your raw magic," Edina surmises, and I wince. The image of the prince engulfed in hellfire and shooting white-hot flames at me dances in my memory.

"I guess I should be grateful," I grumble. Hellfire is typically a death sentence. It devours everything in its path, and no one has survived a direct hit from the magical fire. I'm lucky to be alive.

"Give yourself time to heal," Adriana says softly. "It's only been a few hours since the attack."

I swallow the rising lump in my throat as images of the attack flood my mind. Archer killed so many people trying to protect me...to save me. I didn't tell him I came to the Dark Witches of my own free will, to save Edina from being persecuted when she emerged as Fae. Of course he would lose his mind when he saw me in pain in the center of their lair. And once he was lost to the hellfire...

Archer once described the white-hot fire as a demon, and using it as surrendering to its will. We don't know enough about the element, and I still pushed him to train with it. I blame myself more than I blame him...a sentiment I know won't be echoed by my sister and best friend whose hatred of the prince radiates off them in waves.

I glance down to the bandages wrapping my arm, shoulder, and half my chest, hiding the charred flesh beneath. The Highland Coven comprises only Dark Witches, so they don't have a healer to assess the damage. The wound will scar, but in a weird way, I'm grateful for the reminder.

"Do we have a count?" I ask, flopping back onto the pillows and wincing when the bandages chafe my raw skin.

"Nine," Adriana whispers, tugging on a rogue yellow-blonde ringlet. "One head of a coven. Her second left shortly after the battle to hold an election, but we expect the new leader will return tomorrow."

"The rest?" I push, and Edina moves closer, her freezing fingers interlocking with mine.

"Three children," Adriana whispers, and my hand tightens around Edina's. "Two teenagers who already joined a coven, and three witches who died fighting. We'll have a memorial for those we lost later in the week."

Five children. Edina told me there were children in the area that Archer first attacked, but hearing that he killed them...

A tear slides down my cheek and I bite hard on my bottom lip.

"No one blames you for the attack, Katie," Adriana reassures me. "They were humbled and awed to have you fighting beside them. If you hadn't been there—"

"If I hadn't been there, Archer wouldn't have been either," I remind her grimly. A cough cuts off my self-deprecation, leaving my body shuddering in pain. Adriana opens a cabinet attached to my vanity that's stocked with water bottles, sodas, and some snacks. She crosses the room, giving Edina a water bottle to chill before handing it to me. I drink it greedily.

"What happened on the throne?" Edina asks, and I give her a grateful nod for changing the subject, passing her what's left of my water.

"It felt like my magic was intensified," I say, remembering the power surge coursing through my body as it strengthened my natural magic. I've always been powerful, but that level of strength was heady, addicting. I could have brought the world to its knees with that kind of power. And now my magic is reduced to scraps.

"It was," Adriana says. "The power surge allowed you to receive the vision from Finley." My eyebrows hit my hairline, and she smiles as she saunters over to the edge of the bed and kneels beside it. "Did you think I didn't know?"

According to Adriana and my father, I was supposed to receive a vision from Queen Carman, the last queen of the Dark Witches. But instead, the vision was of Finley, the only other lightning wielder in history. She and I are descendants of the King of Light Magic and were infused with Carman's Dark Magic, which resulted in our lightning. During the vision, Finley told me her death caused the imbalance of power in the Kingdom of Magic, and that I would be the one to right it.

I look at my sister, on her knees, looking up at me expectantly. Until recently, I thought Dark Witches were all evil, my perception colored by the prejudices of Elemental Witches and by my own experience with my father. But Adriana has proven multiple times that she's anything but, and I know in my gut I can trust her with the message Finley gave me.

"We need to restore the balance of magic," I tell her.

"Oh, is that all?" Edina scoffs. "Did your vision indicate how we're supposed to do that?"

"Finley said to form an army, starting with the Dark Witches. Then we need to recruit the Magical Creatures."

"I'll arrange a meeting with the heads of the covens for tomorrow," Adriana assures. "I also know where your werewolf lives. Once things are settled here, I can take you there."

I don't know that I'd call him *my* werewolf, I don't even know his name. But he did save my life before, so he's a smart person to approach for an alliance. I ignore the gentle tugging in my stomach I've come to associate with the bond the werewolf made to take my pain that night we met. It feels more insistent tonight than it has in the past. *Is he close by?* No, that's insane. He lives in

Northern Italy and we're in the Scottish Highlands. There would be no reason for him to be here.

"What else?" Edina asks, pulling me from my musings.

"We need to find the four pieces of the blood oath."

"What the fuck are those?" Edina looks at Adriana, who shrugs.

"The Four Monarchs each used an object to solidify a blood oath. Finley thinks it'll help convince people that I'm fit to rule," I say, trying to recall her exact words. "A person can't carry all four unless they're the rightful ruler or some shit. We already have two of them."

"The diadem and the locket," Adriana says thoughtfully, and I nod.

"Holy shit," Edina breathes. "You felt like the locket was meant to be yours when Archer put it on you."

"The crown was the same way," I add, my finger skittering over the bandages to the hollow of my neck where the locket once sat.

"They're both in a safe under your bed," Adriana says. "The chain for the locket burned, but I saved the pendant."

"What are the other two?" Edina asks.

"A sword and a scepter," Adriana answers for me, and Edina and I gape at her. "I saw a vision of Katie holding them all yesterday, but I didn't know what it meant."

"You saw me holding them all?" I gasp, and she nods.

"Any chance your vision told us where to find them?" Edina deadpans.

"No, but I'll do some digging."

A large crash from the hallway has the three of us jumping to our feet. Ice coats Edina's hands as she steps closer to me, and I toss Adriana's wand back to her. She assumes a fighting stance as the three of us creep closer to the door, the two of them in front. There's another crash followed quickly by a knock.

"No one can know about my magic," I whisper. "They can't know how vulnerable I am until we can determine what's going on with my power."

Edina takes a defensive stance next to me and Adriana cautiously approaches the door. Another knock sounds before she flings it open.

Chapter Two

A WITCH BURSTS INSIDE, slamming the door shut behind her and leaning against it, panting for breath. The woman is small, so small that the black robes the Dark Witches wear slide off her shoulders as she attempts to fix her short brown hair.

"Adriana—" she cuts herself off with a squeak when she sees me standing behind Edina, and instantly drops to her knees. "Your Majesty. I'm so sorry. I didn't know you were awake."

"You can stand," I say uncomfortably.

"Adriana, the wards have been breached," she says hastily, as another crash sounds closer to the door.

"I just fortified them twenty minutes ago," Adriana insists.

"Well..." the girl breathes. "A wolf broke through and is on its way here."

"A wolf?" I repeat. I feel the golden tether pulling at my center like it's guiding me towards an outside force. He *is* close. I was right. I should have known he'd come...he would have felt my pain. "Adriana, I need a robe."

My sister, to her credit, doesn't ask questions. She quickly shucks off hers and tosses it to me, leaving her in a slightly singed gray sweater. The werewolf has seen me in a lot less than the tank top and leggings I'm wearing, but I don't want him to see my bandages. Edina helps me gingerly slide my injured arm into the robe and I zip it up to my neck.

"Is this your wolf?" Edina asks softly.

"I wouldn't call him *my* wolf—" Edina rolls her sapphire eyes.

"I'll protect you, Your Majesty!" the mousy witch proclaims assuming a fighting stance, her wand shaking in her outstretched hand. She yelps as something collides with the door, the wood shuddering under the impact.

"That's not necessary. We should probably open—" the door splinters into a thousand pieces and a gigantic white wolf bounds into the room, "—the door."

He's easily three times the size of a regular wolf, standing at my eye line even on all fours. The wolf snarls at everyone as he looks around frantically, his yellow eyes glowing. When he finds me, I feel the bond between us go taut.

"That was all kinds of dramatic," I monotone, and his responding bark sounds more like a laugh. His body bucks forward, crumpling to the floor, fur and muscles popping and jutting out. When he rises, he's back in his human form and very *very* naked.

"Yes, please," Edina breathes, taking in his tanned muscles. He shakes his dark hair out of his face until it's lying in soft waves that kiss his shoulders. When his eyes return to their usual golden color, he rushes toward me, wraps me in his strong arms, and smushes my face against the crescent moon tattoo just over his heart.

"I ran here as fast as I could," he says, stroking my hair. I stay perfectly still because I can feel *everything* through the thin fabric of my robe and leggings, and the last thing I need is to disturb the freaking cobra between his legs.

"You *ran?*" Edina asks, her eyes trailing over his ass. My teeth gnash together and she gives me a knowing smirk.

"It felt like you were dying," the wolf says, ignoring Edina's question.

"I'm okay..." I tentatively pat him on the back.

"How did you get in here?" Adriana demands.

"You sent me an E-vite with the location," the werewolf says, "after you kidnapped me to deliver the message to Katie."

"Right." Adriana breathes a sigh of relief. "So, the wards recognized you." Appeased, she dismisses the mousy witch, who cannot escape the room fast enough, and sets about cleaning up pieces of my shattered door.

"Umm...dude, what the hell are you doing?" I ask as the werewolf starts nuzzling my neck.

"Making sure you're okay," he says like it's a totally normal thing to nuzzle people who are practically strangers while you're *naked*.

"LOWELL," a deep voice bellows, rattling the picture frames on the hewn rock walls.

One second, it's just the four of us. The next, the door Adriana just fixed is shattered again and a man is standing in the doorway, looking positively peeved. Adriana throws a shield around the room, keeping the stranger confined to the doorway. He scowls at her.

The man is easily as tall as the werewolf, but veins are visible beneath his pale skin. His blonde hair is cut short, and the bags under his eyes make him look half-dead. He's wearing a three-piece suit, in all black, which gives him a "don't fuck with me" vibe. Piercing ice-blue eyes scan the room until he finds the werewolf curled around me.

"Low-ell, we talked about this," he says exasperated, stretching out both syllables of the name and putting his hands on his hips. "After we shift, what's the first thing we do?"

The werewolf...or Lowell, apparently, growls in response.

"That's right. We put pants on." The man turns to me. "I'm so sorry. His emotions are a little primal at the moment. Wolves try to avoid people on the first night of the full moon, but this one got out of his cage. Lowell, come." He snaps his fingers and Lowell snarls and holds me tighter, pinching the sensitive skin on my shoulder. I wince in pain, and the wolf drops me like a hot plate.

"I just hurt you. Where?" Lowell demands, concern tightening his strong, stubbled jaw. His gaze zeroes in on my neck, and he moves so quickly I barely register the movement as he unzips and tears the robe off my body in one fell swoop.

"The fuck?" I exclaim as I'm left in my tank top and leggings.

"What happened?" he snarls.

"Nothing." His large hand reaches up and gently grips my jaw, tipping my chin up so I'm forced to meet his eyes, which are soft and pleading. Such a contrast to the waves of anger I feel radiating off him. "It's just a little burn," I say softly, and the scariest growl I've ever heard emits from his throat.

"Who. Did. This. To. You?" he asks in a quiet voice that's somehow more intimidating than the growl. His muscles ripple and his eyes start glowing again.

"NO," the man at the doorway commands. "No shifting." Lowell snarls but takes a breath and releases it slowly, the shift stopping in its tracks. He nods, and the man must deem that enough because he tosses him a pair of shorts, which Lowell hastily puts on.

"I'm sorry, who are you?" Adriana asks the man in the doorway. "And how did you get past my wards?"

"You had wards?" he asks, and Adriana turns a shade of red I've never seen on human skin.

"Yes, I have wards—" her seething is cut off as the man saunters over to her, walking straight through her shield and stopping close enough that Edina and I both take an offensive stance.

"My name is Vladimir," he says low enough that I almost don't catch it. He snatches her hand, slowly bringing it to his lips and brushing a kiss along her knuckles. "But you can call me Vlad."

Adriana rips her hand from his hold, wiping away the kiss on her pants, but I notice the shiver she tries to hide. Vlad must notice too because he flashes her a dazzling smile, fangs extending over his lips. Edina, Adriana, and I inhale simultaneously.

"You're a vampire," I breathe.

"Thank you for that assessment," Vlad deadpans. "And to answer your question, your shields don't protect against my kind. You may want to rectify that." He pulls his gaze away from my sister and appraises me. Lowell, now marginally less naked, steps between me and the vampire and snarls.

"Relax," Vlad intones, sounding bored. "I'm not going to hurt your witch."

"My name's Katie," I retort, earning me an approving smirk from the vampire. Lowell starts circling me like he's claiming territory.

Of all the fuckery that's happened to us today, Edina sends through our Mind Magic channel, which I'm very pleased is still working, *this is by far the weirdest.* I chortle, and Lowell stops pacing, pulling me so my back is flush against his chest, and throws a protective arm around my waist.

"This...*reaction* is because of the full moon?" I ask as he rests his chin on the top of my head.

"Yes," Vlad answers for the wolf, who is doing a weird rumbling thing that makes me feel oddly at ease.

"And what exactly is your role in this?" I ask the vampire.

"Lowell wanted to stay close to London after he delivered the message to you yesterday," the vampire continues. "He asked me to come and keep an eye on him, make sure he stayed in the woods he picked out for tonight."

"You did great," Edina deadpans. Vlad turns to acknowledge my best friend for the first time, and I think I see surprise flit across his features, but he schools them back into neutrality before I can be sure.

"Is he dangerous like this?" Adriana asks, finding her voice.

"Oh yeah," Vlad scoffs as Lowell nuzzles into the non-injured side of my neck, making me laugh as his hair tickles me. "He's a real menace. Positively rabid."

A sudden wave of dizziness washes over me and my knees buckle. Edina rushes forward, but Lowell scoops me in his arms before she even takes a full step. "Out," he barks at everyone.

"Umm, fuck all the way off," Edina says and the werewolf growls.

"We all should probably get some sleep," I interject.

"You want me to stay here?" Edina asks eyeing the werewolf like she's unsure if she should give us privacy or kick him out.

"I'm fine. You need sleep too." Edina reluctantly nods and gives the werewolf a glare that promises the worst kind of death before she sidesteps the vampire on her way out.

"There are extra rooms," Adriana says to our new guests as she magics the pieces of my broken door back into place again. "If you need a place to stay for the day."

"Thank you." Vlad mimes tipping a hat and I can hear Adriana's jaw tic from across the room as she pulls in her smile. She magically turns off all the glowing orbs in my room, so only the dim light from my bathroom trickles into the room.

They leave, and the wolf throws back my comforter and sets me down on my mattress.

"You can go too," I say softly. Then, when he ignores me, "I don't need a guard dog."

"If you had one maybe you wouldn't be hurt," he says, his eyes dipping to my shoulder again. "Are you going to tell me what happened?"

"Nope." He arches an eyebrow at me, his golden eyes not leaving mine until I acquiesce. "Fine, tomorrow. I almost died today. That takes a lot out of a person." The pause that stretches between us is enough to tell me my joke doesn't amuse him.

"Go to sleep, little witch," he says after the anger subsides a bit. He pulls down his pants, and before I can make a peep of protest, Lowell is back in his wolf form and hopping onto my mattress.

"No. Down boy," I command. He lets out a puff of air and settles himself at the foot of the bed, taking up the entire width of the mattress plus some. Once he's comfortable, he looks at me, daring me to make him leave. "Fine, but you stay down there."

I arrange the pillows to not touch my arms, but it's almost impossible to get comfortable. After about an hour of tossing and turning, I begin shivering, my whole body shaking violently. The adrenaline has worn off and I'm feeling the extent of my injuries.

The mattress beside me dips, and yellow eyes appear an inch from mine.

"I said stay down there," I get out through chattering teeth. The light in Lowell's eyes pulsates, and instantly some of my pain recedes. He lies down next to me, and gently nudges my bad arm with his cold nose.

"You're very demanding for someone who should be in his own room," I tell him, which makes his body shake in laughter. He scootches closer and I sigh before throwing my arm over his back, spooning his giant wolf form. My hand runs through his soft fur, and he makes a rumbling sound in his throat that relaxes me so deeply that my eyes start to drift closed.

"Thank you," I murmur, and somehow, despite the pain, I fall into the best sleep I've ever had.

Chapter Three

I WAKE UP REACHING for Archer.

Not consciously, but in the moments between sleep and waking, I reach across the bed seeking out his warmth, and I jolt awake when I realize I'm alone. Emotions barrel into me with the force of a train when I look around my darkened room, making it hard to draw breath.

He attacked me. He burned me. He killed for me...*again*.

I guess I can't claim to be surprised. He told me from the beginning he would burn the world to keep me safe. And I found that romantic. I spent every moment since my father infused me with Dark Magic feeling like I needed to care for those weaker than me. I made a career from it. So, when someone came along and offered to do that for me...

My lip trembles as I push my emotions down. Today isn't about my feelings. The Dark Magic Covens made me their queen, so today I need to be there for them, for the people who lost loved ones because of me.

A light knock against my door has me blinking tears from my eyes as I call for the person to come in. A witch I don't recognize enters and flicks her wand to magically light the room. She holds the door open for Lowell, who comes in bearing two large mugs and a tray of pastries balanced on his forearm.

"Merry Christmas, little witch," he says. I give him a smile in return, but I know it doesn't reach my eyes, and that he can feel my lingering pain through our bond. *Right. It's Christmas.*

"If that's coffee, you're officially my favorite person under this god-forsaken mountain," I say.

"And if it's tea?" he asks, and I glower at him as he approaches my bed. He breaks with a laugh and extends a mug the size of a small bowl, filled to the brim with black coffee, and emblazoned with the words *Witch, please.* I moan as the caffeine invades my system. "Good?" he asks.

"Better than sex," I reply, greedily drinking three more mouthfuls even though it's scorching.

"Sounds like you need better partners," he mutters, sitting beside me in bed with a wink, and I'm rendered speechless. I stutter for something quippy to respond with as he puts the plate of pastries on the bed between us. My stomach takes that moment to rumble loudly, and we both dissolve into laughter as the tension dissipates.

I awkwardly search for a way to transfer my mug to my other hand so I can eat, but I can't quite move my arm properly with the bandages. Lowell extends a golden, flaky croissant up to my lips.

"I'm not letting you feed—" I start, and he takes the opportunity of my open mouth to thrust the pastry inside. As soon as the aroma hits my nose, I'm helpless to stop myself and take a bite. "Fuck me, that's good."

Lowell chuckles before taking a taste of the same pastry. I gape at him open-mouthed as he extends the croissant back to me. "There's literally an entire plate right there," I say, and he answers by shoving the rest of my pastry in his mouth. "Animal," I grumble.

He chuckles and when the laughter subsides, we fall into an awkward silence. I take a sip of my coffee as I struggle to think of what to say, which seems ridiculous because he was naked and draped over me last night.

"Are you feeling..." *less feral* seems like the most appropriate description, but I opt to maintain some manners and decide on, "better?"

"The first night of the full moon is always the worst," Lowell says with a shrug. "I usually stay in wolf form the entire night, but—"

"But then I almost died, and you lost your shit?"

"It's not funny," he murmurs over his coffee mug. "You have no idea how much that hurt."

"I'm sorry that was so difficult for you," I deadpan. "I'll try not to get hit with hellfire in the future." Lowell goes deathly still, and then very slowly pivots his body to mine.

"Tell me you did not just say hellfire." His voice dips an octave, rumbling through me and making me shudder.

"I did not say hellfire," I respond instantly, wishing I could take it back. Only two people in the mortal realm have hellfire, and I think the werewolf knows exactly who they are.

"Fuck."

A wave of exhaustion overwhelms me. "Can we just have breakfast? And maybe not talk about last night? I'm sure I'll have to go over it all again later." His jaw tics, but eventually he gives me a curt nod. "Thank you." There's a tense silence between us, and I sip my coffee just for something to do with my hands.

"So, Lowell--" he cuts me off with a grimace.

"Low-ell," he corrects, his accent thicker as he separates the syllables. I echo the name, correctly this time, and there's a pulse of something indiscernible down the bond that I choose to ignore.

"Is it French?" I ask, and he nods. "Does it mean anything?"

"No idea," he says, a smile pulling at the corner of his mouth. He avoids my eyes as he extends another pastry to my lips, but I snap them shut, waiting him out. "Fine. It means little wolf."

I laugh, and then immediately try to cover it when he glowers at me. "That's adorable, pup."

"I'm no pup," he growls.

"And I'm no little witch," I respond, straightening my spine and rising to meet him. His face is inches from mine, but neither of us back down.

"No," he says, and I swallow hard as his eyes dip to my mouth. "You're most definitely not."

"You gonna drop my nickname?" I ask, and he smiles slowly.

"Very small chance, little witch."

"Okay then, pup." I pull back and smile over the rim of my coffee mug.

"How is your shoulder?" Lowell asks.

"It's fine." My voice is too cheery. He doesn't buy it for a second. "Okay, it hurts like hell. But don't take away my pain."

"Why?"

"Because..." *Because I deserve this pain. Because there are people who lost a child, and nothing can take away their pain.*

"It's not your fault, you know," he says softly.

"It is, but I appreciate that you're trying to make me feel better." Lowell reaches behind me and wraps his arm low around my waist and our bond gives a soft tug.

"Is that normal?" I ask. "The bond feels even stronger than last night."

"It's most definitely not normal."

As if it's sentient, the bond gives a more insistent prod towards each other. I sigh at the incessant thing and scooch closer so my back rests against Lowell's chest.

"Are you sure?" I ask skeptically. "Wolves are known for being tactile."

"I'm sure," he says, his head coming down to rest on my good shoulder. "I'm bonded with my entire pack, and I've never had this problem."

"And here I thought I was special," I scoff, and he nips playfully at my skin.

"When a new Alpha takes over, every pack member over the age of sixteen swears a bond of loyalty, different from ours, but it's the same premise. I'm familiar with how it should feel, and this isn't it." I hum and accept a bite of the croissant he offers, polishing the thing off.

"I'll ask some of the pack elders why they think our bond mutated," Lowell continues. "My best guess is because you aren't a wolf. Although Vlad isn't either." My eyebrows arch in surprise. "Vlad is an honorary member of our pack."

"How did that happen?"

"I'll let him tell you his story, but the short of it is that after the Four Kings War, the Magical Creatures felt safer teaming up. We all went into exile in groups to lean on each other for protection. Our pack bonded with Vlad and a few other vampires. We ensure they don't succumb to bloodlust and drain entire villages, and they keep us in the woods during the full moon. We also keep an eye on the mermaids who live in the lake."

"Like the one who attacked me?"

"Yeah, she was pissed when I stepped in. Almost started a war."

"I'm sorry?"

"You do get yourself into a lot of trouble, little witch," he jokes.

"It's a new hobby." A knock at the door pulls my attention.

"That'll be your sister with the healer," Lowell says, before calling for her to enter. Adriana opens the door a crack and just her head pokes in. The visual is enough to make me laugh out loud. Satisfied that I'm awake, she and Edina come in.

"Guess who we brought?" Adriana calls, entirely too awake for the hour. Although now that I think about it, I have no idea what time it is. It could be dinner time for all I know.

"A healer?" I guess, and my mouth drops open as an older man pops in, his graying hair cut shorter than I've seen it. His kind eyes are crinkled in the corners as he smiles at me, and he carries a black medical bag that clashes with his all-white uniform. "Coleman?"

"Hey, Captain." Coleman was a healer in the Dragons, one who I requested on all my missions. Adriana coughs loudly and Coleman sputters. "I'm sorry, I meant Your Majesty. Old habits."

"How—?" I look between him and Adriana.

"Your sister can be very persuasive," Coleman says, raising his eyebrows.

"Did you abduct him?" I ask Adriana, who gives me a sheepish smile. "Adriana, no! We don't kidnap people. He has a family."

"I agreed to come," Coleman says, stepping in for my sister, and making his way to the bed. Edina grabs the pastries and puts them on my nightstand, and then motions for me to give her my now empty mug. "My family is being set up in a suite as we speak."

"You deserted the Dragons?" He gives me a wistful smile.

"I thought Archer was different than his father," Coleman says carefully. "But he clearly isn't, so I pledge my loyalty and service to you and your cause, My Queen." Coleman bows from the waist.

"That's not necessary," I murmur. Coleman begins gingerly unwrapping my bandages.

"Katie," Adriana interjects, her tone only mildly self-righteous, "You're going to have to accept that you took the crown last night and are now our queen. Our people will look to you as a leader, and they should bow when addressing you. You need to watch out for the ones who don't." She side-eyes Edina.

"I'm not adding to her ego," Edina teases.

"Because I have an abundance of that right now," I say through gritted teeth as the bandages stick to my tender skin. Lowell takes my hand in his free one and squeezes it gently.

"I know you," Coleman says, looking at Lowell for a moment before returning to his task.

"We met another time Katie almost died," Lowell responds, not taking his eyes off me.

"Right. The werewolf from the lake," Coleman says, and my mouth drops open.

"You knew he was a werewolf?"

"He offered to take your pain away and his eyes started glowing. I might have been focused but I was right there, Cap—Your Majesty. I assumed you knew."

"I did. Did Archer know?" Coleman shakes his head, and Lowell sneers at the mention of the prince. "Relax, pup."

The last of the bandages fall away and a gasp echoes around the room. "Is it that bad?" I ask, afraid to look at my side.

"I'm going to kill him," Lowell responds.

"Get in line," Edina agrees.

I build up enough courage to look down at my shoulder. Most of my skin is blackened, completely charred, and what's not is angry and red. It wraps around my entire bicep and shoulder and spreads to my chest, stopping just shy of my heart.

"Fuck," I groan.

"I'll have to debride the area before I begin healing. A lot of the skin is..." Coleman shakes his head and removes a syringe with water. He turns to Lowell. "You should share in her pain if you think you can handle it. This will be worse than what I did for your leg wound."

"No," I say forcefully.

"Little witch," Lowell warns, his eyes already glowing.

"No," I repeat. "I want to feel it all."

"Babes..." Edina's voice is soft.

"If this is going to be too much, you don't have to be here," I say addressing the room before looking at Lowell. "With the bond, I know you'll feel some of it regardless, but I need to feel all of this." He doesn't respond, but slips his arm around my waist, squeezing gently. I sigh in relief and sink into his side.

"Go ahead, Coleman," I instruct. I get one moment of blinding light as a warning before he digs into my skin.

"You're doing great, Katie," Coleman reassures me.

He's been at it for at least two hours, but the healer has finally managed to peel away the burned skin, leaving me raw and exposed. At some point, Lowell shifted behind me to hold me still, propping me against his chest as he murmured a constant stream of soothing tones in my ear. Edina had to leave once when she was so overwhelmed that it started snowing over Coleman, but she's back now, her icy hands keeping a compress cold, mopping up the sweat that's accumulated on my brow.

Adriana left to finalize the meeting of the coven heads and arrange things for the Christmas banquet tonight. I told her we should cancel, but she waved me off, insisting that it would be the perfect event for me to address everyone before the memorials scheduled for later in the week.

"We're almost done," Coleman announces. "I'm going to start the actual healing...but I'm afraid you'll still scar."

"I understand, thank you, Coleman," I give him as big of a smile I can muster.

"Katie..." Lowell starts.

"I'm fine," I cut him off, anticipating his offer to share my pain again. He hasn't offered since we started, but I heard his teeth gnashing together more often than not.

"You're infuriating," he grumbles but doesn't push it.

Coleman takes that moment to call his Light Magic to his hands again, and starts running them up and down, an inch away from my burned skin. It feels like my body is rejecting the magic, trying to violently purge it from my system. I inhale sharply, and Lowell's muscles tighten beneath me.

"Holy fuck," I breathe, squeezing my eyes shut, ignoring the stars blooming beneath my lids.

I hear the door click open, and open my eyes to see Adriana entering, her face pale and worried. "How's it going?" she asks in a falsely cheery voice.

"Just wonderful," I grumble.

"Are you almost done?"

"What's wrong?" I grit out. Edina sits at attention and Lowell tenses behind me. Adriana's face flits with indecision before she approaches the bed.

"We need to move the meeting up," she announces as her eyes glass over momentarily. "Yeah. Sometime in the next twenty minutes will be best. Will you be done by then? I could have them meet us in here, but it won't be the desired effect."

"Why are we moving the meeting up?" Edina asks.

"We need the heads of each coven to swear fealty to Katie before dinner. I'm not sure why, but I can feel it." Adriana closes her eyes, searching for an answer but then opens them and shakes her head in defeat. "I can't see exactly what will happen if we stay on our path, but it's not good."

"Is someone plotting something?" I ask.

Adriana simply shrugs "I'm sorry I wish I knew more."

"We need to get you a clairvoyance teacher," I huff in frustration. Any information is better than nothing, but we could use some details.

"I'm almost done, Your Majesty," Coleman says.

"Okay, fine, move the meeting up," I say. "I need to shower but have everyone meet in the war room in twenty minutes. I want Lowell and Vladimir in on this meeting as well. Is it sundown?"

"It is," Edina says. "I'll go wake the vampire daddy." The glare Adriana gives my best friend could kill a lesser person, but Edina just flashes her a taunting smile.

"I should go," Lowell responds before Edina can move too far. "Vampires don't respond well to being woken up. Are you—" He looks at me like he'd rather do anything than leave my side.

"I'm fine," I assure him. Lowell hesitates, then carefully extracts himself from me and disappears from the room using his insane werewolf speed.

After he leaves, Edina fixes me with a stare that has me squirming. "Are we gonna talk about that?" She gestures to where the werewolf was just sitting.

"Nope," I respond.

"Mm-kay, but if it's too much, just say the word, and I'll freeze him out."

"We're stooping to ice jokes now?" Edina blows an icy wind in my face, and we both laugh.

"How does he know where he's going?" Adriana asks, concerned.

"Scent?" Edina offers and I wrinkle my nose.

"Can you smell a vampire?"

"Babes, I can smell everything," she says miming a gag. "It's fucking gross. Did you know some emotions have a scent? Like seriously, I never needed to know what arousal smells like."

"Oh, dear god. Who—"

"You so don't wanna know."

She's right. I don't. "We need to find you a teacher too," I say after a moment.

"One step at a time," Edina responds logically. "Let's get you off the operating table and your magic all sorted before we go there." Adriana shoots her a glare and then looks to Coleman, who is doing a great job pretending he didn't hear anything we just said.

"You can kidnap the man and bring him into a secret underground bunker, but you don't trust him to know about my magic?" I snort.

"Well, when you put it like that..." Adriana's cheeks pink, and she motions for me to go ahead.

"My magic has been...uncooperative since I was hit with the hellfire," I tell Coleman. "No one outside of this room knows."

"I understand, Your Majesty," Coleman responds. "I won't say anything."

"Have you ever heard of anything like that happening?"

"Well," he says thoughtfully, his magic absorbing back into his hands, "I've come across toxins that block a witch's magic, much like the mermaid venom did to you. I can perform an assessment, but it takes some time."

"Tomorrow then," I respond, pushing to my feet and stretching, testing the elasticity of my new skin. "Thank you so much, Coleman." He dips into a slight bow and scuttles out the door.

"Adriana, pick out whatever you want me to wear," I instruct, and she's already on the move to the wardrobe. "You and Edina are also joining us for the meeting, a show of unity and all that. Give me five minutes to shower and then we'll go."

I cross into my adjoining bathroom and pause at the mirror, only mildly afraid of what I'll find. My chestnut hair is mussed, but it's not the worst bedhead I've ever had, and surprisingly none of it is burnt. Deep black circles are under my eyes, but Edina knows a spell that can remove those, and my skin is a bit pale.

I finally force myself to look at my shoulder. The new skin is a mottled pink and red, with deep rivets that run the length of my arm, where the worst burns were. The edges are jagged at the base of my neck and across my chest and look remarkably like flames reaching for my face and heart. There's no mistaking the fact that I was burned, branded by Archer's fire.

The thought of him makes my stomach sink as I turn on the shower and step into the tepid water, trying not to focus on the fact that the last time I showered was with the prince. I can't bring myself to make it hot like I prefer. My nerves are still too raw. I run a loofah over my scarred skin as gently as I can, barely feeling the course material against my arm. I move the sponge aside and trail my fingers over the divots, but even when I scrape my nails against my skin, they feel like they're buried beneath multiple pairs of gloves. I don't know why the nerve damage hits me harder than the look of the scar, but suddenly I'm struggling to breathe.

I can't fall apart yet. I can't examine the betrayal, the worry, the gut-wrenching heartbreak I'm feeling, not when I need to play the part of a queen in three minutes. So, I grit my teeth, shoving it all down as I go through the motions, grateful that the pain from earlier has faded into an incessant itching. When I return from the shower, I have my queen mask firmly in place.

I am Kathryn Carmichael, the Heir of Carman, and Queen of the Dark Magic Covens. Time to show them who they're dealing with.

Chapter Four

I JOG DOWN THE carved, rock halls, my heels echoing against the stone floors as we wind through the labyrinth that is the Highland Coven. The magical green light gives the place an eerie, foreboding look, though that might be me projecting. I'm nervous about this meeting, and Adriana's constant stream of warnings hasn't helped.

"Remember," she says as I struggle to keep pace, "you need to show strength. Everyone there is looking for an excuse to blame you for yesterday's attack." Edina swears as she magically curls my post-shower hair into perfect spirals.

"Don't give them that opening," Adriana instructs before turning, plopping the tiara on my head, and handing me a black robe that all coven members wear. "If you start apologizing—"

"Which coven leader did we lose?" I ask as we continue our trek.

"Shanghai, but they're not back yet. There was internal fighting." I slide the robe over my shoulders and Edina throws a spell at me to zip it up over my dress.

"And the head witch who lost her sons?" I ask, and Adriana stops so quickly that I almost fall over her. She steadies us with a hand against the rocks.

"Katie, it's a bad idea."

"My favorite kind." I push past her through the wooden doorway that leads to the war room.

Twenty witches stand as we enter, their black robes billowing around them in the flurry of movement. The "war room" is not a room as much as it's an open cavern with a board room style table in its center. Maps are magically tacked to the walls, and the green light is almost fluorescent in its brightness. But the most impressive feature of the room is the giant mirror that has a dozen live feeds of various Kingdom strongholds. I gasp when I see my mother and Marcus arguing in the dungeon underneath the palace.

How--? I mentally ask Adriana. *Did you do this when you were captured?*

Of course, I hear her scoff echo in the recesses of my mind. *Focus, I'll explain another time.*

I pull my gaze away from the mirror and scan the room. The atmosphere is tense, and there's a wariness that didn't exist yesterday.

"Kathryn," my father coos from his position at the head of the table. He extends his bony arms out to the side, flashing a smile full of yellowing teeth courtesy of his years at the magical prison. "It's so wonderful to see you up and about. Surviving hellfire...it's the stuff of legends."

I ignore his praise as my eyes fall on an older woman sitting at the table's far end. Her eyes are puffy, and I can see a small piece of tissue crammed into her hand. I approach the grieving mother and she immediately dips into a bow.

"Ms. Andrews?" I ask gently.

"Cecelia, Your Majesty," she responds as she rises.

I take her hands in mine, squeezing gently. "Words cannot express my condolences. I am so truly sorry."

"Thank you," she whispers, her voice raw. "My boys are--were so excited to see a Dark Witch ascend the throne. My oldest was enlisted in our Chicago Coven. He was ready to go to war to assure you would rise to your rightful place."

"I will do my best to honor their memory, and the memory of all that were lost yesterday," I vow and release her hands with another squeeze.

I motion for everyone to be seated and take my place standing at the unoccupied head of the table, with Edina and Adriana flanking me. I take a moment to look at each coven leader, noting the empty seat reserved for the Shanghai leader and the two empty seats along the wall for Vlad and Lowell, both yet to arrive.

"Before we begin," I start, summoning all the power I possess in my voice. "I would like to say a few words." My eyes lock on my father. His eyes, auburn mirrors to my own, regard me curiously. "There wasn't time to address you after I was crowned, and the vision was bestowed upon me. I want us to be able to move forward with full transparency." *For the most part*, I add mentally to Edina and Adriana.

"When I arrived yesterday, I wasn't ready to be your queen." Eyes of the coven members dart around the room, some look down at their hands, avoiding my gaze completely. "I didn't believe your cause to be the noble one. I'm sure you know I refused the position on several occasions and know of my relationship with Archer Baran." At the mention of his name, the atmosphere in the room thickens with tension.

"What changed?" a red-faced witch I haven't spoken to before asks. Sweat glistens along his receding hairline even though it's freezing in this room.

"On the throne," I respond, keeping my tone level, "I was informed of my misinformation. And then Archer..." I swallow hard. "I won't tolerate attacks on the innocent."

"And somehow, it's happened twice on your watch," the witch retorts.

I take a deep breath through my mouth as memories of burned husks on an altar join the images of the battle last night. My father shifts forward in his seat, steepling his hands in front of his mouth, which I'm sure is meant to hide a smirk.

"We've discussed the incident in Sicily," Adriana snaps, coming to my aid. "We decided to place blame solely on the prince. There's no need to drag it up now, Sanderson."

"I think yesterday's incident is enough of a reason. How do we know the prince won't return, looking for her again? She might be able to survive hellfire but the rest of us sure can't." He jabs a stubby finger in my direction as questions about my miraculous survival bounce around the table.

In black robes of their own, Vlad and Lowell enter and take the seats set aside for them as the order in the room dissolves. Adriana hastily tries to explain their theory about the combination of magic stopping the hellfire.

I hold up a hand and am surprised when the entire room falls silent at the simple gesture. "I can't change what happened," I say, steeling my spine. "But I will work to make sure it doesn't happen again. The Kingdom of Magic is broken and has been for centuries. I now understand that it is my calling to restore the balance destroyed during the Four Kings War."

"By taking the throne?" one of the Coven Heads asks gently.

"By restoring the Four Monarchs." The gasps that ensue at my declaration are better suited for a mortal courtroom drama than for a coven of Dark Witches. "Dark Magic is not the only faction that has been egregiously wronged since the Four Kings War."

"Let them start their own war," my father sneers.

"Do I need to remind you what we're going up against?" I assert. "Even if we neutralize Arch—the hellfire, they have the most sophisticated military in the Kingdom. We would be massacred in minutes without a proper army, without allies. We need to work with the other factions of magic.

"My plan—" I glance at the vampire and werewolf at the back of the room, "—is to approach the Magical Creatures first. They have been treated as poorly as Dark Witches in the centuries since the war. I hope to secure a meeting with the Count and Council of Vampires and the Pack Master for the European Werewolves. Then we'll approach the Fae and any others we find, including any Light or Elemental Witches who understand that the Kingdom is imbalanced."

"You expect us to work with *Elemental Witches*?" my father hisses. "During the war *and* after?"

"If you're with me," I say to the room, ignoring him, "then I expect you to swear a binding vow of fealty immediately."

After the longest silence of my life, Cecelia stands. "The Chicago Coven swears it's fealty to Queen Kathryn." She pushes her chair away and kneels.

Her declaration opens the floodgates, and soon everyone kneels except my father.

"Kathryn," he starts, shaking his head like he's disappointed, his silver hair glowing green under the lights. "The prophecy showed us that you'd be the sole queen."

"Or so Queen Carman led you to believe," I inform him. "I am simply following through with her plan as dictated to me on the throne."

My father's eyes widen when he realizes I've blocked any move he can make by invoking Carman's name. And it's not a total lie. It just wasn't Carman who gave the instruction.

He sucks on his teeth before sinking very slowly to his knee. "The Highland Coven swears fealty to Queen Kathryn," he says through gritted teeth. My sigh of relief isn't full. I might have been able to check his king, but the game between us is far from over.

"Adriana," I direct, taking a seat in the swivel chair at the head of the table. "If you will please perform the ceremony."

ADRIANA TAKES ALMOST AN hour to perform the ritual, which involves the head of each coven reciting a portion of a spell and then using Dark Magic to seal the vow. The vow will transfer magically from the heads to every member of their covens, so we won't have to do this with each witch fighting for us. Adriana also assures me that there are consequences if anyone breaks the fealty vow, but she didn't go into details.

When the heads of the covens leave, Adriana and Edina take seats on my left as Vlad and Lowell stand and amble towards the board room table.

"Isn't this quite the group?" Vlad chides as he sinks in a swivel chair, rocking back and forth, his ice-blue eyes staring me down. "I'd love to discuss how you know so much about vampire politics, baby queen. Not many people know about the council, let alone the Count."

"Katie is fine," I respond. "And I was the youngest ranking officer in the Dragons, on track to be a general by the time I turned thirty. I studied magical politics like it was my job."

"But you don't know *who* the main players are," Lowell states, taking the seat between me and Vlad.

"That was above my clearance level. Can you get me a meeting?" I ask them both.

"It will take some time to convene a council," Vlad says carefully.

"But you can do it?" I press.

"Hypothetically." He gives me a sly grin.

"What can you offer in return for an army?" the werewolf asks.

"A balanced Kingdom isn't enough?" I joke, but Lowell just arches his eyebrows. "You know I plan to restore the Four Monarchs—"

"Yeah, you remember how that ended right?" Vlad interrupts. "It was a fucking mess. Trust me. I was there."

"How old are you?"

"Old," Lowell and Vlad respond in unison.

"Which means I'm an invaluable source of information," Vlad gloats.

"What would you do differently then?" I ask, and Vlad just shrugs. I look exasperatedly to Lowell who smacks Vlad on the arm.

"Don't be a dick," he chides.

"But that's my best feature," Vlad says with a wink. "She's not ready. Let the baby queen go ahead with her plan. She'll figure out that it's destined for disaster soon enough."

"Not loving the nickname. Or being talked about like I'm not in the room."

Vlad turns to me. "You're not ready. Go ahead with your plan. You'll figure out it's destined for disaster soon enough."

"This bodes so well for the future of the Kingdom," Edina deadpans, and I pinch the bridge of my nose.

"Anyway," I huff. "Is there something you think the Pack Master will specifically ask for?"

"Yes," Lowell says, looking to Vlad, who nods in approval. "The weres will be your largest force and will most likely suffer the highest casualties. We'll need someone in command, both in the army and in the new government."

"Vampires will follow the werewolves before they follow the witches," Vlad adds.

"You want the wolves on board?" Lowell fixes his golden eyes on me and gives me a predator's smile. "I'm your second."

"You?" The realization washes over me with the force of a tsunami. "You're the Pack Master."

"I am."

"And you can make these promises without conferring with the other Alphas?" He nods, waiting for my decision. "Adriana is my second. I won't tempt fate by going against a vision from a clairvoyant."

"Actually," Adriana interjects, "I just saw myself by your side. I'm happy to be your third."

"I'm the third," Vlad responds. "And Tinker Bell is the fourth."

"Tinker Bell?" Ice shoots from Edina's fingers across the table, but the vampire moves out of the way just in time.

"Sorry, sweetheart," he says to Adriana without skipping a beat. "But since our queen has Dark Magic, you're redundant."

"Don't speak to her like that," I snap in my sister's defense. "None of us would be having this conversation if it wasn't for Adriana."

"I'll be your advisor," she says, her eyes locking with the vampire, daring him to question her decision.

"That's settled then," Lowell says. "What's next?"

"Ideally, we'll also get the support of the vampires, and maybe some of the other Magical Creatures. But I don't know where to even find them," I tell him honestly.

"You'd be better off going to the Fae," Vlad says. "But they'll drag their feet, so you want to send her to Faerie as soon as possible." He jabs a finger in the direction of my best friend.

"No," I say flatly.

"Babes—" Edina starts.

"Absolutely not." I turn and stare her down. "The whole reason we came to the coven is so you didn't get shoved into a portal in a world full of vicious—"

"I swear to god Katie, if you finish that sentence." Edina stands leaning over the table, fuming at me. "If you can get over the idea that the Dark Witches aren't all evil, why can't you understand the Fae aren't either?"

The silence in the room is deafening.

"In all fairness, ninety percent of the Fae *are* vicious," Vlad says. Edina and I glare at him in unison.

"I'm sorry," I say to Edina. "You really want to do this?"

"I don't think we have much of a choice." Edina sinks back into her seat with a heavy sigh.

Vlad clears his throat and props his hand under his chin. "So, when did you emerge?"

"Yesterday," Edina answers, keeping her eyes on me.

Vlad hums and taps a long finger against his lips. We watch him, waiting as he swivels back and forth in his chair, intently staring at my best friend. After a long silence, he says, "I've been to Faerie. Quite a few times." Another beat. I swear he's more dramatic than me, Edina and Adriana combined. And that's saying something. "Even if I hadn't been, the scandal of your kidnapping reached this realm. In fact, the man responsible was killed by someone in this room."

I pale, my hand shooting out to grab Edina's. I killed a man who was wanted for stealing Fae children when I was with the Dragons. He's the only man I ever killed and, even though it was in self-defense, it tore me up inside.

"So, you know who my birth parents are?" Edina asks the vampire. The temperature of Edina's hand drops, and ice starts spreading over the table as Adriana grabs her other hand, silently lending support.

"Your mother's name is Gwyneira," Vlad says, expression softer than I've seen it. "She's the queen of the Winter Court."

"What?" Edina squeaks.

"Holy shit," Adriana breathes.

"It makes things more complicated." Vlad says the word *complicated* like he means *interesting*. He leans back in his chair, crossing one long leg over the other. "If the princess shows up in Faerie unescorted, she'll be kidnapped. The Winter Court has a lot of enemies looking for a good bargaining chip against the queen. She'll need an escort who can protect her and won't be killed on sight. Someone they know not to fuck with."

"Is that you?" I ask.

"I would need a few days, and you don't have that kind of time."

"Why can't you take her tomorrow night?"

"Because, baby queen," Vlad says, his fangs lengthening. "I haven't fed in a week, and if I go into Faerie in bloodlust, it won't end well for anyone."

"You haven't fed in a week?"

"I'm old," he responds. "I don't require as much blood as a younger vampire—"

"But he'll be in bloodlust by tomorrow if he doesn't feed," Lowell finishes. "We're leaving after this meeting and heading home or looking for a blood bank."

"And he can't feed on you?" I ask. Lowell shakes his head.

"I need human blood," Vlad responds, "Magical Creatures may appear human, but they're a different species."

"And Vlad stopped attacking humans centuries ago," Lowell adds. "There are a few humans who know us back home who will feed him."

"You don't feed on someone unless you have their consent?" I ask, and Vlad nods. "Wow, that's...noble." Vlad shrugs. I look him over silently for a long time before extending the wrist on my good arm.

"No," Lowell responds, swatting my hand away.

"Vlad can't drink a witch's blood?"

"He can, but he's not drinking from you," Lowell grumbles.

"That's not your decision, pup," I bark. "If we're working together, we need to establish trust."

"Katie, you've been through a lot today," Edina says gently.

"He can drink from me," Adriana offers, but I wave her off.

"No," I fix my gaze on Vlad's piercing blue eyes. "You'll drink from me. Lowell will monitor my pulse and be there to step in, just in case."

"Why?" Vlad asks, tilting his head and eyeing me intently.

"Tons of reasons," I respond. "But you're hungry, and you need to feed. So..." I thrust my wrist closer to him and he swallows thickly.

"Wait," Adriana says, her eyes glassing over with a vision. "You need to do this at the banquet."

I look to Vlad, who is impossibly paler. He nods. "That's settled then," I say, trusting Adriana's clairvoyance.

"How many of you can teleport?" Vlad asks, and Adriana raises her hand. "Right, then you should teleport us all to my house tomorrow."

"Why?"

"Because I have a portal," he says like that's something completely normal and not crazy illegal.

"How in the hell do you have a portal?" I demand.

"And from my house," he continues ignoring my question, "you can go see the mermaids about your magic problems." My mouth drops open, and Edina and Adriana mirror my sentiment.

"How did you—" I start.

"What's wrong with your magic?" Lowell says over me.

"I have excellent hearing," Vlad answers. "It sounds like your magic is blocked. The mermaids might be able to help you."

"Why didn't you tell me?" Lowell demands.

"I was trying to keep the fact that I'm vulnerable quiet."

"And she's met you like twice," Edina adds.

Lowell growls but doesn't press it. "And it has to be the mermaids?" he asks through gritted teeth. Vlad nods and Lowell pushes his hands through his dark hair. "They're not going to be happy to see us."

Vlad barks a loud laugh. "Nope."

"These are the same mermaids who tried to kill her?" Edina asks.

"They wouldn't have killed her," Vlad says. "They just would have tortured her a little, and then maybe drowned her afterward."

"Fucking great," I grumble. "So, that settles it. I'll ask the murderous mermaids for help—"

"Nice alliteration," Vlad teases.

"Thank you."

"I'll go with Katie and then meet with the Alphas to issue their orders," Lowell adds.

"Edina and Vlad will go to Faerie—"

"I'll call a meeting with the Council so they'll be ready when I get back," Vlad interjects.

"And I'll move up the memorials to tomorrow morning so you can be there," Adriana says. "What else do you need me to do?"

"I need you here," I tell her. "I don't trust Father, so keep an eye on him. And you can gather the covens." She bobs her head excitedly. There's a long silence as we all stare at each other, the weight of the moment settling over us.

"That's it?" Edina asks.

"What were you expecting?" Vlad asks.

"It just seems a little anticlimactic for forming a multi-species alliance." She flips her hair over her shoulder.

"Should we make a blood oath?" Vlad monotones. "Declare a death pact? Have an orgy?"

"I think we should just go to the banquet," I respond, and Adriana nods enthusiastically.

"Lead the way, little witch," Lowell says.

Chapter Five

AFTER WE'VE DISCARDED OUR robes, our group heads towards the training room where the Christmas banquet is being held. I smooth down the satin, burgundy gown Adriana picked out for me, wishing she chose something with sleeves rather than thin off-the-shoulder straps that don't cover my scar. My stilettos clack against the stones as we walk down the hall.

"I never understood why witches celebrate Christmas," Vlad says absently, breaking the silence. He's wearing a tux tailored so perfectly that I'm not sure where he got it on such short notice. His blonde hair is swept back in a way that makes him look like an old-Hollywood movie star.

"We've had to blend in with mortals for centuries," Adriana calls over her shoulder. Her blonde curls are pinned high so her neck is bare in her strapless mauve dress. "It was easier to adapt to their customs, especially in regions heavily influenced by religion."

"Witch families started creating their own traditions, so even when it became more accepted to celebrate pagan holidays, we kept the other holidays around," I finish.

"My family celebrates Hanukkah too," Edina says, spinning around so her powder blue gown flutters around her legs in time with the beat of her wings. "We have one giant rager from Thanksgiving to New Year's that encompasses all the holidays."

Vlad seems appeased by the explanation and drops back until he's matching my stride. I look at him expectantly. "May I have a word?" he asks, slowing his pace to a meander, and linking his arm in mine to slow me down.

"What's up?"

"Have you ever been bitten before?" he asks after a long pause. The group moves ahead, disappearing behind a corner and we slow even further. I shake my head. "I thought as much and wanted to see if you had any questions."

"Will it hurt?" I ask playfully. "I mean I can handle it, but you saw pup's reaction to my pain yesterday."

"Briefly." Vlad reaches over with his other hand and his thumb tenderly caresses the vein in my wrist. "But I've been told it's also quite a pleasurable experience."

"Really?"

"Feeding a vampire is a very intimate act," his voice dips to a whisper. "It often leads to more carnal activities." I stop in my tracks, glowering at him.

"And you agreed to do this in *public*?" My indignation breaks his melancholy, and his laughter fills the empty hallway.

"It was your sister's idea, not mine," he reminds me, holding his hands up. "And I thought you knew the tradition."

"What tradition?"

"When Queen Carman asked the Count for his aid in the Four Kings War, she offered to feed him. It became symbolic of an alliance."

"I think you're full of shit," I deadpan, and he smirks.

"About most things, maybe. Not about this. It will be a meaningful gesture to your coven."

"Mhmm," I tsk, grabbing his arm again and pulling him along the corridor.

"I just wanted to give you a fair warning," he adds. "If you feel aroused, it's normal. It's just the bite."

"Got it." We walk for a moment in companionable silence, our arms still linked. "Can I ask you something unrelated?" I whisper as we approach the training room.

"Of course."

"What do you know about the pieces of the blood oath?" His ice-blue eyes flick immediately to my necklace.

"You seek the remaining two," he surmises. "It's a smart play. Rumor states owning all four will intensify your magic."

"I could use that right about now," I grumble. "When I sat on the throne, I was given a vision of a spirit. She told me to find them but not where they're located."

"Was the spirit Finley?" A hint of emotion I can't place fills his voice, and upon my confirmation, a strangled laugh escapes his lips. "She always did love a dramatic quest."

"Of course, you knew her," I laugh. "Any idea where they could be?"

"Possibly," Vlad says with a smirk. "An idea."

"Care to share with the group?"

"Not here."

Adriana holds the door and ushers us inside the training room. The room drops to a knee and Vlad releases my arm to follow suit. Gone are the standard attire of black robes in the coven. Instead, everyone wears tuxedos and gowns in festive colors. I give the room a warm smile and an incline of my head, and Adriana motions for everyone to stand and take their seats.

My sister outdid herself, transforming the gym-like space into a formal dining room adorned with crimson and gold accents. A long table runs the hall length, covered from end to end in succulent dishes that make my mouth water. There's even light Christmas music playing through the air via some magical amplification system.

"Princess," my father approaches, his eyes scrutinizing. His silver hair is still tied back, and he wears a dark gray tux that washes him out.

"You probably should think of a new nickname," I tease, but the levity is missed. He holds out his arm for me to take and I can't hide the involuntary shudder that passes through me. Adriana, seeing my discomfort, swoops in and grabs Father's arm in my stead.

"I wasn't sure who you wanted as your guests of honor," she says quickly, "but I arranged for our vampire and werewolf to sit at your side. Father, I have you at the opposite head of the table."

Thank you, I mouth before we walk in opposite directions. Everyone remains standing behind their seats, waiting for me to sit first. Lowell pulls out a chair for me at the head of the table, but before I get the chance to sit, my father opens his mouth.

"Before we begin the celebration," he begins, basking in the attention as all heads swivel to him. "We would be remiss not to acknowledge those missing from tonight's festivities." My father hangs his head in an over-the-top attempt at empathy. A murmur moves across the crowd, but I stay still, watching what he's planning.

"We're so fortunate to have the unrivaled power of our queen to lead us in this inevitable war." He raises a glass to me. "With Kathryn and her lightning at our helm, I have no doubt the Dark Magic Covens will emerge victorious against the Elemental Witches."

Everyone cheers except the five of us who know better. I eye my father warily. His sugar-coated words leave a bad taste in my mouth. *Does he know about my magic?*

My father stares me down as he takes a long pull of his wine and I wait until the applause dies naturally to speak.

"Thank you, Seth, and the heads of every coven for their vow of fealty," I say, the hint of a threat lacing my voice before I cover it with a sickly-sweet smile. "I am honored and humbled to be chosen as your queen."

As I continue, Adriana gives me a nod of approval from the other side of the table.

"I would like to introduce my guests of honor for the evening." Lowell and Vlad flank me, looking downright intimidating in their matching tuxedos. "I am pleased to announce that we are on the way to securing alliances with the Magical Creatures that have been banished under the rule of the Elemental Witches."

"What?" my father hisses, clearly upset that I'm stealing whatever attention he hoped for. I open my mouth to respond, but Lowell tugs gently on the bond between us, and I halt.

"As Pack Master of the European Werewolf Packs," Lowell says with booming authority, "I publicly swear fealty to Kathryn, Queen of the Dark Magic Covens. Our packs will fight alongside *her* and the Dark Witches in our joint goal of restoring the balance to the Kingdom of Magic." The way he says *her* makes no question that their alliance is conditional on my reign.

Lowell steps closer until he hovers over my shoulder. "Now," he whispers in my ear.

"Vladimir," I call above the din. Vlad steps to my side, another direct message that neither he nor the werewolf guarding my back are beneath the Dark Witches. "Thank you for your help in arranging a meeting with the Council of Vampires." I extend my wrist to him. Someone gasps dramatically, and I fight the urge to roll my eyes.

Mention Queen Carman, Adriana says through our Mind Magic connection.

"I will not have someone go hungry at our banquet," I continue. "In the tradition set by Queen Carman, please accept my blood as a sign of our alliance."

The crowd murmurs and Vlad gives me an impressed look before sinking to his knee in a flourish. "Thank you, Your Majesty."

Lowell steps behind me, his hand discreetly coming up to my neck on the side away from the table to monitor my pulse. Vlad places a feather-soft kiss on my wrist before his fangs scrape along my vein and he inhales deeply.

"Kathryn, that's quite enough," my father rages at the end of the table, but I ignore his protests and nod to the vampire at my feet. In one swift motion, Vlad winks and sinks his fangs into my wrist.

I hide my flinch expertly, but I can tell by the way Vlad pauses and Lowell's grip on my pulse that they feel my tension. Vlad suckles my wrist, his eyes closing as the blood rushes out to meet his waiting lips. The pain fades almost instantly, replaced by a warmth spreading up my arm. The world falls away, narrowing to the pulling sensation that shoots from my wrist straight to my core and the light pressure at my neck.

My breathing quickens, and my head spins as Vlad groans against my skin, sending vibrations through my entire body. Lowell adjusts his grip on me, his other hand falling to my waist to hold me upright as my legs turn to jelly. His hands are warm through the fabric of my dress, and it does nothing to quell the arousal coursing through me.

"You all right, little witch?" Lowell chuckles in my ear, his breath brushing against my sensitive skin, making me shiver. I nod as my eyes flutter closed, and I grab Lowell's hand as the pleasure intensifies.

"Open your eyes," Lowell growls. "Unless you want the entire room to know how aroused you are." I note his words, but then Vlad sucks again, turning the pulling in my core to throbbing need.

"Fuck," I breathe, my head tipping back and landing against the hardness of Lowell's body as my spine arches. The pleasure is intense, so fucking intense that a strangled moan leaves my lips.

"Archer."

Chapter Six

MY EYES SNAP OPEN, meeting Vlad's as he extracts his fangs and I jerk back upright. Lowell goes rigid behind me.

I just said Archer's name as I was about to come.

FUCK.

I look wildly to the crowd to see if anyone heard my slip, but everyone seems riveted by the show we just put on. Slowly, the witches applaud, calling out thanks to the vampires for aiding our cause. I'm vaguely aware that Vlad is brushing a thumb over the wound on my wrist but I'm too embarrassed to look at him.

What happened? Edina asks through our channel.

Did you hear? I ask.

Hear what?

"Thank you so much, Your Majesty," Vlad says loudly, kissing the back of my hand, and forcing my attention back to him. The color of his skin is pinker, not as translucent, and the bags under his eyes have evaporated. He squeezes my hand reassuringly before jumping to his feet and moving to stand behind the seat allotted for him.

"Breathe," Lowell whispers, as he slowly turns me back to the waiting crowd, and I realize I haven't been. I manage a half-smile and a nondescript hand motion, which Adriana thankfully interprets and sits. The rest of the table follows suit.

"What do you need?" Lowell asks softly as he guides me into my chair.

My pulse pounds in my ears, making the world around me sound far away. Lowell fills my plate with some red meat and a few other items, murmuring something about needing iron.

I take a few bites, not tasting anything, but resolutely swallow past the lump that won't dislodge. I half-listen as Vlad tells Edina stories about Faerie, and she asks question after question about her people. Occasionally his eyes wander to me, but the fake smile plastered to my face seems to appease him. Lowell, on the other hand, isn't convinced, and his eyes never leave me as he eats in silence.

My hands shake as I reach for my wine glass, so I fold them in my lap instead. When someone finally comes around to clear the plates and bring dessert, I stand and excuse myself, walking evenly from the training room without another word. I hear someone call after me, and someone else inquires if they should be standing as I leave, but I make it to the door without further interruption.

The training room doors close behind me as I walk in a fog through the underground labyrinth. I keep moving at a steady pace, even as the world around me blurs, the edges of my vision going black. I don't know how long I walk, or how I make it back to my room, but as soon as I see the familiar door I barrel inside and run into the attached bathroom.

I crash to my knees and yank open the toilet a second before the bile rises in my throat and I empty the contents of my stomach. I manage to catch my tiara before it slips into the mess, and I toss it aside. Salt from my tears trickles into my mouth, making me gag and sputter.

It feels like I'm suffocating inside my own body.

My heart pounds, the thudding ricocheting from my rib cage into my skull and filling my ears. The pendant of my necklace thumps at my throat, confusing my heart as it races to try and keep up with the irregular beat.

I claw at my neck, trying desperately to unlatch the new silver chain with my shaking hands. It feels like an iron collar, reminding me I'll always be tied to the man who almost killed me. *The man I thought would never hurt me.*

I feel him everywhere, his touch on my skin, his kiss on my lips, his fire seeking to destroy my soul. My nausea surges again even though there's nothing left. I dry heave as my body tries to purge the memory of the prince from my very being. But no matter what I do, I see his face, the flames flickering over his hazel eyes as he attacks me.

Two sets of footsteps enter the bathroom, one pausing at the door and one moving closer. A cold hand scrapes across my scalp as Edina holds my hair back.

"I've got you," she says. I reach up and flush away the evidence of my episode, trying to calm my breathing, but that stupid necklace is choking me. I feel my body react to the lack of air as my hands flutter to the chain and I start tugging. "I need you to breathe, babes."

"Get it off," I gasp. Edina guides me back towards the center of the bathroom as her fingers start working the clasp. She swears as it sticks, and my entire body seizes.

I double over, wrapping my arms around my middle trying to hold myself together. My body is wracked with tremors as the world narrows to this feeling. *This helplessness.*

The scent of rain and earth washes over me as a warm hand gently grips my chin, tilting it up. Lowell crouches before me, his calloused fingers brushing down the column of my neck. He grabs the thudding pendant and tugs sharply, the metal biting into my skin before it falls away. My heart rate slows as soon as it's off, as if remembering how to beat to its own rhythm.

Edina pulls me back against her chest, one arm wrapping around my chest and pulling tightly as the other rests against my stomach. "From here, babes, deep breaths." I inhale deeply, my diaphragm rising at her hand's suggestion. Her signature rosewater scent replaces the smell of vomit and sweat and with each breath, I feel like I'm returning to my body, the panic receding like an ebbing tide.

Lowell moves out of my line of sight, but he returns quickly with a damp washcloth. Very slowly, so I see each second of his movements, he presses it to my clammy forehead, the cool temperature soothing. He slides it to my cheeks, wiping away the mascara before he flips the cloth and dabs the corners of my mouth. His touch is light and tender, very un-wolf-like. When he's done, I lift my eyes to meet his golden gaze, and he offers me a small smirk.

"There you are," he says, his thumb catching a tear falling from my lashes.

Edina's arms tighten around me and I sag into her embrace, my hands gripping her arms to return the affection. I can't form the words to let her know what happened while Vlad was feeding on me. How do I tell anyone I had a fantasy about the man who attacked me? *I can't.* I need to focus on the next steps, mainly getting my damn magic back so I'll feel like myself again.

"No, you don't," Edina snaps, spinning me in her hold. "Don't you dare shut me out."

"What is it?" the werewolf asks from behind me.

"She's going to shove this down until she literally explodes," Edina says, not taking her eyes off me. "She does that."

"E—"

"No, he has to know the type of bullshit to expect from you," she insists. "I'm going to another realm and I'm not leaving you on the verge of collapse without some decent backup." She points behind me. "He's your second, which means he's the new me."

I scoff, but Edina looks over my shoulder and the werewolf wraps his arms around me like my best friend held me just moments ago. Unlike with Edina, I go rigid in his hold. My stomach clenches and my breaths quicken.

"Eyes on mine," Lowell says, turning my head to meet his glowing eyes. My lip trembles as I feel him start to take some of my pain. "Breathe," he murmurs, and I inhale sharply as more of my anxiety bleeds down the bond. When I can stand the feel of his touch, I slump back against his chest and his arms tighten.

"You don't need to shoulder this alone," Lowell murmurs. "I'm here if you need to break."

"And what? You'll hold me together?"

"You can do that yourself. I've seen it," he says, softly. "I'll be there to catch the pieces so they're easier to find when you're ready." His sincerity pierces the shell I've used to surround my fragile emotions.

"What was the panic attack about?" Edina asks.

"I..." I swallow down nausea as I try to form the words. "I said his name." Lowell grunts in understanding, but Edina still looks confused. "Archer. When Vlad...when I was..."

"When she was aroused from the bite," Lowell finishes for me.

"It's only been a day, babes," Edina says soothingly, taking my hand and squeezing.

"But what does that fucking say about me?" I counter.

"That it's only been a day," Lowell reassures. I wriggle free of his hold so I can look at him. I can't imagine what he thinks of me, but I find no judgment in his eyes. I only feel an overwhelming sense of concern.

"Do you love him?" Lowell asks, his voice remaining steady despite the swirling emotions I can feel through our bond.

"I think I could have," I say, watching his reaction for judgment that never comes. "Before he killed nine of my..."

"Nine of *your people*?" Edina finishes for me.

"Fuck, when did that happen?" I ask as the realization crashes over me. Sure, I took the crown and made moves to secure an alliance because it's what I was ordered to do. But at some point since the battle, the Dark Magic Covens became my people. My responsibility.

The weight of my tiara presses down on my head, even though the actual accessory is in the corner of the bathroom. These people have been persecuted for hundreds of years, and it stops with me. But as much as I need to restore the balance, I'll do everything in my power to make sure none of my people are hurt. Even if that means negotiating with the King. *Even if that means agreeing to a political marriage.*

I realize Lowell and Edina are staring at me, waiting for me to say something in response, but I can't share that with them. I don't think either would understand. I'm saved from coming up with a reply as Vlad appears in the doorway.

"Hey baby queen," he says, his eyes crinkled in concern. "I'm so sorry. I shouldn't have—"

"What are you apologizing for?" I ask, and he swallows hard, looking between me and the toilet. "I didn't get sick from the bite. It was because of..."

Realization crosses over Vlad's features. "Thoughts of the prince would make me nauseous too." He winks and I roll my eyes emphatically as he sits on the floor across from us.

A second later, Adriana comes in, holding ginger ale and a sleeve of crackers. "Why are we all in the bathroom?" she asks, and I can't help the laugh that escapes my lips. Lowell's arms tighten slightly around me at the sound, and I lean my head into his chest, sinking into the warmth. I catch Edina giving me an approving smirk.

Adriana pushes past the vampire and sits beside Lowell and me on the floor. She offers me the crackers, and I shake my head, but Lowell takes them on my behalf.

"You should eat something," he murmurs. He opens the package and offers me a cracker as the others start talking. I shift slightly so I sit sideways across Lowell's lap, and his free hand instantly moves to support my back.

"Do you get off on feeding me or something?" I ask before clamping my mouth shut in protest and making a face at him. He chuckles darkly and leans in.

"Food isn't what I picture in that pretty mouth when I get off, little witch," he purrs in my ear. My mouth drops open in shock and he quickly pops a cracker in it. He laughs loudly as I sputter, around the dry crumbs, finally reaching for the ginger ale to help me swallow.

"Asshole," I choke out, as his laughter continues. "That wasn't very friendly, pup."

"Who said I only want to be your friend?" he says, amusement still dancing across his features, making it hard for me to think straight. Suddenly the space between us seems minuscule, the air thickening as the bond between us pulls taut and I find myself staring at the flecks of bright yellow in his irises. I lick my lips, trying to return moisture to them, and his throat bobs in response.

"If you two are done..." Vlad's voice is a shock of ice water. "We're having an actual political conversation over here."

"How are your past sordid relationships with Fae a political conversation?" Adriana grumbles.

"One was a king," Vlad smirks. "And two were princesses, though they weren't in line for the throne so I'm not sure if that counts."

No matter how hard we try, we never end up discussing anything of importance. We just laugh and enjoy each other's company on my bathroom floor, and for a moment, I can forget the weight of the world on my shoulders.

Chapter Seven

THE MEMORIAL SERVICE MIGHT be the hardest thing I've ever done. Adriana advised me to be compassionate, but not over-emotional, but I barely make it through one speech before I'm sobbing. When the services are over, I spend more time than we have scheduled listening to stories and offering hugs when condolences just aren't enough. Luckily, Adriana is right, and most people don't blame me for the attack. They seem honored when I say a few words about our casualties.

When the Shanghai coven leader arrives, Adriana pounces on him, not even allowing him to enter the coven before she makes him swear the vow of fealty to me. She told me last night that she's worried about father and Sanderson making a play to get the new coven head on their side, so she had to act fast to ensure that we wouldn't be at a disadvantage.

Once all that is finished, Coleman comes to my room to assess my magic. Just like Vlad predicted, my magic is intact but is being suppressed by something. Unfortunately, Coleman can't tell what that something is, but he suspects the mermaids' antidote will help.

I spend the rest of the day trying out different spells with the new wand Adriana procured for me. In addition to the hellfire impeding my raw magic, it appears to have severely weakened my strength and stamina, putting me at the level of an ordinary witch. Which is fine. It's only an eighth of my usual power. *It's fine.*

A few hours after sundown, we teleport to the woods outside Vlad's house. Adriana's gray magic swirls around our little cadre and we hold hands as our lungs are squeezed and compressed until we're out of the Highlands and in the center of a wooded area that's covered in a light layer of frost. It's dark despite the full moon, the clouds blocking out the light and casting the area in shadow.

"Katie, a light please," Adriana instructs. I have half a mind to use my new phone's flashlight, but I refrain and grab my wand instead. The little orb of light sputters twice before sticking and illuminating a small circle around us. Adriana gives me an approving smile before she wraps me in a hug, telling me to be safe and disappearing in a cloud of gray smoke.

"My house is just over this hill," Vlad announces as he picks his way through the brambles covering the forest floor.

We walk in silence until I feel the kiss of a magical shield against my skin. We pass through the barrier and the forest gives way to a large sloping hill. The perfectly manicured lawn is a lush green despite the frost and runs unobstructed up to a modern mansion that's pristine white with black shutters. The house, illuminated with spotlights, is a beacon in the darkness. Vlad cuts across the grass, and we follow as he leads us to a heavy, red door.

"After you." He holds the door open, and Lowell pushes inside first, flipping on the light in the foyer before zipping off to do a security check of the enormous property.

Much like its exterior, the foyer is pristine. White walls with ornate wainscotting meet white marble floors with veins of black that match the dark iron chandelier that hangs from the vaulted ceiling. Every door off the foyer is closed, but I see a sitting room behind the grand curved staircase. Edina glares at the iron railing like it's personally offended her, and I wonder if there's any truth to the rumors about Fae and iron.

"Welcome," Vlad says, shutting the door behind us all. "Kitchen is through there." He points to a swinging door at the back of the foyer that blends into the white walls. "The bedrooms are all light-tight, not that you need it, and they each have their own bathroom attached."

He pushes the wall to the right of the front door and a hidden closet door clicks open. Vlad takes my bag before helping me out of my coat and storing both items in the broom closet. "The portal is through there."

He leads us into an office, which is all dark cherry wood and lit in a soft yellow glow. A large desk takes up most of the space, sitting in front of a wall of built-in bookshelves that are neatly organized with old tomes. There's also a blood-red fainting couch, a large wingback armchair in front of a fireplace, and a wall covered in clocks with plaques underneath indicating the location. My eyes snag on the one for Faerie which is motionless. I'm about to ask if it's broken when the second hand finally ticks.

"Oh good," Vlad says, following my gaze to the clock. "The sun just set in Faerie."

"Does that mean we're going now?" Edina asks, her face paling.

"Yep. Let's get you home, princess." Vlad pulls on a candlestick that sits on the mantle of the unlit fireplace. The whole thing swings open to the side, revealing the swirling purple mist of the portal.

Lowell enters and walks right up to Vlad, pulling him into a tight embrace that has the vampire releasing his breath in an *umph*. "Be safe, brother," he murmurs as Vlad stiffens.

"Fucking full moon," Vlad grumbles, making Lowell laugh and hug him tighter, and I'm pretty certain I see him nuzzle his neck. Vlad rolls his eyes and pats the werewolf on the back. "All right, enough. I'll only be gone a week."

"A week?" I squeak. "I thought you'd be back tonight."

"One full night in Faerie is roughly a week here," Vlad tells us. "I'll stay long enough to get Edina settled and then I'll be back. I called the Council and they'll arrive within the next four to six days. There should be enough blood in the fridge, but if not--"

"I'll take care of it," Lowell says.

"If they ask, she's my human." Vlad jerks a thumb in my direction, and my mouth pops open. "Don't get excited, baby queen. It's so they won't eat you. If they know you're mine and they still try something, I'll tear out their fangs and give them to you as earrings."

"That's...sweet?" I look at Edina, who is just staring listlessly at the portal, clutching her duffle bag like it's a life raft. I grab her shoulders and hug her tight, ignoring the bite of her freezing skin. She drops the bag between us and trembles as she returns my embrace.

"I'm meeting my birth mother," she whispers.

"I know." I squeeze her tighter. "Word your promises carefully and don't get kidnapped."

"Don't die in the lake," she responds, pulling away, and we both laugh.

"Love you," I say, cupping her cheek in my hand.

"Love you most, babes." She repeats my motion before we hug again. She backs up and sets Lowell in her sights. "If she gets hurt, I'll freeze your dick and cut your balls off."

"You really are Fae," Vlad laughs, but Edina doesn't take her eyes off the werewolf.

"I'll protect her with my life," Lowell promises. She gives him a once-over before nodding in approval.

"All right, vampire daddy," she says, tilting her head back. "Let's do this." If Vlad thinks anything about his nickname, he doesn't say it. He just grabs her bag and holds out his free arm for Edina to take.

"See you soon," I call after them as they step into the swirling mist of the portal and vanish.

Lowell and I stand silent in the study, staring at the portal for a moment before he swings the fireplace back into place. He'll have to leave it open when the council starts arriving, but for now, it's better if it remains sealed.

"Now what?" I ask.

"How much do you know about mermaids?" He heads over to one of the bookshelves, removing two large tomes bound in colorful leather and embossed in gold writing.

"Umm...their claws hurt like a bitch?" I offer, and he shakes his head, crossing the room to hand them to me.

"You study," he instructs, running a hand through his dark hair. "I'll make dinner."

I STUDY FOR MOST of the night. The information I learned about mermaids in school is minuscule and completely inaccurate, and unfortunately, the books Vlad owns are outdated. The politics have changed significantly since the Elemental Witches forced them into freshwater after the Four Kings War. Lowell does his best to fill in the gaps with what he knows, but I still feel woefully unprepared for any sort of official meeting.

Lowell hopes his position as Pack Master will allow us to meet directly with the elders, the rulers of the merpeople. We go over strategies for the meeting into the early hours of the morning but ultimately decide on a simple plan. The merpeople need to return to the oceans because their species is slowly dying in freshwater. By offering them access to the oceans, we hope to gain a remedy for my magic and allies in the war should we need them.

At dawn, the werewolf and I head into the forest towards the lake. Lowell is back to being shirtless despite the freezing temperature. He keeps running his hands through his long hair and the nervous habit has me grasping the wand in my jean pocket. He mentioned he *had* a good relationship with the mermaids in this lake, and he said something about an almost war when we were in the Highlands.

"On a scale of one to ten," I say, breaking the chilly silence of the morning, "how bad is this going to be?"

He pauses as the grass gives way to sand and we approach the lake. Sitting on a rock is a mermaid. Her back is to us, but her seafoam green hair seems to sparkle in the early morning sunlight as it cascades in gentle waves. Her creamy skin is bare to the small of her back, where iridescent black scales begin, ending in a large fin that looks like a spill of oil in the opaque water.

"Twenty," Lowell says softly. The mermaid's shoulders tense as he speaks. "Delmare?" he calls, his voice turning honied, which makes me bristle in a way I don't have time to process.

"Fuck off, Lowell," she responds, her voice melodic and seductive even with the harsh sentiment.

"I need your help," he says, moving closer to the water.

"Set one foot in my lake, and I will fucking kill you," she snaps, turning her head so we're treated to her profile and the delicate curve of her long neck.

"Del..." Lowell starts, but she dives off the rock, disappearing with a flick of her tail.

"What now?" I ask, turning to face him as the water stills, putting my back to the lake.

"Give it a second," Lowell says, and I turn back just as the mermaid resurfaces close to the shoreline in front of us.

Her unnaturally large blue eyes connect with mine and she gives me a warm smile before opening her mouth and sighing in a way my body mimics. Up close, she's even more beautiful than I thought. She has a button nose that's spattered with green freckles and plump, pink lips. Her skin has just the faintest tint of green, several shades lighter than the hair that artfully covers her bare breasts. I sigh with her again and the worry bleeds from my shoulders as I step closer to the water.

"Back down, Delmare," Lowell warns, stepping between the two of us, breaking the spell. I shake my head, clearing her residual magic from my brain. Lowell warned me that her voice could cause hypnosis, but I figured my mental walls would be strong enough to fight it.

"Are you kidding me?" she demands, the melody dropping from her voice. "You fuck up my plan for this *witch*--" she spits the word like it's a curse, "--and now you won't even let me play with her?"

"It was a terrible plan." Lowell sounds like he's had this conversation a thousand times.

"She was with the *prince*," she shrieks, and the sound makes my eardrums feel like they're about to burst. "He was in love with her! She was the perfect ransom."

"That makes you as bad as them and you know it," Lowell snaps, and Delmare pouts.

"I wouldn't have killed her," she says with a sinister smile, flipping her hair back to expose her breasts like they're some sort of prize.

"You've always been a bad liar," Lowell chuckles but doesn't lower his eyes. She sticks her chest out farther and a guttural noise spills from my lips.

"Don't you dare *growl* at me," Delmare hisses, baring her teeth which sharpen into razors. Her skin darkens to a putrid shade of green and she lifts her webbed hands from the water, revealing nails with pointed barbs attached.

The sight of the black needle-like barbs makes me see red. I reach for my wand but Lowell's hand snaps out, his fingers intertwining in mine as calming energy flows down our bond. I glare up at him as he steps in closer, tucking me protectively behind his body.

"Delmare," Lowell barks, and I'm surprised when she backs down, the barbs retracting and her teeth receding into her gums.

"Sorry, Alpha," she purrs. "So, you're fucking the witch now?" Lowell runs a thumb over my clenched knuckles in a soothing motion.

"We need to see the elders."

"That wasn't an answer," the mermaid pouts.

"You lost the right to ask me that when you fucked my Beta. We need to see the elders."

"You or her?" she asks, her voice edged with disdain.

"Both of us. We have a proposition for them." Delmare considers it before disappearing under the surface of the lake. As soon as she's gone, Lowell's shoulders drop and he releases my hand, sitting down on the beach with his eyes fixed on the water.

"She'll ask them to come up," Lowell says, answering my unasked question. I nod and sit beside him, watching the sun rise in the distance. "That was reckless," he whispers so low I barely hear him.

"What was?"

"Baiting a Siren," Lowell says. "What would you have done if I hadn't stepped in?"

"Probably nothing," I say honestly. "My magic isn't strong enough to hurt her."

"Reckless," Lowell repeats, swiping a hand down his face.

"Thank you for the input, but I don't need you to protect me," I snap. "That's not your job, pup."

"That's exactly my job, little witch. Not to mention your best friend threatened to freeze my cock off if anything happened to you."

"That *would* be a shame." Out of the corner of my eye, I see Lowell trying to fight his own smile, his anger fading to amusement. We sit in silence, watching the lake's surface, but the amusement never fades. "You have something to say?" I ask.

"You growled," he says with a chuckle.

"I don't know what you're talking about," I retort, my cheeks heating.

"Were you jealous, little witch?"

"No." My traitorous voice squeaks too loudly to be convincing. "I'm just curious. You've obviously slept with her, and I don't know how that would work with the tail and everything."

Lowell smiles fully, bringing his hand up to scratch his stubbled jaw, and then leans closer to me, his arm brushing against mine. "You're sexy when you're jealous," he breathes.

"I'm not jeal—what?" My heart jumps into my throat. Lowell starts laughing, a full-bodied sound that is impossible not to return.

"I hate you," I whine, but there's no real malice behind it.

"Lies," Lowell says. "You growled for me. I'm your new favorite person."

"Keep telling yourself that pup," I quip, turning my attention back to the lake. "How long should we wait—"

I'm cut off when a webbed hand wraps around my leg and pulls me feet first into the water.

Chapter Eight

"KATIE!" Lowell screams from the shore as I'm dragged beneath the lake's surface. The strongest sense of déjà vu plays through my mind as I thrash in the hold of my captor. The water swirls around us, but their hold on me is firm.

A figure covered from head to fin in purple scales hovers by the surface. The water swallows my warning scream, and as soon as I see Lowell's legs breach the waterline, the mermaid grabs him and drags him under with me.

I struggle, trying desperately to get to the werewolf. The water around me churns as I reach out and connect with his fingertips one second before I'm stabbed in the arm with something sharp and my body stills. I can't move, not even my eyes which burn as the lake water rushes into my open lids. Lowell must have been stabbed with the same substance because his face is set in an unmoving mask of rage.

We're dragged at a sickening pace towards the bottom of the lake. I can't see who has hold of me, but a school of mermaids circles us, guiding the two that have us held captive towards pitch-black depths. Delmare floats beside me, her beautiful features completely gone, giving way to the monster she is. She reaches up and draws a barbed fingertip down my cheek, and with speed that shouldn't be possible under the water, slaps me, her leathery green skin making my cheek heat despite the cold. She smiles sinisterly, flashing rows of sharp, blackened teeth as I can do nothing but hold my breath.

My vision blurs, the edges turning black as my lungs burn with the desperate need to breathe air. The water presses down on me, but I'm still dragged down. We're almost at the bottom, we have to be. I hold onto consciousness as long as I can, begging my body not to breathe in. Just as I feel sand brush against my outstretched fingers, my mouth opens, and I suck in water. Stars burst before my eyes, and I slip into the darkness.

I WAKE SPUTTERING, LAKE water working its way out of my stomach as I heave onto a damp stone floor. It's cool wherever I am. A faint wind raises goosebumps on my skin, but I can't observe more than the floor. I pant, gulping down air into my sore lungs.

"There, there," a slimy hand lands on my back, slapping it hard and forcing more water from my body. I push the wet strands of hair out of my face and find Delmare back in her beautiful form next to me, but she has legs instead of her tail. They're curled beneath her, completely bare. Her hair is somehow dried, even though mine sticks to my face in a sopping mess.

"How do you have legs?" I choke, my throat raw. She pushes to her feet and walks her naked body into the shadows surrounding us.

"I'm a Siren, you arrogant bitch," she coos in a way that makes me want to follow her even though she's insulting me. "We have three forms and can change between them at will."

She slams something in front of her, and it takes me a minute to see the bars. I rush at her, throwing myself against the mildew-encrusted cell door, but she holds her ground, safely two inches out of my grasp.

"Where's Lowell?" I demand, straightening my spine, and glaring at her.

"Oh, did you want to see him?" Delmare asks sweetly. I snarl at her, reaching for her again and missing. "Sorry, witch. He's standing trial for interfering in my territory when he saved you. He'll probably be executed for it." Her melodic voice has a cruel edge of laughter, and she pads down the hallway away from me.

"Wait!" I call desperately, and she halts but doesn't turn. "What do you want?"

"From you?" she laughs. "Only your body. Which we'll send to the prince in pieces if he doesn't give us access to the oceans." And with that, she disappears into the darkness.

"WAIT," I shout fruitlessly, slamming my hands against the bars and kicking it violently when I don't get a response. I gasp as pain radiates up my shin and flop onto the floor, rubbing my sore toes.

Breathe and think. I swipe my hand over my face and take a deep breath before opening my eyes again.

My cell is small, barely ten steps in each direction, made of thick stone on three sides. It has a mattress that's sopping wet in the corner, under a window a few feet above my head, and sealed shut. I can't tell for sure but based on the light coming in from the slit, I think we're at the bottom of the lake. It certainly would explain why everything is damp and smells of mildew.

I spend an indeterminate amount of time screaming Lowell's name, hoping he's being held in a cell near me. When that doesn't work, I try and tug on the bond we share, hoping that maybe I'll feel him on the other end. I know it doesn't work like Mind Magic, but I try anyway. At least I know he's not in pain.

When my eyes finally adjust to the darkness, I see a line of similarly built cells across the way. I can't tell if there are people in them, but any attempts at contact I make are met with resounding silence. I can hear running water, which makes me believe some of the cells are submerged, and I think there's a canal down the center of the hall. Thick wooden doors mark the end of the space, which I assume leads to the rest of this underwater structure.

My wand is missing from my pocket, so either someone confiscated it, or it fell out on the descent. I try to call my magic to the surface of my skin again, reaching for any bit of my power. I imagine my lightning flickering at my fingertips, something I took for granted until a few days ago, but it doesn't respond. I look for my Light next, for that kernel of sunshine that I was born with, and then finally focus on my Dark Magic. Nothing comes.

I slump down against the wall, alone with my anger and no one to take it out on but myself. I bang my head against the wall behind me enough to hurt but not enough to knock myself out while I try to figure out how not to die in this underwater prison.

THREE DAYS. BY MY estimation, that's how long I've been down here. Twice a day--I assume, but again I'm just guessing--someone floats down the canal and shoves a tray of food into my cell. They open a small slot within the bars to give me a meal, which is typically some sort of seaweed. Once, someone gave me an apple and I ate that shit up. Never did I think I'd be so happy to have a fucking apple.

Delmare also visits once a day to taunt me and tell me details of Lowell's trial. The mermaids are really pissed about him pulling me from the lake a few months ago. She tells me the whole sob story about their race dying off, which I empathize with until she starts listing how mermaids like to kill their victims. Her favorite, and what she's hoping for the werewolf, is a harpoon.

Even with her taunts, I try desperately to negotiate with her. I offer her anything and everything I can think of, money, jewels. I even tell her our plans for the Kingdom of Magic and promise her the oceans if we win the war. She just laughs and tells me she'll be back after the trial to take one of my toes to send to Archer.

I spend the rest of my time going through my non-magical training, pushing my body to its max with fighting drills and punching the air to expel some anger. When I trained with the Dragons Army, we spent a fair amount of time on hand-to-hand combat. Letting my body slip into familiar fighting routines makes me feel slightly more in control and a little less helpless.

In the middle of a set of pushups, a commotion beyond the dungeon door has me scrambling to my feet and assuming an offensive stance. I hear a distinct thud that sounds a lot like someone being thrown into a wall before everything goes quiet again. Tentatively, I press myself against the bars of my cell, straining to see farther than is physically possible.

The wooden door at the end of the cell block is thrown open, and light streams in from the hallway, temporarily blinding me. I squint and step back as a silhouette blocks some of the light and then is on the move towards my cell. Shrouded in shadow, the figure stops at my cell door, something jingling in his hand, and then the bars are thrown back.

"Hey, little witch," Lowell croons in his smooth baritone. His golden eyes catch the light from the hall, and I see them narrow as he takes me in looking for signs of injury.

My breath catches in my chest, relief seeping through me slowly. *He's okay.* Part of me wants to run into his arms and make sure he's actually here and not some weird phantom hallucination, but instead I just gawk, my mouth opening and closing like a fish.

"Pack Master," a female voice calls from the water. My eyes flit to her, and I recognize the mermaid as the one who gave me the apple. Her hair is a beautiful royal blue, and the same color of the small scales coat every visible part except her eyes. Her voice is rougher than Delmare's which means she's not a Siren and explains why she hasn't gotten out of the water. My guess is she's a water sprite.

"Katie, we gotta go," Lowell tells me, extending his hand to me. I reach out, and his fingers lace in mine as he tugs me past the other cells and into the light.

We enter a chamber that is completely made of glass save for the sand-colored stone floors. *We really are at the bottom of the lake.* Water presses all around us, only slightly illuminated by the daylight that softly trickles down through the depths. A school of fish with silver scales drift by, seamlessly avoiding the glass as they pass us and swim through an archway that bridges the glass room with a giant sandstone palace. A large wall surrounds the palace, blocking the bottom half from view, but the top is coated in a thin layer of bioluminescent algae, making it glow with a soft green light.

"Where are we?" I breathe as I watch mermaids swim into openings in the stone.

"Atlantis," Lowell says.

"Seriously?"

"No," he chuckles, shaking his head. "But I think the palace was modeled after the lost city."

I take a step forward to attempt to see the top of the tall spires when a large arm wraps around my waist and yanks me back a step. I look back at Lowell in confusion, and he simply points down at the polished stone pathway beneath our feet. Two inches from where I'm standing it abruptly ends, opening into a large central pool, where the blue-scaled mermaid waits, impatiently clicking her tongue.

"Take the hall to the right," she instructs. Lowell holds up a hand, silently telling me to wait as he creeps up to the mouth of an above-water hallway branching off the atrium. He peeks around the corner before extending his hand again, which I take.

We silently scurry down the open-air hallway, winding around curves until we reach another chamber. Unlike the previous one, this one only has a small sliver of the stone walkway, most of the room taken up by the pool in the center. With our backs to the polished stone, we inch towards the center until Lowell motions for me to wait.

"Were you found innocent?" I whisper. "Delmare told me about the trial."

His golden eyes meet mine and he gives me a mischievous smile. "Not quite." A sudden wailing of an alarm fills the hallway and Lowell's eyes widen. "Do you trust me?" he asks, and I barely have a moment to nod before he tosses me into the pool.

The water is freezing, but it washes away the dirt that coats my skin from three days of being in the cell. I breach the top swiping the remaining droplets away from my face just as Lowell pops up next to me, spraying me with water as he flings his long hair back.

A second later, the mermaid who directed us down this hall surfaces. "This is Marella," Lowell says. "She's going to get us out of here."

"How—" I gesture to the ceiling. Because literally every escape plan I devised ended with *and now we're trapped under a thousand feet of water.*

"No time to explain. Do you trust me?" he repeats and again I nod.

He motions to Marella who leans over and kisses me. Okay, *kiss* might be the wrong word...but she brushes her lips to mine and then blows air into my lungs. I balk, and suddenly I can't breathe at all. I look wildly at Lowell, who is having the same process done to him. He motions to the water.

"Under the water," Marella instructs as I sputter, and when I don't respond she shoves my head down. I open my mouth to protest and air rushes in, filling my lungs beneath the surface.

Lowell wraps his arms around my waist as Marella swims behind us and begins pushing. We kick our feet, giving us more momentum as we wind through dark, water-filled passageways, Marella guiding us the entire way.

Bursting through a large gate and out of the underwater palace, a large crowd of merpeople waits for us, hovering between the palace and the outer wall. They say something to Marella that I can't hear with the water pressing on my ears, and then they join her, forming a barrier around us. With fire-red hair and scales, one of the merfolk grabs my hands and begins pulling as Marella continues to push. Lowell has two merfolk on him as well as they tug us straight over the wall and towards the surface.

We make it halfway up when something streaks by our pack in my peripheral, followed by a bone-shattering shriek. I peek behind us and see Delmare's monstrous form directing other Sirens as she sits perched on the palace wall.

"Fuck," I swear, which comes out in a stream of bubbles. Something else is launched at us, taking out the mermaid to my left. I turn back again to see Delmare loading a cannon ...*a fucking cannon.* How does she even get a cannon to work under the water? I don't get an answer to my mental question before another cannonball takes out the mermaid directly to my right.

Several of our pack drop back to meet the problem head-on, but Marella keeps pushing us forward. She says something to the crowd and another two begin pulling us as well, doubling our speed as we rush towards the surface. There's a scream behind us, but I don't dare turn around.

Sunlight is streaming into the water, and the surface is getting closer. When we're barely feet from breaking through, one of the other mermaids grabs my face and kisses me again, sucking the breath from my lungs and causing them to burn. Someone else does the same for Lowell just as we break through the waterline, and I gulp down fresh air.

Marella surfaces behind us as we streak frantically for the beach. I pump my shoulders hard, swimming as fast as I can even though the mermaids are helping us. Another underwater shriek rises to the surface in a stream of bubbles, and I feel something brush against my foot. I inhale sharply as it wraps around my ankle, but Lowell is faster. Using strength I didn't know possible, he hauls me over his shoulder and tosses me the extra few feet to the beach. I land hard on my shoulder, rolling further onto the land, keeping an eye on the water until I see Lowell stand and run onto the sand.

"Pack Master," Marella calls and throws something that Lowell catches. "You remember how to make this?"

"Yes, thank you, Marella," he says, not stopping his backward descent.

"GO. Get to the forest. She won't be able to breach Vlad's shield." Lowell throws me over his shoulder and runs using his werewolf speed without further prompting. He doesn't stop until we reach the sloping hill in front of Vlad's house. A scream of frustration sends a flock of birds scattering from the dead branches of the forest.

Lowell and I stand on the lawn, doubled over, panting. "You think they'll join us in the war?"

I ask between breaths.

Lowell slowly turns to me, one eyebrow raised and then we dissolve into hysterics. We keep laughing even as Lowell slings his arm over my shoulder and guides me toward the entryway.

He closes the thick red door just as another bone-rattling scream echoes in the winter air.

Chapter Nine

AFTER THE LONGEST SHOWER of my life, my skin is scrubbed pink and I finally feel like I've washed the dank prison cell off my body. Wrapped in a towel, I head back into the room Vlad designated for me, which reminds me of a hotel room in its simplicity. The walls are a nondescript beige, the floor carpeted in wine with gold diamonds spotted at random intervals. There's an oak desk and a dresser, but no artwork, unless you count the full-length mirror that hangs on one wall. The large bed is made with military precision, the white and cream striped comforter tucked in without the hint of a wrinkle.

I haven't poked around, but I have a feeling the rest of the rooms in this long corridor are the same. Lowell mentioned that Vlad hosts the Vampire Council whenever they have meetings, so it makes sense that the rooms are treated like a hotel, and explains the full stock of toiletries in the bathroom.

I grab some clothes from my backpack, leaving most of my things tucked away in the magically enhanced depths. After throwing on an oversized gray sweater, leggings, and fuzzy socks, I leave the room and head down the endless hallway of identical doors until I reach the giant double staircase. After much slipping and sliding on the sleek marble, I make it to the first floor and cross behind the stairs to meet Lowell in the kitchen. I don't even get the door open before I'm overwhelmed with the scent of Italian herbs and spices that make my stomach growl appreciatively.

The kitchen is beautiful given Vlad doesn't eat food, and is complete with stainless steel appliances and black granite countertops. The white cabinets somehow stand out from the chevron patterned white-tile backsplash. There's a large island in the center with leather stools that's already set with two place settings. It's clinically pristine, and somehow still homey.

Lowell gives me a half-smile over his shoulder before turning his attention to the amazingness on the stovetop that he's already started preparing. His long hair is tied back in a low ponytail and he's predictably shirtless, but has a navy apron on over his chest and jeans. He's moving around the kitchen with ease like he's done it a hundred times before.

"That smells great," I tell him as I head over to the large fridge and open the French doors. The thing is completely stocked with fresh produce, bottles of white wine, and pouches of blood on the top shelf. "White wine okay?" I ask because I don't trust anything red in a vampire's home.

"Perfect. I'm making carbonara." Lowell turns with a spoon and holds it out for me to taste. The cream and cheese flood my tastebuds and I groan obscenely.

"Thank you for making carbs," I say as he chuckles and returns to our meal.

"Not a fan of seaweed?" I scoff and start opening drawers looking for a corkscrew when it appears in front of me, held out in Lowell's outstretched hand. "You're in Italy, I figured pasta was appropriate."

"Did you make homemade pasta?" I ask almost dropping the damn bottle of wine. "How long was I in the shower?" He chuckles, stirring his sauce while I grab the glasses off the island. They're so large they look like they can hold the entire bottle, which I take as a personal challenge. I empty the bottle between the two and deposit Lowell's at his seat before hopping up on the counter closest to the stove.

I watch Lowell work, sipping my wine as he moves around me. He reaches behind me and definitely goes out of his way to brush his knuckles along my arm as he returns with a spoon. The small bit of contact has me all tingly and I take that moment to look away, hiding my reaction with my glass. When I turn back, Lowell is directly in front of me. His hands braced on the counter on either side of my hips.

"I need to get into this cabinet," he murmurs, tapping the one beneath my legs.

I could hop down, but the way Lowell's caging me in, I'd wind up in his arms if I move any closer. Instead, I lift my legs, planting my feet on the counter and hugging my knees to my chest. He smirks and bends down, opening the cabinet beneath me, his eyes not leaving mine as he drops to a knee and reaches forward. My breath hitches and I suck my bottom lip between my teeth. Lowell slowly rises, a colander in his hand, and closes the cabinet again, leaning in closer than necessary as he does.

"Thanks." His voice dips an octave before he retreats to the stove. I release a breath, shaking away that particular bad idea and taking a large gulp of my wine.

"So, what happened with the trial?" I ask as Lowell dumps the pasta water into the sink.

"That's complicated," he says, not turning back to face me. I can see the tension in his shoulders and the bond between us give a sharp tug. I hop off the counter and circle to the seat at the island, waiting expectantly. "They decided I had cause for saving you. Which is when Delmare threatened to kill us both regardless." He continues putting the plates together.

"She did seem pretty convinced they'd vote for execution," I mumble.

"She came to your cell?" Lowell spins around, a feral look in his eye. "If she laid one finger on you—"

"She didn't," I assure him. He stares me down, unconvinced, but finally huffs out a breath of frustration and grabs the bowls of pasta, putting the steaming dish down before he takes the stool beside me. He chugs a mouthful of wine as I bite into the creamy goodness and moan in appreciation. "So good." Lowell cracks a smile and digs into his food.

"Is there any chance Marella would be able to get us the antidote to mermaid venom?" I ask, before taking another bite. Obviously, we can't count on the water sprites to align with us unless we're fighting in their lake, but that was a secondary part of this mission. The main focus was to find something to fix my magic.

"Actually, she already did." Lowell tugs something out of his pocket and slides me a sapphire scale that shimmers like it's still wet. "Water sprite scales are the antidote to Siren venom. But—"

"But?" I ask, wondering how the hell a scale is supposed to help me.

"Marella said it works like a stimulant, helping your body process the venom at an impossibly fast rate," Lowell explains.

"But you don't have venom in your system, and when there's no venom to counteract, it could make a person high."

My mouth opens and closes as my brain works around this tidbit of information. "So, I'm supposed to snort a mermaid scale--"

"Water sprite," Lowell interjects. "And you grind it up and put it in water. You shouldn't even taste it. We don't have to try, but you wanted options. And it's just us here, so if you do get high off your ass, I'll be here to take care of you." He gestures to the scale with a movement that says, *what could go wrong?* I jab my pasta with my fork, using too much force. "What is it?"

"Nothing."

"We're bonded, little witch," Lowell says simply. *Right. He can read my emotions.* I sigh heavily and grab my wine, downing half the glass in one go.

"We don't even really know each other," I say finally. "We keep getting thrown together because of a series of ridiculous, life-threatening events, but I didn't even know your name until a few days ago." Lowell considers this as he takes another bite of pasta.

"What do you want to know?" he asks, turning to me, ensnaring me with those freaking golden eyes that see straight through to my soul.

"Everything." He smiles. "I mean if you're going to be my second, we should know everything about each other, right?"

"Ask away," he instructs, not looking away even as he sips his wine. My entire body tightens as I watch his throat bob and my mind goes blank.

"Well now I can't think of anything," I grumble. "Okay start from the beginning. What's your last name?"

"Dubois," he answers.

"Are you close to your family?"

"Very. Werewolves are pack animals; we tend to be close. You?"

"Well, you met my dad," I roll my eyes and he laughs. "And I thought Adriana was dead for most of my life, so it was just my mom and me growing up. We have a...strained relationship."

"Why?"

"She expected a lot from me," I answer. "She always pushed me to be better, work harder, achieve more. She never said it, but I think she was worried I'd turn out like my father. She must be shitting a brick knowing I went to him willingly." I haven't thought of my mother's reaction to my crossing over to the dark side, but I know even if she understood my decision, she'll be worried.

"I get that," Lowell says softly, tugging his hair from its tie and then tousling it with his hands. "My father was tough on me." My eyebrows tick up at his use of the past tense. "He died when I was fifteen."

"I'm so sorry." I reach across the island and grab his hand. "Did you become Alpha after he died?"

"Just my pack," he shrugs. "I didn't become Pack Master until a few years ago. But between becoming the Alpha and helping my mom raise my sisters, my childhood was over when my father died." A heavy silence sits between us.

"You have sisters?" I ask, trying to lighten the mood.

"I have four," he says, smiling. "I'm in the middle. My oldest sister, Luna—"

"Of course her name is Luna," he pinches the hand still holding his, and I jerk it away, laughing.

"Luna is six years older. She has a husband and three pups. Then there's Lyra, who's my Beta—"

"The Beta who slept with Delmare?" I ask with my mouth full, and he nods. "Okay but seriously," I lean into him. "What did you see in Delmare? Was it the green skin? The tail?"

"Totally the tail." I laugh so hard my cheeks hurt, and Lowell joins me, humor lighting up his eyes. "You'd like Lyra," he says after we've calmed down. "She's a lot like Edina."

"Lord help us if they ever become friends," I chuckle. "And your younger sisters?"

"Twins. Laura and Leanne."

"Mom ran out of wolf names?" I tease and he leans over, grabbing my jaw using slight pressure to turn me towards him.

"That mouth is going to get you in trouble soon enough," he says. His eyes dip down to my mouth, and suddenly the humor is gone and I'm on fire.

"I've never had any complaints." I wet my lips and watch as he tracks the movement.

"Anyone ever tell you you're a tease?" he murmurs, his voice dipping to a rumble.

"Nope," I clap back, dropping my voice in the same way and drawing out the word, popping the p in a way I know he notices. He swears and lets me go, clearing his throat.

"You're going to be the death of me," he groans, and I laugh as I take another bite of my pasta.

I know logically I shouldn't be flirting with Lowell. I have a "true love" out there. But whenever I'm around him... He helps me forget the enormity of my situation. I can just...flirt and have fun.

But that's not fair to him.

I sigh, trying to ignore the creeping wave of guilt that rises.

"So, the twins?" I ask, trying to sound just as light-hearted. I know Lowell can feel the shift in my emotions but doesn't bring it up.

"They were a mistake." He laughs, bringing a genuine smile back to my lips. "They're ten years younger than me, so they were only five when my dad died. My mom had a tough time after losing him, so I basically raised them. What else do you want to know?"

I hum as I think. "How old are you?"

"Twenty-six. You?"

"Twenty," I say sipping my wine. "Have you always lived in these woods?"

"Yes. My parents moved from Provence when my mother was pregnant with me."

"That's why I couldn't place your accent," I murmur. "It's like a French/Italian hybrid. Do you speak French then?"

"Oui," he responds, and I scoff.

"Come on, pup. Even I know oui."

Lowell takes my hand and proceeds to say something that could be just a bunch of meaningless words, but the emotion behind them has my breath speeding up and my thighs clenching. When he finishes, he winks, leaving me dazed. And I know from his smirk he knows exactly how much that display affected me.

"I—" I clear my throat and finish my wine as Lowell chuckles.

"Do you know me well enough to try the scale yet?" he asks, motioning to the sprite scale.

"Not nearly. But let's grind that shit up."

"WHY ARE YOU HARPING on this?" Lowell asks, lounging in the armchair. We moved into Vlad's office so we'd be more comfortable after I drank the mermaid scale, which tasted like ass, for the record.

I huff and spin in Vlad's leather desk chair, my head hanging off the side. I had to move it out from behind the desk after whacking my skull on the corner. *Not fun.*

"Because it was a cannon! In the water!" I remind him. "How did it work? Why didn't the gunpowder get wet? Where did she get the fucking cannonballs?"

"Katie," Lowell says, suppressing a laugh at my purely legitimate query. "You're a witch who shoots lightning out of her fingers. I'm a werewolf. And currently, you're high on a mermaid scale—"

"Water sprite," I correct.

"--but 'water cannon' is too unbelievable for you?" He shakes his head.

"It just doesn't seem fair," I pout. I'm still a little salty that the water sprite scale didn't re-activate my magic. I am *not* salty about the fact that it made my whole body feel alive and invincible and--

"Ow, fuck." The world tilts on its axis. I tumble from the chair, and it dares to land on top of me. I whimper in my helplessness.

"Okay, time for bed," Lowell says, righting the asshole chair and scooping me into his arms. I'm about to protest that I can walk, but he's so warm, so I let my body go limp and loll my head into his chest.

"I'm sorry I'm a mess," I mumble against his skin, which I'm totally not shoving my face into.

"It's adorable," he responds, carrying me up the stairs to my bedroom.

I take the opportunity to study the werewolf up close, unabashedly staring at his strong jaw covered in dark stubble. His skin is tan, even though it's the middle of the winter, and where my head is resting, is a tattoo of a crescent moon. I start absently tracing the shape and I feel him tense under my hands, before relaxing into the touch. The bond between us gives a sharp tug that feels like... approval? *So weird.*

"What's so weird?" Lowell asks. *Fuck, I guess I said that out loud.* "Yes, you did," he responds to my inner monologue, which is apparently not so internal.

"The bond," I say, moving away from his tattoo to play with the ends of his dark hair resting on his shoulders. He grunts in agreement as he nudges the door to my room open and carries me over to the bed, tossing the comforter back. He lays me down gently, but my arms have a mind of their own and they stay linked around his neck as he tries to get back up.

"Little witch," he chuckles, trying to dislodge my spider-monkey grip, but I hang on. He lifts his face and he's so close that his nose brushes against the tip of mine. The air between us thickens like it's electrically charged, and his eyes darken as I feel a wave of longing pour through the bond.

"What is it you want?" he asks in that husky tone that makes my insides clench and my toes curl. I pull my bottom lip between my teeth.

What I want. What I want is for him to kiss me, to give in to the chemistry between us, damn the consequences. What I want is for him to make me come so hard that I can't remember my name, let alone the fact that I have no magic and am leading a group of people into a war that I can't help them win. What I want is the reassurance that if I admit any of this, he won't hurt me the way Archer did. And most of all, I want to know that I would still feel the same even if I was sober.

But I don't know that, so I just say, "Stay. Just for a bit?" My voice is small and cracks over the words. As if he feels every one of my mixed emotions, and he probably does, he brushes his nose against mine in a tender gesture that instantly calms me down.

"Scoot over," Lowell murmurs, and I remove my arms so he can slide into the bed next to me.

He props himself up, leaning back against the pillows, and stretches his arm out in invitation. I curl into his chest, tucking my body against his and throwing my one leg over his so we're completely intertwined. His arms fold around me and his head dips so his chin rests on the top of my hair. It's so natural. Like we've done this a thousand times before.

"Delmare told me you were going to be killed," I tell him softly as his calloused fingers idly trace the lines embedded in my scarred skin.

"You were worried about me?"

"Yes." I sink further into his arms. "It's my fault that you were on trial. That you could have been harpooned to death."

"It wasn't your...did you say harpooned?"

"That's what Delmare kept saying she was going to use to kill you," I say, propping myself up so I can look at him. "Why did you save me?"

"I would never have left you there—"

"Not today. The first time we met. Did you know it was against the rules?"

"I did," he says, his jaw clenching.

"So...why?"

"Honestly? I don't know," he says, releasing a breath. "I knew I wasn't supposed to help you. I knew Delmare planned to use you as leverage to get the mermaids out of the lake. But the second I saw you I knew I couldn't let them do that. I can't explain how or why. I just knew. So, I jumped in the water."

"What did you say to the mermaids to get you out of the trial? You never told me."

"I didn't," he responds with a sly smile.

"Oh, come on. Aren't we supposed to tell each other everything?" I say with a bounce that makes Lowell groan.

"Little witch, I need you to stop moving," he murmurs, and I furrow my brow because I have no idea why my moving would be an issue. He pointedly looks down, and I follow his gaze, realizing at some time I literally hopped on top of him and am now straddling his waist.

"Oh," I breathe with a chuckle and a not-so-accidental wriggle of my hips. I feel him harden beneath me and my mouth pops open. Lowell's hand snaps up and grabs the base of my hair, tugging me down so we're only inches apart, our bodies flush against each other.

We stay like that, breathing each other in, just one second away from blurring that line we've been treading since he pulled me from the water. Everything in my body screams at me to close the distance between us, to get swept up in the tornado of desire coursing through my body. I can feel the lust pouring off him too, I know this is something we both want.

But this wouldn't be a distraction. It couldn't be a one-time thing or even a friends-with-benefits thing. The bond between us would make it heavier, more serious.

And how can I do that to Lowell when I have a true love?

He pulls me down a little further, until our foreheads touch. "Not yet," he murmurs, his voice rumbling through my chest where we're still connected. "Not while you're high. Not while you feel that guilt that follows your arousal every time you look at me."

I swallow hard, not bothering to deny my feelings as I push myself back off Lowell and he switches positions so that he's hovering over me.

"Goodnight, little witch," he whispers and kisses my freaking forehead. "My room is right next door if you need me." And with that, he leaves the room, and I bury my face in the pillow, trying to ignore the tears burning my eyes.

Chapter Ten

SLEEP EVADES ME FOR most of the night, so I spend the rest of my buzz trying to call forth my raw magic to no avail. I don't even have my wand, so it's not like I can see if the scale enhanced the iota of magic I still possess. My high finally wears off around the same time the sun rises, leaving me wide awake with a massive headache.

Resigning myself to no sleep, I slip out of my room, still wearing the same ensemble from the night before. I carefully tiptoe past Lowell's room and down the marble stairs to head into the kitchen for coffee. I locate the grounds and the mugs with minimal issues only to spend ten minutes poking and pulling different levers and buttons until the fancy-ass coffee maker starts to work.

Once my coffee is brewed, I take my mug and explore the first floor. I pass by a dining room with a table large enough to sit twenty and continue my trek behind the stairs where there's a formal sitting room. I sit on the uncomfortable couch for one second before abandoning the room, slipping out the French doors to a covered patio that overlooks the backyard and the forest in the distance. The patio is at odds with the rest of the modern feel of the house, but the swinging wooden bench is exactly what I was looking for.

I sip the life-affirming liquid, letting it seep into my brain and clear the fog that lingers from the sprite scale. When I feel like I can tolerate the sound of other people, I dislodge my phone from my bra and open a message to Adriana telling her to call me when she can. Two seconds pass before the phone vibrates in my hand.

"What's wrong?" she demands, not stopping for pleasantries. I wince at her tone and lower the volume drastically. "I had a vision of you in jail. I've been trying to get away, but things have been so crazy here and I couldn't--"

"What's happening there?"

"—Oh, I just knew it!" she laments, not hearing me. "I knew you were in trouble. I'm on my way."

"Adriana," I shout, and she quiets. "Lowell and I are fine. The mermaids held me in a cell for three days while Lowell was on trial, but we're back at Vlad's house now. What's wrong at the coven?"

"How did you get out?" she asks.

"It wasn't the cleanest exit, and I don't think many allies were made." I pinch the bridge of my nose.

"Did you get the chance to ask about your...*problem?*" she whispers the last part.

I quickly explain the water-sprite scale debacle, leaving out the part where I mounted Lowell. "Oh, and I lost my wand," I finish as I the last of my coffee.

"I'll send over a messenger this afternoon."

"Now," I say with authority. "What aren't you telling me?" She exhales loudly into the speaker.

"You need to stay at Vlad's house for a while," she finally whispers. "Father is resisting my authority here."

"Then shouldn't I come back?"

"NO!" she bellows, making me tug the phone away from my ear. "No, Katie, every vision I have of you coming back here ends in death. You need to stay there and focus on getting allies who are loyal to you."

"The council meeting is in a few days," I tell her. "And I think Lowell has a meeting with his pack and some of the other Alphas today."

"Good," Adriana says. "Work on your stamina with the wand once it comes. I'll check with Coleman and see if he's found anything on removing the magical block."

"Thanks. Adriana if you need me, I need you to promise you'll call. You don't have to deal with Father alone." She assures me she has it handled before we end the call, but somehow I feel worse. I hate that I can't help her.

I wish Edina was here. As much as Lowell and I have developed a...whatever this is, he didn't know me at my full power, so he can't understand how debilitating this feels. I know I still have magic. I know I'll be able to get my stamina up to be competent. But I was never just competent...I was *extraordinary*. Edina would understand. She'd tell me to get off my ass and find a way to be useful, but she'd understand why it was such a blow that the sprite scale didn't work.

I put my empty mug beside the wooden bench-swing and trot down the steps into the lush green lawn to start a workout. I can at least be strong physically if I can't be strong magically. I stretch out, doing a little light yoga to wake up my spine and warm up my muscles before going through my hand-to-hand combat routine. The temperature is freezing for December, but I'm soon sweating and have discarded my sweater so that I'm only in my purple sports bra and leggings.

"You know there's a gym in the basement, right?" Lowell appears on the porch about an hour into my workout, sweatpants slung low on his hips and giving me a show of all his muscles.

"I did not know that," I pant, pausing my assault on the air. Flashes of me throwing myself at him last night flit through my mind, making me want to bury my head in the ground. "Lowell, about last night—"

"It looks like you need a partner," he says before hopping off the porch and gliding over to me. He takes up a defensive stance. "Show me what you got, little witch."

"You want to spar?" I ask, and he beckons me closer. I hesitate for a second before bouncing on the balls of my feet. "Okay, but don't go easy on me." I make the first move, which Lowell easily blocks and returns, lightly tapping my stomach as he lands a blow.

"Don't pull your punches," I insist as I get in a solid jab to his ribs. His breath releases in an *oomph* as I dance back.

"Oh, that's how it is?" he taunts and launches his fist at me. I deflect his blow, but he uses his momentum to wrap an arm around my waist and take me down to the grass. I struggle against him, but Lowell pins my hands above my head. "Now what are you gonna do?"

I inhale deeply, my chest rising and brushing against his. Lowell glances down and I capitalize on the momentary distraction to kick my legs out, wrapping them around his waist and flipping us so that I'm straddling him. I pin his arms to either side of his head. The position has our bodies flush against each other and our lips inches apart. We both pant, our breaths mingling. I know he could use his superior strength to get out of this hold, but he doesn't.

"Look at you going all Alpha," he purrs, sending vibrations through every inch of where we're connected.

"You sound surprised, pup."

"Impressed. Not surprised." I laugh breathlessly, trapped in this moment as Lowell and I stare at each other. Lowell cocks his head to the side, a silent question, but doesn't make any move to dislodge me.

"I should have guessed," a cold, familiar voice deadpans from the forest beyond us.

I look up, still pinning Lowell beneath me, and meet my mother's piercing green eyes. Her hair is in her usual tight bun, but she's wearing a simple black sweater and jeans instead of her uniform. My father and sister, both in their usual black robes, stand beside her.

"I'm sorry," Adriana says off my look. "She just showed up outside the coven screaming your name." I push off the ground, releasing Lowell and approaching my mother, aware that the werewolf is a few steps behind me the entire time.

"And now I'm bringing her home," my mother announces, and Adriana's mouth pops open. My father looks unphased, which is odd considering his lengths to ensure I was his queen.

"Hi mom," I say sweetly, looking down at my shoulder to the burn mark. "Oh, this? I'm fine. I was just attacked with hellfire. No big deal. How are you?"

"Archer said he had a mishap..." my mother trails off.

"A mishap?" I grit my teeth and Lowell snarls.

"Did you say hellfire?" she asks, her usual mask of cold indifference slipping.

"Misty, Archer attacked innocent people," Adriana says softly. "He killed children. And when Katie stepped in to stop him, he turned on her."

"Did. You. Say. Hellfire?" she demands, her body shaking. "He said he burned you, but he didn't say—"

"It was hellfire," I respond. My mother's hand drifts over her mouth and she looks like she's about to be sick. But as quickly as the emotion came on, it's gone, her mask firmly back in place.

"Where's Edina?" she asks, her eyes scanning my scar like she's seeing it for the first time. "I'm taking you both home."

"She's in Faerie."

"Foolish girl," she chastises, but it doesn't have her usual venom. Now that I'm looking for it, I can see the bags under her eyes and the grayish color of her skin. "Why didn't you come to me when she emerged? Edina is like a daughter to me. Do you think I wouldn't have helped--"

"You would have been implicated," I say simply. "If you were caught harboring a Fae, you could have lost your job, been sent to jail."

There's a heavy silence as a million unsaid things cross my mother's face. "Get your things then," she orders. "It's time for you to come back to your life."

"No." I square my shoulders, and Lowell's arm brushes against mine in silent support.

"Kathryn, perhaps you should go with her," my father says.

"Excuse me?" I demand as Adriana says, "What?" and comes to stand at my side. Anger rolls through the bond with Lowell, amplifying my own.

"You went through hell to get me here," I seethe. "Tortured me relentlessly when I was a child, all so I could lead your covens. And now you want me to just leave?"

"But you're not leading," my father intones. "You're...recovering in this..." he gestures to the mansion behind us with disgust.

"I've been gone less than a week," I growl. "Trying to find allies for a war *you* started."

"I'm just saying, your mother has access to some of the best healers in the Kingdom," he says raising his arms. "They should look you over."

"She's already been healed," Adriana spits.

"Really?" He eyes my scar. "Then why was she fighting with her fists just now and not using her magic?"

Lowell steps in before my father can realize he's close to the truth. "I'm training her to spar," he says smoothly. "You need many tactics when fighting in a war." My father's eyes narrow, but he doesn't say another word.

"Mom," I breathe, meeting her gaze again. "The balance of the Kingdom is all screwed up. It has been for centuries. You know this. You're the one who first told me."

"I never said align yourself with—" she breaks off and steps away from my father as if his mere presence is toxic.

"Seth," I hiss, turning my attention back to the man who sired me, "You can go now. Adriana will take Mom back to Headquarters." He looks like he's about to protest but thinks the better of it and turns on his heel, walking past the invisible shields before disappearing in a puff of black smoke.

Adriana breathes a sigh of relief, scraping her hand along her face as soon as he's gone.

"Can you handle him?" I ask softly, and she nods. "I'm coming back right after the Vampire Council meeting. We're not letting him get any more ideas I'm hiding because of my magic."

Adriana's eyes glaze over. "That should be fine. But if I get any visions that change—"

"Then she'll stay away," Lowell answers, and I roll my eyes. My mother watches the three of us talking curiously. I turn my attention back to her.

"The night we went to the Highland Coven," I start, "the daughter of King Baran visited me in a vision. She told me the prophecy Father always used to spout referred to me restoring the balance of the Kingdom. She gave me instructions, and the first step was aligning with the Dark Witches and Magical Creatures.

"But I need your help too," I say, walking closer to her. "You said you wanted to find a way to protect people with all forms of magic. This is it, Mom."

"A war isn't the way," she says softly.

"Neither is sitting back and not changing anything." My mother's jaw tenses and I feel Lowell take a step closer. "I don't need an answer from you now. You can think about it. But I'm not coming back with you."

"Katie..." she breathes.

"I need to do this, Mom." After a long beat of scrutiny, she nods.

"Did you bring the wand?" I ask Adriana, who looks at my mom cautiously before handing it over. My mom watches the entire exchange but doesn't speak. "The hellfire weakened my magic."

"I'll look into it." My mother turns her attention to Lowell. "Pack Master."

"General," Lowell responds, remaining firmly at my side.

"You know each other?" I ask, and Lowell nods as he and my mother continue their stare down.

"You always did have a fascination with werewolves," she says in my direction, and Lowell's eyebrows hit his hairline.

"Excuse me?" I hiss, and my mom hums derisively. "I'm not sure what you think is happening here, Mom, but a week ago the man I thought was my 'true love' attacked me. The Pack Master is my second in command, and my friend, not—"

"I didn't say a word, Kathryn," she sighs. "Adriana, take me home."

Adriana looks at me, and I nod wearily, the exhaustion of dealing with my mother hitting me in waves. They start walking towards the barrier in the wards, and I turn back to the house, beckoning Lowell to come with me.

"Kathryn?" my mom calls, and I turn to face her. "I know of factions within the Dragons that are upset with the imbalance of the Kingdom. I'll see if they're willing to help when the time comes. Is your Mind Magic still working?"

"My existing connections are fine," I tell her.

"Then I'll be in touch."

"Thank you," I say, and she gives me a small smile.

"Don't trust your father," she adds sternly.

"I don't," I assure her. Then, she and Adriana are wrapped in gray smoke, disappearing from the woods. I look back at Lowell, who has a cheeky smile on his face. "What?"

"A fascination with werewolves?" he asks with a wide grin.

"*That* was your takeaway?" I ask, rolling my eyes.

"That," his face falls slightly, "and you think Archer is your true love."

"I used air quotes around 'true love.'"

"Doesn't change anything," Lowell responds.

"That's literally what air quotes do," I point out. "They change the meaning."

"I assume 'true loves,'" he overemphasizes his now imposed air quotes, "are the witch version of mates?"

"I don't know," I answer honestly. "It's not something I heard of until I found out I had one." We reach the door, and Lowell grabs the handle, pulling it open and motioning for me to enter first.

"How do wolves know?" I ask, pausing at the threshold. "When you meet your mate?"

"I wouldn't know," he says, which causes my gut to twist in a way that I can't explain. "My sister said she felt drawn to her mate, but she only knew for sure when they slept together. It was like something snapped into place the first time they had sex, like a piece of her soul that she didn't know was missing was found."

"I don't think I've ever felt anything that profound," I admit.

"Then maybe he wasn't it. Maybe you're destined for someone else," Lowell says, offering me a small smile. I can't bring myself to tell him about the locket, tucked in the safe back at the Highlands, probably still thumping away in reminder.

"I've never been one to believe in destiny anyway," I say with a shrug.

"We're starting a war based on the words of a dead woman and a centuries-old prophecy," he deadpans.

"Other than that, *obviously.*" His laughter follows me into the house, making me feel lighter as I push the thoughts of my 'true love' away.

Chapter Eleven

I SPEND THE REST of the afternoon scouring the giant tomes
Vlad keeps in his library. One titled *Unique Elements* sounded
promising, but it said the same thing every other resource material
said on hellfire, that it's a death sentence. An entry from a past
king said the hellfire felt like "another entity with its own soul
and twisted agenda." It said he never used that facet of his magic
for "fear that it would overtake him." But then I found an article
that said the king was a raging alcoholic, so it's hard to rely on his
testimony.

When the sun starts to set, I realize that Lowell said he'd be
back from the meeting with his pack in time to cook dinner. I
wouldn't mind taking turns but I burn things in the microwave. I
barely figured out how to make coffee this morning, and that skill
is a matter of survival.

I head into the kitchen and open the refrigerator, finding a
covered dish that takes up an entire shelf. I cautiously pull it out
and see a post-it stuck to the top.

Little Witch,

Heat in the oven for 30 minutes or until cheese bubbles.

--Pup

That shouldn't make me smile.

It does anyway.

I drag the tin to the island and preheat the oven, one task I actually know how to do. As it comes up to temperature, I peek under the foil. *Lasagna.* I do a little happy dance while I refasten the tin foil and pull off the post-it before popping it in the oven. As I set the timer, I hear the front door open and slam shut.

"Hey," I call, rounding the island and heading to the kitchen door. "You're early, I just put the lasagna in the—"

I stop in my tracks as I enter the foyer. Standing in the center is a blonde woman, her hair pulled back in a bun so tight it hurts *my* hair. She wears a black pantsuit cut in a conservative style, complete with a string of pearls. She inhales deeply, then slowly smiles, revealing her fangs.

"Oh, hi," I say, trying to remain calm even though my pulse skyrockets. The vampire definitely hears the increase in my pulse because her black eyes zero in on my neck.

"Vladimir left me a snack," she says, licking her lips.

"No, I'm—" Before I can say another word, she's holding me by the throat. I scrape at her hands as I struggle for breath. She lifts me straight in the air, holding me aloft as I squirm and try to use any momentum I can to kick her.

"Fuck, you smell good," she moans, inhaling again and bringing me closer to her mouth. She licks up the length of my cheek and I swipe at her face, even though I'm starting to see black spots. "I can smell your power from here. You must taste like a milkshake."

I abandon my attempt to rip her hand off and reach into my pocket to grab my wand. With a flick of my wrist, I cast a stunning spell that hits her square in the face. It's not strong enough for her to lose consciousness, but it zaps her, and she drops me. I land in a crouch and take off running, desperately gulping down air as I go. I sprint toward the back door, vaulting over the uncomfortable couch in the formal sitting room and practically crashing through the glass.

I hear the vampire swear behind me just as I open the door. I can't outrun her, but I need to put as much distance between us as I can. I bolt down the porch stairs and take off across the open lawn, heading for the forest. Lowell's pack is somewhere out here. If I can get close to them maybe they can help me.

I make it halfway before something collides with my back and forces me down with a thud.

"I was just going to have a taste," the vampire hisses, flipping me over so I'm staring into her soulless black eyes as she straddles me, pinning my hips beneath her. "But now I'm pissed, so I think I'll drain you dry. Vladimir will have to get over it."

She rears back, her fangs exposed again and aiming for my neck. This time she's pinned my arms to my side, so no matter how hard I thrash, I can't get them free to punch her.

She's inches from my neck when a bolt of white streaks over my head and tackles her. I gasp as the vampire is thrown off me, and a giant white wolf pins her to the ground. She hisses and curses at the wolf, thrashing her body from side to side to try and escape his giant paws.

Lowell's wolf form jerks and bucks as he shifts back into a human, his muscles rippling with the effort to keep the vampire pinned. "Sybil, enough!" he bellows. The vampire pauses, looking at the naked werewolf with disdain. "She belongs to Vlad, and he'll take your fangs if she's harmed."

She huffs before her face reconfigures into a sickly-sweet smile. "Well, why didn't she just say so?"

"I fucking tried," I sputter, scrambling to my feet. Lowell abandons the vampire on the grass and looks me over.

"How did you get into the house?" I ask the vampire, who is standing and readjusting her clothes as though nothing happened.

"I took my jet," Sybil says with a dismissive roll of her eyes. "Vladimir is expecting me. Is he not awake yet?"

"He'll be back in a few days," Lowell tells her, his eyes still on me.

"I guess I'm the first," she shrugs. "Well, more should be arriving tonight. Rex at the very least. Is the portal open?" Lowell finally tears his eyes from mine and turns to our guest.

"I'll open it now. Let me get you a blood bag." Sybil heads back to the house, and Lowell puts his hand on my lower back. "Are you alright?" he asks, leaning in close. I nod and feel a wave of relief through our bond.

"I'll open the portal," I tell him when we reach the back door. "You go put pants on."

"I'll do both." He winks before disappearing in a burst of his enhanced speed, leaving me gaping after him. I loiter in the sitting room, not wanting to make small talk with the bitch vampire who just attacked me when I smell smoke.

I hear Lowell swear a second before the alarm goes off and I run into the kitchen. Sybil is sitting at the island with a crystal goblet full of dark red liquid in her hand and Lowell is swatting a dish towel at the smoke detector, either trying to knock the thing loose or dissipate the smoke around it. I'm not entirely sure. He arches an eyebrow at me and gestures to the burnt lasagna on the stovetop.

"I'm not sure whether to be concerned or impressed that you ruined this so quickly," Lowell says, a smirk ticking up the corners of his mouth.

"How?" I ask... because honestly, this is a record even for me.

"What did you set the oven to?" Lowell asks, and my face falls.

"Fucking metric system," I grumble, folding my arms over my chest. "Technically, the cheese *is* bubbling." It just looks more like tar than cheese.

Sybil scoffs. "She's funny," she says to Lowell like I'm not in the room. "I'm almost sorry I tried to kill her."

"I'm almost sorry I didn't use my wand as a stake."

"Would have been more effective than that weak-ass stunning spell you used." She bares her fangs at me, and I take a step closer, refusing to back down.

"Behave," Lowell barks just as the smoke detector stops blaring. "Both of you."

Sybil rolls her eyes but returns to her glass of blood. I pointedly sneer in her direction but walk over to the pantry, grabbing a cereal box. I take the stool farthest from the vampire and reach my hand into the box, pulling out the sugary goodness and stuffing a handful in my mouth. Lowell grabs a bowl from the cabinet and slides it over to me, but I ignore it and take another handful.

"Sybil, this is Kathryn Carmichael," Lowell says, "Queen of the Dark Magic Covens. And this is Sybil Grimwald. She owns the blood banks that supply vampires with bagged blood."

"And I'm part of the Council," she adds haughtily.

"Right." Lowell grabs the cereal box from my hand and pours himself a bowl before passing it back. "How's business?"

"Booming," she says, her cold eyes lighting. I become very engrossed in the cereal box while she prattles on about her *progeny*, business affairs in Asia, and other countless topics while Lowell nods politely. I swear she must talk for half an hour straight without pausing for a breath or a sip of blood.

"Any idea why Vladimir called the meeting?" Sybil asks Lowell. I note how she keeps calling him Vladimir instead of Vlad, so they're clearly not as close as she likes to believe.

"He'll tell you himself," Lowell responds, which makes Sybil purse her lips. "Katie, can I have a word?" He deposits his bowl in the sink and motions to the door. I bring the box with me and lead the way into the hallway. He follows on my heels, bending close to my ear and directing me to the stairs.

"My room," he instructs, and I let him lead the way upstairs to the room next to mine.

Where my room looks like a typical guest room, Lowell's is anything but. It's very clear he has made the space his own. The midnight blue walls are covered with pictures, paintings, and posters. It's all very eclectic but suits him. His bookshelf is overflowing, he may have more books than I do, and his desk is cluttered with various papers. Despite the lived-in feel of the space, the whole thing is very neat and impeccably clean.

Lowell sits on the edge of the bed, rumpling the gray comforter. "My room is soundproofed," he says by way of explanation.

My feet guide me to the oak dresser that is covered with photographs. Most are of Lowell and women who all share his dark features and olive skin tone. "Wow, you really do have a lot of sisters," I muse, putting down the cereal and picking up a photograph of the five of them.

"Speaking of," Lowell appears at my side, "go pack your things. Luna is expecting you."

"What?" I ask, putting the photo back where it came from.

"You're going to stay with my sister until the council meeting."

"Like hell I am," I shoot back at him.

"It's not safe here," he says. "You already almost died and that was only with one vampire present. There will be over twenty by tomorrow."

"But you'll be here the entire time."

"I have to play host to them until Vlad returns from Faerie. Besides, there's no room for you." There's an edge to Lowell's voice. "Even with the coffins in the basement, we have just enough room for everyone."

I decide to sidestep the 'coffins in the basement' comment, not wanting to lose momentum, but I make a mental note to return to it later.

"You're staying though," I reiterate, and Lowell nods. "Then I'll stay in here with you."

"Katie..." Lowell exhales like I'm infuriating.

"Look, these people are the leaders of the vampire community. I get the impression they're not going to follow my rule under the best of circumstances, let alone if they think I'm hiding from them." I arch my brow, waiting for Lowell to contradict me, but he doesn't.

"You stay away from the portal." He sticks his finger out like I'm a child he's scolding. I grab it and twist.

"Make no mistake, pup," I say, dragging out my scary queen voice. "You don't order me around. I might not have my magic right now, but I know my limits. And I'm still your queen." Lowell jerks his hand closer to his body, tugging me along with it. He cranes his neck down so our faces are inches apart, but I don't back away.

"Make no mistake, *Ma Reine*," he purrs, and the French floats over my skin like a caress. "As your second, it's my job to keep you safe. Even if it pisses you off."

Somehow in this exchange, he's wrapped his hand around mine, cupping it and using light pressure to keep me close. I loosen my grip on his pointer and watch as our fingers lace together, seemingly on their own accord. I'm mesmerized as his thumb brushes against mine, scoring a line of fire up my skin with each passing stroke.

"Fine," I concede, finally meeting his molten eyes. "I'll stay away from the portal."

"Good girl," he croons, still not letting go of my hand. That simple sentence sends a jolt through me that warms my cheeks. It makes me feel powerful and sexy. Lowell's pupils go wide, eclipsing his golden irises and the mix of emotions down our bond runs from amusement to pure unadulterated lust.

"I like *Ma Reine* better than *little witch*," I say. He chuckles darkly as he leans into my ear.

"Is that so, *Ma Reine*?" His voice drops so low that it feels like thunder rumbling into me, charging the air around us and making me tremble as electricity explodes from where our hands are connected. My teeth sink into my bottom lip, and I nod slowly. Lowell hums in approval and everything below my waist clenches.

"Hello? Anyone home?" a male voice yells from downstairs. Lowell sighs, dropping my hand and stepping back. I miss the closeness instantly, and I release the lust churning in my chest with a slow breath.

"Go get your stuff," he says, appearing much less rattled than I am. He crosses to the door, holding it open for me. "I'll be back in a bit."

"Do you need my room right now?" I ask, and Lowell's eyes narrow. "Great, then I'm gonna come meet some vampires."

I don't give him a second to protest before bounding past him through the door and heading downstairs.

Chapter Twelve

I STAND IN THE doorway of Lowell's room, chewing on my bottom lip as I stare at his bed. The bed we'll be sharing. I was so focused on convincing him to let me stay that I didn't think through the fact that we'd be sleeping in the same bed. *Together.*

No matter how hard I try, I can't seem to stay away from the werewolf. *It has to be the bond.* That's the only logical reason I'm feeling this pull. Under normal circumstances, I wouldn't feel so drawn to someone so quickly. Under normal circumstances, I wouldn't trust someone to this degree after everything that happened with Archer. Under normal circumstances, I wouldn't be ready to jump into bed with another man for a very long time.

But here I am. With a heavy sigh, I step into the bedroom, ignoring the way it smells like Lowell, and that his scent instantly calms me. I grab a tank top and pair of shorts from my bag and head into the attached bathroom to wash up and change.

In contrast to the small but functional bathroom attached to my room, Lowell's is huge. The white tiles are perfectly pristine and snake halfway up the wall to meet pale gray paint. The shower on the opposite side is simple, nothing special compared to the jacuzzi-style tub that sits along the back wall. If it wasn't already dawn and I wasn't exhausted, I would be tempted to hop in the tub right now, but tomorrow will suffice.

The vanity with his and hers sinks is bare, so I poke around the drawers underneath until I find a spare toothbrush and some facewash. After grabbing a towel from the full linen closet, I wash up and change into my pajamas, determined to survive this night with at least fifty percent of my dignity.

I exit the bathroom at the same time the bedroom door opens. Lowell and I stare at each other across the room, the space feeling infinitely smaller, taken up by the surmounting tension. He shuts the door, the click of the lock echoing in the silence.

"Where do you want me—" I start and Lowell points to the side of the bed closest to me. I slowly pull the comforter down and sit on the edge of the mattress.

"Are you uncomfortable, little witch?" Lowell asks, sounding truly concerned. He stands at the other side of the bed like he's afraid coming closer will make it more awkward. "I can sleep on the floor."

"No," I say too quickly. "I mean...it's fine. Unless you're not comfortable. I know you didn't want me here."

"When did I say that?" Lowell asks, mirroring my position on his side of the bed.

"Before," I say, scooting towards the center of the mattress.

"I want you to be safe, I never said I didn't want you in my bed." *And...speechless.* My heart leaps like it's trying to climb through my throat, and I'm simultaneously too hot and shivering.

"Just...stay on your side," I manage, not at all smoothly. Lowell chuckles and leans in closer.

"No promises," he whispers before grabbing a pair of sweatpants from his drawer and heading into the bathroom.

This is a terrible idea. Lowell was in my bed for thirty seconds last night and I made a fool of myself. How am I supposed to keep any sort of dignity when I spend the entire night?

I make the snap decision to take some excess pillows on my side and put them down in the center of the bed. I don't know how many Lowell thinks girls use but he gave me about ten, so the wall is high. When I'm done, I settle back on the remaining two pillows, lacing my fingers behind my head, proud of my solution.

Lowell reemerges in nothing but a pair of gray sweatpants and stares at my pillow wall. "Afraid you won't be able to keep your hands off me, little witch?"

"Hardly," I scoff, and he gives me a smirk that I immediately want to slap off his face. He doesn't say anything else as he slides into his side of the bed and starts playing on his phone.

My eyes drift closed until I feel fingers brush a stray piece of hair away from my face. I open them, finding Lowell on top of all the pillows. He leans down and his lips brush against my cheek.

"Goodnight, *Ma Reine,*" he purrs against my skin, and then with a wink, he rolls over and turns the light off, leaving my jaw on the floor.

"Goodnight," I squeak. I roll away from him, sure that I'll be up over-analyzing that moment for a good hour. But as soon as my head hits the pillow, I fall asleep.

I WAKE UP IN Lowell's arms.

No, that's wrong. *In his arms* implies that he's the one holding me when in reality, we're completely intertwined. My head is resting on his chest, my hand splayed on his stomach, and my one leg is thrown over his. And his arms are wrapped around me, holding me like he never wants me to go.

I'm a romance novel cliché.

And honestly, I'm so comfortable and I slept so well that I don't even care. You'd think the ridiculous muscles would feel like sleeping on a rock, but it doesn't. It feels like the spot I'm nestled into was made for me. Like my body was meant to be molded to his in this way.

Lowell's arms tighten, pulling me impossibly closer. He nuzzles into my hair, his eyes still closed in sleep and I'm suddenly hyper-aware of every place our bodies touch. The bond between us feels like it's singing, urging me to relax in his arms, to stay longer. But he was so sure we'd wind up in this position while I adamantly refused, and I'm not ready for him to be right about this. Or to admit what that means.

I stretch, closing my eyes and pretending to be back asleep as I attempt to roll back to my half of the bed. Lowell's arms tighten their hold and pull me right back into place. I try again, and the same thing happens when I notice his stomach gently shaking in laughter.

"Asshole," I grumble, pushing away with force as Lowell drops the façade of being asleep.

"I knew you'd have trouble keeping your hands off me," he laughs.

"How do I know you didn't initiate this? Hmm?" I ask, propping myself up on my side once I'm a safe distance away.

"I might have if you didn't do it first." Lowell runs a hand through his sleep-mussed hair as he turns on his side, his impressive biceps flexing with the motion. "Five minutes after you fell asleep, you threw the pillows across the room. You were on a mission."

"Shut up, no I..." I trail off, looking around and finding the pillows scattered around the room. Lowell laughs again and I grab the remaining pillow I have and swat at him, muttering a curse under my breath.

Lowell's phone chirps from his nightstand and he rolls to grab it as I get one more good hit with a pillow.

"Hello?" he says into the phone, his accent noticeably thicker. He starts speaking in French and I use the excuse to spring up from bed. I stretch out my back, waking my spine before grabbing clothes from my bag. I spend a little more time than necessary bent over my backpack, and the blast of lust I feel down our bond tells me Lowell definitely takes notice.

"You're drooling," I mouth as I saunter towards the bed. Lowell shakes his head, his phone call forgotten as he watches me snag my phone off the nightstand and slip into the bathroom, shutting the door behind me. I hear him mutter a curse through the wall before switching back to French on the phone, and I chuckle in my small victory.

I decide to indulge in a bath, since Lowell's is the size of a small pool, turning on the taps and adding some products lining the white tiles' edge. As the tub fills, I put a mellow playlist on my phone before heading to the sink to brush my teeth.

My reflection in the mirror stops me dead in my tracks. My hair is tousled, my cheeks are pink, and my auburn eyes are bright. I look...really happy. I watch my face fall in the reflection.

I shouldn't be this happy.

Not because of another man. Not when a week ago people died because of my romantic choices. *Nine people.* Five *children* will never get the chance to live their dreams, fall in love, and feel anything ever again. I shouldn't even be alive, let alone be happy.

I brush my teeth, refusing to look at myself again, and get in the tub as quickly as possible. I try to focus on the song playing, letting the words soothe the ache that's blossomed in my chest, but my breaths are coming in too quickly. I don't want to fall apart in front of Lowell again. I can shove this down until I have a minute to process it. I inhale as deeply as I can and sink beneath the water.

I'm bombarded with visions of people falling beside me, devoured by flames. Archer's fiery gaze floats before me in the water, the hellfire streaking in a perfectly targeted attack. An attack I taught him and was proud that he mastered. It all circles back to me, the blame is all on me. If I hadn't left my phone on so he could track me, if I hadn't mentioned I was leaving, if I hadn't been falling for him--

The scent of burnt flesh replaces the eucalyptus soap, choking me and making bile rise in my throat. My lungs burn from the smoke, the hellfire creeping in my veins. I should let it destroy me, tear me apart. It's what I deserve.

I hear my name called, but it's drowned out by the blood-curdling screams. They're dying and I can't help them.

Large hands grab under my arms and jerk me up. Cold air rushes in my lungs and I blink as water drips down my forehead and into my eyes. The world around me crystalizes, the bodies and fire replaced by tile and bathwater.

"Katie," Lowell gasps, his hands cupping my face. I shake him off, pressing my palms into my eyes, trying to shove all the pain back inside. Trying to hide from the werewolf whose terror I feel in my gut like it's my own. But the wound is exposed, freely bleeding, and I can't stop the tears.

"What happened?" Lowell demands.

"Nothing," I say, lowering my hands and wrapping my arms around my chest, trying to hold in my heart, which feels like it's about to burst through my ribcage.

"Don't bullshit me, Katie. I can feel your emotions."

"Then find a way to fix the bond," I snap, and Lowell balks.

"What do you need?" he asks softly, and I'm hit with the helplessness he's feeling. "What can I do?"

"Just leave," I rasp. "Please."

"I'm not leaving you like this."

"Fine." I stand, not caring that I'm covered in soap or completely naked. "I'll leave."

I climb out of the bathtub, wrap a towel around myself and flee into the bedroom, slamming the door behind me. Lowell doesn't follow.

I hastily dry off and dress in a warm sweater and leggings, throwing my boots on as I sprint down the stairs. I need to get out of here, to get some space and quiet my mind. I stop at the hall closet on my way, aiming for my jacket, but I find a broom instead. My fingers wrap around the wooden handle, and as soon as I get the front door open, I mount it and take off into the sky.

The sun is already on the decline, we slept through most of the day. Images of waking in Lowell's arms flash in my mind and I swear as a fresh wave of tears streaks from my eyes. I shouldn't have lashed out the way I did, but I can't deal with that guilt right now. I need to let myself go numb, so I fly higher and farther away.

Being in the air helps. The wind is strong, so I have to focus on the currents. It pulls me from my mind and lets me center myself on something real, something happening right now. It doesn't make the pain go away, but it recedes enough that I can breathe.

I don't go far, making wide circles around the mansion and the surrounding forest. I find the old campsite where I stayed with Archer and the rest of the team on his mission. The night I met Lowell. I can't believe how close we were to Vlad's house without ever knowing it was here. I didn't even register the shield when I flew over it that night, but then again, I was focused on finding the prince.

"Fucking hell," I swear, switching it up and flying away from the memory of that night. I pass over a small town, the center crowded with celebrating mortals. The sound of music and clinking champagne glasses drifts up on the winter wind. *It's New Year's Eve.*

Edina believes that the way you spend New Year's Eve will dictate how the rest of your year goes, so we always spend the night together. That way neither of us will be alone. I miss her so much that I ache; it hasn't even been a week. Even when we lived a continent apart, we were never this cut off from each other. She's my silent strength, my biggest cheerleader. And now she's in another realm for God knows how long and I've never felt so alone.

Once the sun dips beneath the horizon, I'm sufficiently numb, physically, and emotionally. My hair is still wet, and I never did get a coat or gloves. I don't trust my magic enough to attempt a warming spell while holding onto the broom, so I go back to the mansion, seeing blurs of colors flying into the door as more vampires arrive for the meeting tomorrow night.

I land on the hill and make my way inside, storing the broom in the closet and heading to the kitchen, hoping no vampires will be in the room since they don't eat food. I push the swinging door open and collide with a wall of muscle. I'm enveloped by his scent even before I look up to see his golden eyes peering down at me. A wave of relief washes through our bond as Lowell's hands grip my arms, steadying me.

"You're freezing," he says, reaching to cup my cheek in his hand. He stops himself an inch from my skin, stepping back and withdrawing his hands.

"Yeah," I say, not meeting his scrutinizing glare. I gesture to the kitchen. "I was just going to..." He steps aside, and I slide past, heading right into the walk-in pantry to look for cereal or something.

"That was awkward," Sybil intones from her perch at the counter, startling me. I look to the door, noting that Lowell is gone before I shrug. There's an Asian vampire with the strongest jawline I've ever seen sipping a glass of blood beside her.

"Why are you so sad, human?" he asks. I meet his dark brown eyes and have the strangest urge to tell him everything. Warmth spreads from my chest, urging me to go to this man, and my feet move on their own accord.

"She's Vlad's," Sybil hisses, and the man sighs in frustration as the feeling disappears.

"What did you just do?" I demand, and he chuckles over his goblet.

"Just a bit of mind control. Did you not know vampires can do that too?" he smirks. "I couldn't resist. You smell delicious."

I storm from the kitchen, slamming the door behind me. "Fucking vampires," I mutter, knowing they can hear me with their superior senses. I stalk down the marble hallway looking for a place to hide for the evening.

Chapter Thirteen

I SETTLE ON HIDING in the office, which you think wouldn't be smart since the portal is still open, but most of the vampires have been coming in through the front door, so it hasn't been bad. Though I have heard how good I smell more times than I can count.

I'm lounging on the fainting couch tucked in the corner of Vlad's office, facing the portal and the door just in case anyone comes through. The spell-book I was searching through earlier is now discarded on the floor, replaced by one of the romance novels I found tucked behind the history books. Disappearing into someone else's love story makes me feel closer to normal.

The grimoires didn't have anything useful to restore my magic, but I did find one spell that electrically charges the air around you. It's completely useless, but it might fool my father and the other coven members into thinking I still have my lightning.

The door opens, letting in a stream of fluorescent light from the hallway, contrasting with the soft yellow light illuminating the office. Lowell finds me instantly like his eyes are magnetized to my presence. He runs his hands through his hair and releases a sigh as I comically hide behind my book.

"You're avoiding me," he observes, my attempted levity not working, and I drop the book on my lap.

"Not intentionally," I fib. The silence between us stretches, and the awkwardness I feel is mirrored in the bond.

"Are you—" Lowell cuts himself off. "I'm sorry if I crossed a line."

"I'm..." I'm about to say that I'm fine but I stop myself. I'm not fine. I know I haven't dealt with all the feelings that surfaced earlier. I know it's not healthy. But honestly, I'm so wrung out that being numb is fine for now. "I'm not mad at you," I say instead.

"I won't push you to talk about it," he says. "But I'm here when you need to."

"Thank you."

"And you shouldn't be in here by yourself," he says sternly.

"Because of the vampires or because of the panic attack?"

"Both."

"So, sit with me." I sit up and scoot to the edge of the couch so he can join me. He zips to my side faster than I can register and leans against the back of the singular arm.

"Do you—" he extends his other arm along the back behind me without touching. An invitation. I nod, moving to slide closer. "Wait," he says, swinging his legs up on the couch and maneuvering me so I'm between his legs, my back leaning against his chest.

"Is this okay?" he asks, still barely touching me even though I'm lying against him.

"Yes," I admit and relax into his hold as his arms wrap around my waist and tighten around me. "I'm sorry I snapped before." He nods, keeping his promise to not talk about it, but I feel his concern through the bond as he leans forward to rest his chin on my shoulder.

"Are you this tactile with everyone?" I ask as he nuzzles into me in a way that's so wolfish and oddly soothing.

"Sure," he says unconvincingly. I chuckle and I feel the tension he's still holding drain at the sound.

I open my book, picking back up where I was as I melt into Lowell's arms, trying not to think about how freaked I was about this very issue hours ago. For whatever reason, Lowell can calm my mind and comfort me with just a simple touch. And without my usual support system, I need him. So, I'm not going to think about it too deeply, and just accept the comfort and friendship he offers.

"The fuck—" he snatches the book from my hand and his eyes skim the page. "This is dirty as hell," he says finally.

"I know, right?" I laugh. "It's Vlad's." He hands me back the book.

"Remind me to make fun of him for that later," Lowell laughs behind me. "And tell me when you get to the bottom of that page."

He leans closer, now reading over my shoulder as the couple in the book leave the bar and are hooking up in the cab. I'm not one to balk at a romance book, but something about having Lowell's hard body behind me and reading over my shoulder has a blush creeping up my neck. I turn the page and it only gets hotter as they make it back to a hotel room.

"Katie?" Lowell murmurs my name softly against my skin.

"Hmm?" I hum, turning so that our faces are inches apart.

"Happy New Year," he whispers, and my eyes find the clock, which indeed says midnight.

"Happy New Year, Lowell." I lean forward and kiss his cheek, his skin so soft and smooth right above the start of his stubble. His head tilts slightly and he brushes his nose against mine tenderly before pulling back.

The portal starts glowing, purple and blue mist swirling around as someone approaches our door. "Fucking vampires," Lowell grumbles.

"How are they even getting into the portals? They're so heavily guarded—"

Lowell scoffs. "The ones you know about."

"The ones I...how many are there?" I demand.

"Hundreds," a sarcastic voice intones, and Vlad steps through the portal. He's wearing the same suit he left in, although it's only been a few hours in Faerie and not the full week it was here. He runs his hand through his blonde hair, melting snowflakes that have gathered in his locks. His blue eyes narrow as he looks over the position Lowell and I are in. "You better not be fucking on my couch," he monotones.

"We're not," Lowell snaps.

"Just in your bed," I tease, breaking the tension. Lowell laughs, a full sound I'm helpless not to join in with. He gives me a little squeeze before I hop to my feet.

"Smartass," Vlad scoffs, and I skip over to him and throw my arms around his neck. He tentatively returns the hug, his body remaining completely stiff and making me tense in return.

"That was weird," I say pulling away.

"Yeah, don't do that again," he says with a smirk.

"How's E?" I ask, stepping back into the center of the office so he can exit the portal's threshold, but he doesn't move.

"She's..." he sighs heavily. "She's in Faerie. But she's in the palace, with her mother. So, she'll be safe as long as she can control her mouth." I swear and drag my hands through my hair. I feel she may make some enemies in Faerie before she makes friends.

"I brought you a present," Vlad announces, giving me a sly smile. "Well, two actually." He reaches into his suit jacket and withdraws a small hand-held mirror, the antique glass smudged around the edges. My fingers trace over the familiar swirling snowflake pattern etched into the back.

"How—" I start, and Vlad smiles widely.

"Edina had it," he says. "She said she'll call you when she wakes up, which should be in about three days in our time."

"And it'll work between realms?" I ask, and he nods again. I throw my arms around his neck again, a single tear falling from my cheek. "Thank you."

"We just said we're not doing this," Vlad intones, but his arms wrap around my waist much more naturally this time.

"Blame the wolf," I murmur. "He's made me all touchy-feely."

"Fucking werewolves," he deadpans, and I laugh breaking away from him. "And your other present..."

Vlad steps to the side, and a Fae male exits the portal. He is easily six feet tall and has blonde hair so pale it's almost white. His ice-blue eyes narrow at the surroundings until his long, white eyelashes obstruct them. He's all hard angles from his face to his wings, which remind me of a bat's wings if bat wings were white and glittery.

"Thanks?" I look from the Fae to Vlad, who is beaming at me like a mom on Christmas morning. Lowell steps forward, putting a protective arm around my waist as he and the Fae study each other.

"This is Eirwen, the Winter Court healer," Vlad says, gesturing to the Fae, who inclines his head slightly in acknowledgment. "He's here to fix your magic."

"What?" I gasp, finally returning Vlad's smile.

"Attempt to fix her magic," Eirwen clarifies, looking at me like I'm something that crawled out of the sewer. "I need to assess the damage. Lay on the couch."

"If anyone can help you, it's the Fae," Vlad assures me with a wink.

"Why?" I ask as I move to the couch. If looks could kill, Eirwen would have murdered me at that moment.

"Because *we* are the origin of your magic," Eirwen snaps. I look between Lowell and Vlad, who are both looking at me like I'm the crazy one for not knowing this.

"Sit, witch," Eirwen demands. His bedside manner left little to be desired before I insulted him. Now, he's just hostile. "Vladimir can fill in the gaps of your education while I work."

I lie down on the couch and Eirwen kneels on the floor behind me. He places his hands on both temples and closes his eyes. The crown of my head starts tingling before the sensation slowly spreads down to the tips of my ears. Lowell sits at the far end of the couch, lifting my legs and placing them on his lap. He kneads the arches of my feet as Vlad scans his shelf, removing a large tome.

"About a thousand years ago—" Vlad begins.

"One thousand and seventy-two years ago," Eirwen interjects, not opening his eyes. Vlad glares at him, which goes unnoticed, of course.

"One thousand and seventy-two years ago," he repeats caustically, "The Fae created the first portal from their realm into the human realm. They were searching for compatible races to breed since the Fae had fertility issues."

"To *breed?*"

"The Fae discovered humans were a compatible race that could produce half-Fae children who could live in Faerie. They also found that humans could retain magic if given to them."

"Do I want to know how they found this out?" I ask.

"No," all three men answer in unison.

"The Fae made a deal with several rulers at the time," Vlad continues. "The rulers offered male and female servants of breeding age. In exchange, Fae from each court came to the human realm and bestowed two males and two females with their magic. They also brought Magical Creatures as a sign of good faith, hoping the leaders would leave the portals open and allow the Fae to return in the future."

"And there are six courts, aren't there?" I confirm.

"The Night Court came first, bringing vampires and bestowing Dark Magic. Then came Day Court, with Light Magic and Harpies. Then the seasonal courts brought their form of Elemental Magic."

"Is that why Edina appeared to be a water elemental before she emerged?" I ask.

"Of course," Eirwen answers. "Until a Fae becomes of age and their magic manifests in full, they appear human, and their magic is weak."

"The seasonal courts are pretty self-explanatory," Vlad continues. "Spring brought centaurs and Earth Magic, Fall brought Air Magic and werewolves, Winter Court brought Water Magic and mermaids, and Summer brought Fire Magic and dragons."

"Are there really harpies?" I ask in awe. I've heard tales of the other creatures, the ones I haven't met. Centaurs guard the prison for the kingdom, and dragons live in the mountains somewhere. It became illegal to hunt them after Archer's father killed one for his Moment of Valor...not because he cared, but because he wanted to be the "last dragon-slayer."

"The harpies went into hiding about five hundred years ago," Vlad says.

"Five hundred and forty-five years ago," Eirwen interjects, and Vlad looks torn between tearing his head off or letting him finish his scan on me.

"They usually live around mountain tops. They don't love humans," Lowell adds.

"Why aren't witches told about the origin of our magic?"

"Did you ever ask?" Eirwen asks, and he's got me there. I know that magic is a dominant trait...so if I were ever to have children with a mortal, my offspring would still have magic. But I never thought to question how it got here in the first place, or why the magical community is so small. Now it makes sense.

Eirwen pulls his hands off me and hisses. He stands, moving nimbly over to where Vlad has pulled another book out of the shelves.

"You said she was struck with fire," he growls.

"She was," Vlad says with a smirk.

"Hellfire," Eirwen hisses again.

"Which is a type of fire."

"It's not," he says, looking back at me with venomous eyes. "It's not natural."

"What do you mean, it's not natural?" Lowell asks, his grip on my legs tightening as I sit up.

"There was a Summer Court Queen who wanted more power," Vlad tells me. "She manipulated her fire by--"

"She extracted magic from children," Eirwen responds. "Before a Fae emerges, their magic can be taken, but it kills them. All children are sacred, but Fae children are revered in our realm. Harming a child is the worst offense a Fae can commit. The queen gained unrivaled power by killing them, but she also damned herself."

"She was one of the Fae that came to the human realm," Vlad explains. "But she only gave hellfire to one of the males. His line was royal, so the hellfire stayed contained."

"Archer said the hellfire felt...off. Like a demon."

"It's not a demon," Eirwen says, looking at me like I'm the one who drained the magic from a child. "But it is dangerous. Especially when the caster is emotional."

"What happened to this queen?" I ask the men in the room. "You used the past tense."

"Queen Gwyneira killed her," Eirwen responds simply, motioning for me to sit back down, and then putting his hands on my head again. The tingling starts back up as his magic invades my body.

"Edina's birth mother," Vlad supplies.

"The only recorded thing to have any effect on hellfire was Queen Gwyneira's ice magic," Eirwen says. "Which is how the princess was able to save your life."

"So, it had nothing to do with the fact that my sister and I used our Light and Dark Magic at the same time?" He thinks about that. "Because my sister is clairvoyant, and that's what she saw happening."

"Regardless," he scoffs, "the princess's magic is containing the hellfire, keeping it from spreading, but it is alive within you still."

"It's what?" I breathe, feeling like someone punched me in the stomach.

"Princess Edina's ice magic surrounds the hellfire, which in turn is surrounding your Light and Dark magic. Neither form of your magic is strong enough to break through layers."

"Would that explain why she can't use her raw magic, but can use a wand?" Lowell asks, and Eirwen nods.

"So, what do I do?" I ask, looking around at the men surrounding me.

"Nothing. If the Princess removes her magic, you'll die," Eirwen says simply. "I must return to Faerie. Good luck, Queen Kathryn." He disappears through the portal without another word.

Chapter Fourteen

THE THREE OF US stare at the empty portal, reeling in the revelation the healer just gave me. I sit up and swing my legs out of Lowell's grasp.

"Katie?" I hear one of them call me, but it's like their underwater.

"Give her a minute," the other one says behind me as my feet carry me out of the office and upstairs. I'm vaguely aware of vampires moving around me in a flurry of movement, some brush against me, I think one sniffs me, but I ignore it as I retreat into the sanctuary of Lowell's room and close the door behind me.

My magic, my power...it's who I am.

It's really gone.

I rip my sweater from my body, the high neckline suddenly suffocating, and pull my leggings off. Instead of going through my bag, I open Lowell's drawers and grab one of his shirts. His scent wrapped around me makes me feel a tiny bit calmer.

I flop down on the bed, curling around myself, staring blankly ahead. I don't know how long I lie there, completely numb, but I hear the door open after a while. Quiet footsteps pad around the mattress to my side, but I don't look up. Legs come into my eye line as a body lowers to the floor, and I'm mildly surprised to see Vlad, crossing his legs as he sits on the floor in front of me.

"Lowell thinks he'll make everything worse if he comes in here," he says, his blue eyes meeting mine.

"I freaked out on him earlier," I say, my voice sounding surprisingly even, albeit devoid of warmth. We fall into silence, Vlad just watching me as I avert my eyes.

"I've been alive for a long time," he says softly. "Immortality seemed great when I was a human whose life expectancy was thirty. But no one expects the sheer amount of downtime, where it's just you and your mind. I've seen more death than you could imagine, a lot of it at my own hands." He grows quiet, organizing his thoughts.

"Do you know why I don't glamour humans into letting me feed on them? Why I only feed on a select few who give consent?" I shake my head. "A few hundred years ago, give or take, I was lost to bloodlust, and I slaughtered an entire village. When I woke, I had a child in my grasp. I hadn't drunk from her yet, but there were others—"

He breaks off, his eyes haunted. "I wanted to stake myself that night," he admits quietly. "It took a long time to come back from that. The child's face staring at me in horror, the scent of her urine mixed with her family's blood, still haunts my dreams."

"Why are you telling me this?" I ask softly, and he reaches out and awkwardly pats my head.

"When I pulled out of that darkness," he continues, "I realized I had the opportunity to make a difference, to ensure that no one else felt that level of pain at my hands or the hands of my kind. I've spent every day since devoting myself to that mission.

"People died in the Highland Coven," he continues. "It might have even been your fault."

"This is helpful," I deadpan.

"It's what you do next, baby queen, that defines you."

"What can I do without my magic?" I ask quietly.

Vlad grabs my chin, tilting it slightly so I'm ensnared in his gaze. "You lead." He releases me and stands to his full height. "I'm sending in the pup now. I can't listen to him pace outside the door anymore."

"I'm glad that nickname caught on," Lowell says from the door, and a ghost of a smile flits across my lips. I roll over to face him as he tentatively approaches the bed and sits on the edge farthest away from me.

"I know this information hurts, but tomorrow is the Council meeting," Vlad says, pausing. "I'll need you both to have your game faces on. We need to present a strong front. I'll send something for you to wear." He nods to us both and then leaves. Lowell regards me for a minute, before stretching out on his side to face me.

"I promise, Katie," he whispers, reaching out to gently brush my arm. "I will find a way to fix this for you."

"Don't make promises you can't keep," I say softly, rolling back over so that he doesn't see the tear breaking free of my lashes and trickling down my cheek. The numbness has faded and in its wake is crushing loss. Even with Vlad's words, I can't help but dwell on what's gone. Missing the comfort my lightning provided me whenever I felt this weak.

Lowell's arm slips around my waist a second before I feel the warmth of his chest press against my back. He leans forward and kisses my scarred shoulder.

"I wish I could take this pain from you," he murmurs against me. My breath catches in my chest, the pressure pushing down on me begging to be released. I hold it in, I don't want him to see me fall apart again.

"We will figure this out," he vows. My hand begins to shake where it's curled in front of me, and he threads his fingers between mine as if he senses it. His thumb strokes my knuckles and I give his hand a small squeeze, afraid that if I open my mouth to thank him, I'll end up sobbing again.

We lie in silence for so long that I think Lowell must have fallen asleep. Gingerly I roll over, and his golden eyes find my tear-streaked ones. He doesn't say anything but pulls me in closer. My head tucks in against his chest, my leg slides between his, and my non-scarred arm wraps around his waist so that I fit into his body like a puzzle piece. He kisses the top of my head before resting his chin against me. We simultaneously inhale, breathing each other in, and our bodies go lax when we exhale.

I fall asleep completely cocooned in his arms.

I CAN'T GET OUT of bed. I've been here all day, sometimes Lowell joins me but mostly I'm alone while he prepares for the Vampire Council meeting at sundown. I feel raw. I can't wrap my head around anything, but I also can't seem to compartmentalize and put it aside. The whole thing is exhausting, so I do the only thing I can manage to focus on, read the romance novel I started yesterday.

I'm just about to get to the third-act breakup when Lowell opens the door with a bang. His eyes bounce between me, in the same position I've been in, and the cup of coffee and sandwich he brought me earlier, both of which are untouched.

"Time to get up," he says, dropping the two garment bags in his arms and a bag full of cosmetics at the foot of the bed. I groan, throwing the blanket over my head and he yanks it off me in one sharp tug. My head dives under the pillow while he disappears into the bathroom and starts running the water.

"I'll get up," I murmur as he rips the pillow away from my face and tosses the rest to the floor so I'm on an empty mattress. "Just—" I sigh heavily.

"Nope," Lowell says sternly and grabs me around the waist, swinging me over his shoulder in a seamless move that no regular human could pull off.

"Lowell," I scream and start thrashing. He smacks my ass, which is on full display since I was only wearing his shirt and underwear. I start punching his back, kicking my legs. "Fucking. Alpha. Asshole," I grunt between strikes.

"That's right, little witch," he says, his grip tightening around my midsection.

"Fuck you," I hiss, and I hear the slide of the glass shower door a second before he steps under the hot water.

"Only if you ask nicely," he chides, lowering me to my feet and caging me against the cold tiles. I have half a mind to knee him in the balls, but he must sense my intention because he presses his body flush against mine so I can't move. Lowell grips my jaw, tilts it up to meet his, and gives me a slow smile.

"Go ahead, hate me," he taunts. "Fight me. Give me your worst."

"What the hell is wrong with you?" I seethe.

"I'm not letting you turn into a fucking zombie." My anger recedes slightly when I realize what he's trying to do. He knows I won't deal with my emotions, and rather than letting me shut down, he's poking the bear.

"I'm too tired to fight you," I murmur. My fight slips away like water down the drain as the spray from the shower soaks my shirt, and plasters my hair to my head like strands of limp spaghetti.

Lowell sighs as water droplets drip down his face, but he makes no move to brush them away. "Do you remember when you passed out in my arms the first night we met?"

"Yeah, you splashed water on me then too," I grumble.

"You threatened to chop my hand off," he says with a chuckle. "You were tired that day. Ready to give up. But you came back swinging."

"I was an arrogant bitch."

"Maybe a little," he pushes the hair away from my face, his hands following the curve of my face until they fall to my neck. "Some might call it fearless."

"But I had the magic to back it up," I say. "I wasn't..." I squeeze my eyes shut, not wanting him to see the truth in my eyes, the cracks in my façade rapidly turning into chasms.

"Finish that sentence," Lowell murmurs, softer, his thumb gently skating over my jawline. I shake my head, holding my breath, trying to keep everything down. "Tell me."

"Damaged," I whisper, and Lowell's chest caves in like I just punched him in the heart. He wraps his hand through the hair at the nape of my neck and pulls me closer, bending down until our foreheads are touching.

"You are not fucking damaged," he growls.

"I am. I'm broken." I can't control the sob clawing at my throat.

"You're perfect," he whispers. "Do you hear me? Magic or none, you're perfect, Katie."

I bite down on my lip to stop it from trembling, and Lowell drags his thumb across it, freeing it from my hold before pulling me into his arms and under the showerhead's spray. The water is warm, but it has nothing on the warmth radiating from the werewolf as he holds me and I fall apart again in his arms. He doesn't push, doesn't try to get me to stop crying. He just holds me until I feel strong enough to step away, and even then he cups my face in his hands and stares into my eyes. Positivity and comfort flood through the bond until my emotions feel less brittle.

"We need to get ready," I murmur, closing my eyes and releasing a deep breath. "Give me a minute to get my mask on."

"You don't need a mask."

"Vlad said—"

"I know," Lowell cuts me off. "But *you're* enough...just as you are." I swallow hard as his words seep into my skin with the water. I've never had anyone who's had such unshakable faith in me.

My spine straightens and I roll my shoulders, keeping our eyes locked the entire time. "Okay," I say, my voice sounding stronger. It's not an act. It's not my captain voice or my queen voice. It's just...me. "Okay."

"We have twenty minutes," Lowell says. "I'll leave you to get ready." He slides the fogged glass door open, and I watch as he steps out and slings a towel around his waist, leaving his wet sweatpants in place. I don't ask where he's going to finish getting ready now that he knows I'm feeling more like myself and I don't ask him to stay even though I still want him here.

"For the record, little witch," he says, turning over his shoulder once he reaches the door. "I really like you in my clothes."

"Of course you do," I snicker. "You're a fucking Alpha asshole." I launch his wet t-shirt at his face before shutting the textured glass so he can only see my silhouette.

His laughter echoes off the tiles in the bathroom as he grips the t-shirt in his hands. "There you are," he whispers before disappearing into the bedroom and closing the door with a click.

Chapter Fifteen

NINETEEN MINUTES LATER, I'M scurrying down the stairs in a black gown that fits me like a glove. It's a sleeveless sheath dress that flows seamlessly to the floor and has a high halter neckline. I used a drying spell on my hair, tied it into a sleek ponytail, and popped my tiara on top of my head at Vlad's request. I kept my makeup minimal, but added dark red lipstick, making me the picture of a Dark Queen.

I descend the stairs, my strappy black stilettos clacking on the marble. Slowly making my way to the back of the house, I hold my head high as I approach the heavy wooden door that signals the dining room. I enter the meeting with a less than graceful heave, and twenty sets of eyes turn to face me.

This room has more color than most of the house. The walls are green, brocaded with an intricate pattern that snakes around the crown molding. A large crystal chandelier hangs over the center of the large wooden table, that's surrounded by matching chairs. A cream area rug covers the hardwood floors, ending right before a large, brick fireplace.

The vampires have a three-tiered system for their 'government.' The lowest level is the monarchy, kings and queens who oversee a region. The fifteen or so monarchs sit on all sides of the table except next to Vlad, who sits alone at the head. The next level is the Council, the five vampires sitting directly behind Vlad in a row before the fireplace. While everyone in the room feels important, these five exude power. Finally, there's the Count, the one with the final say and ultimate ruler.

"Welcome, Your Majesty," Vlad says with a smile and directs me to two empty seats off to the side of the room beside Sybil, who has a laptop set up on a small travel tray. I learned that she isn't a political figure, but because she's such a powerful businesswoman in the vampire community, they allow her to attend meetings and keep their minutes.

I take the seat farthest from her and look around, waiting for the Count to arrive.

"Thank you all for coming on such short notice," Vlad begins, rising to his feet. "As you all know, we have a few matters to discuss regarding the future of vampire kind."

"Count Orlov?" Sybil says from beside me, raising her hand like she's in school. Several of the vampires in the room roll their eyes. "Might I ask why there's a human present for our meeting?"

"You may not," Vlad responds. *Of course, he's the Count.* I feel like I should be more surprised, but I just chuckle as he winks in my direction. "I called this meeting to discuss the timeline for revealing ourselves to the mortal world."

My mouth pops open. There's some murmuring amongst the monarchs, but the council remains stone-faced.

"Perception of vampires has never been more favorable in the mortal media," Vlad continues. "Aleksander can you please tell the council of your experiments in New York and Los Angeles?"

Aleksander is a vampire I met briefly two days ago when he was assigned to my room. He's a freaking giant and built like a brick house. He didn't confirm my suspicions, but I think he was a Viking in his mortal life. He actually looks very similar to Vlad, but his blonde hair is longer, coming down past his shoulders, and his eyes are lighter. He stands, adjusting the jacket of his blue suit and running his fingers through his long, blonde locks. "Sure thing, brother."

Well, that makes sense. I wonder if he means actual brother or if the same vampire made them.

"Since the 1980s, we have been experimenting by telling mortals of our existence in the nightclub scene," Aleksander says, probably more for my benefit than for anyone else's. "We gauge their reactions and then glamour away the information."

"Most of the time," Sybil scoffs beside me, but naturally with vampire hearing, everyone in the room turns to her. Aleksander's fangs pop out and Sybil returns the gesture with a hiss.

"Enough," Vlad intones, bored, and Sybil retracts her fangs immediately.

"In the past ten years," Aleksander continues, his eyes blazing in fury at the woman to my side. "The primary reaction has moved from fear to curiosity, and even arousal."

"You'd be surprised how many humans want to be bitten when they learn of our existence," the Asian king I met in the kitchen the other day adds with a cocky smile.

"What's the ratio, Alek?" Vlad asks.

"Three out of four react positively," Alek responds sitting back in his chair and extending his long leg to rest on the opposite knee.

"Holy shit," another monarch breathes.

"Good. My goal is to reveal ourselves to the media within the next two years," Vlad announces.

"There's one problem," the Asian king pipes up again, arrogance dripping from every word. "The agreement with the Kingdom. They leave us be as long as we don't draw attention to ourselves."

"That is where Queen Kathryn comes in," Vlad says forcefully, and all eyes turn to me again. "Her Majesty is planning on restoring the balance of the Kingdom of Magic."

"And she needs soldiers," Aleksander states rather than asks.

"And you would allow us to come out to the media?" Sybil sneers, and again all eyes turn to me. I swallow thickly. I really wish Vlad had given me a heads up about all this.

"I don't have an issue with it, as long as you don't out the entire Kingdom," I say carefully. "Though it would have to be discussed with the other three monarchs."

"You're restoring the four monarchs?" A brunette vampire with a Boston accent asks. "Because we all saw what a dumpster fire that was." The room chuckles.

"She'll realize her mistake soon enough," Vlad says patronizingly. "She has named me her third in command for the war and after we succeed."

"Who's her second?" someone asks. "Some witch no doubt."

"I am," Lowell says, striding into the room. He's dressed in a black suit with a black shirt molded to every inch of his muscles. He runs his hands through his unbound hair and sits next to me. I'm unabashedly staring, watching as the vampires murmur hello to him and he greets them before stretching his arm along the back of my chair.

The Boston vampire leans in closer to Vlad. "Have they fucked yet?" she asks and my mouth pops open.

"Not yet," Vlad responds with a glimmer in his eye.

"Is there—"

"A calendar pool is posted in the study beside the portal so you can place your bets on the way out. A thousand dollars per date."

"Excuse me," I sputter. Lowell just laughs like the entire room of vampires isn't betting on if we're going to have sex. No, not *if*, when. Like we're inevitable.

"Any other information?" the Boston vampire asks, ignoring my protests.

"I personally peg them as a slow burn," Vlad says off-handedly. "But no other hints."

"Vlad, seriously?" I say in a very un-queenly way.

"Sorry," he smirks, sounding anything but.

"You have to understand," Aleksander chimes in, "Immortality can be dreadfully dull if we don't find distractions. Lowell knows, he's been around us long enough."

"They did the same thing to my sister," Lowell says. "I think Vlad was the only one who guessed she'd be mated to her husband."

The room descends into commotion as they discuss their past bet. "Well forgive me if I don't want them discussing our sex life," I grumble under my breath.

"So, you admit you'll have a sex life," one of the vampires says, and I throw up my hands giving up. Lowell chuckles and leans closer to me.

"We could just go upstairs now and prove them all wrong," Lowell breathes in my ear.

"I already claimed today," Sybil tells us, taking a break from her furious typing. "I took the whole week."

"Well, I know what week it's not going to happen," I deadpan to Lowell. "Is this what all their meetings are like?"

"Pretty much," Lowell says, his thumb brushing along the back of my bare arm. "It's all pretense so they can gossip. No one will vote against Vlad when he says he wants to join a war."

"Then why—"

"He still likes to ask," Lowell says. "And he doesn't trust technology with sensitive information like this."

I watch as the vampires chat and laugh like old friends. Even the stone-faced council members have joined in. When I look back at Lowell, his eyes are on me, and I can't place the expression on his face. "What?" I ask.

"You look beautiful," Lowell says softly, and I fight the blush that creeps up my neck and over my cheeks.

I hum, pursing my lips to keep them from turning up. "Your compliments need work. Someone told me I was perfect today so...beautiful pales in comparison."

Lowell gives me a slow, sexy smile before leaning in, to whisper in my ear. I shiver as his breath tickles the shell of my ear as he opens his mouth to speak, but then he stops. My eyes open, they closed at some point, and I realize every vampire is watching us like we're their favorite reality television show.

"You sure about that slow burn?" someone asks Vlad, and the room dissolves into laughter.

"Can I assume this means you'll fight with us?" I ask, desperately trying to save some face.

"Right," Vlad coughs. "Sybil will you please call a vote."

"Monarchs," Sybil intones, puffing her chest out. "The issue is twofold. Aiding Queen Kathryn and her Dark Witches in their contest against the Elementals and beginning the process of revealing our existence to the mortal media. Raise your hands if you vote 'Yea.'" A majority of the hands raise in the air. "Nay?" A few stragglers are left. I'm not surprised that the Asian king is one of them.

"Council members, same question. Yea?" All five Council members and Vlad raise their hands in the air. "The 'yeas' have it."

"Wonderful," Vlad says. "I want all vampires over a century old to report to the Highland Coven headquarters in two months for training alongside the witches and werewolves. You'll receive the location one day before from a witch named Adriana. I hope to have a portal up and running directly to their base by then, but please make appropriate travel arrangements just in case. This meeting is adjourned."

All the vampires start getting up, breaking into little groups to chat. "Oh, one more thing," Vlad calls, and everyone stops where they stand. "Queen Kathryn is in search of the pieces of the blood oath."

A few vampires exchange glances. "Who has the scepter?" Vlad asks. No one answers and Vlad rolls his eyes. "I know it was two hundred years ago, but don't tell me you've forgotten." No response. "Sybil, can you find the minutes from that meeting?"

"It was given to me," the Asian king growls, "And I delivered it somewhere safe, as promised."

"Where did you bring it, Rex?" Vlad asks, his teeth gritted.

"To the dragons."

You could cut the silence in the room with a knife.

"I'm sorry," I intone dramatically, standing up and putting my hand out to stop the vampires from leaving. "When you say dragons, do you mean the Magical Creatures or the military I just deserted?"

"Why would I give an artifact that we're trying to keep out of the hands of the king to his military?" Rex asks with a roll of his eyes.

Vlad slumps in his chair and rubs his temple. "I told you to keep it safe."

"Tell me a place safer than a dragon's hoard," Rex counters.

"You have a fucking vault!" Vlad shouts. "How are we supposed to get it back?"

"Retrieving it wasn't one of the requirements. You said to keep it safe," Rex goes to leave again but Lowell blocks his way, looming over the vampire king like a mountain.

"Which. Dragon. Hoard?" Vlad asks through gritted teeth.

"Romania," Rex says, and Vlad slowly releases a breath.

"Thank you all," he manages once he's composed himself. "See you on March first."

Lowell steps into the hallway, allowing the rest of the vampires to trickle out of the dining room and head to either their transportation or the portal. I sit beside Vlad, my eyes glaring until he looks up at me.

"Yes?" he drawls, his brow still furrowed.

"I thought you didn't know where the pieces of the blood oath are?"

"I didn't know where they are," Vlad responds with a smirk. "I knew *who* knew where the scepter is, but that wasn't what you asked."

"Damnit, Vlad," I smack my hand down on the table in front of him. "This whole thing only works if we're honest with each other."

"Wrong," he grabs my hand, his thumb brushing over my knuckles. "This whole thing only works if we trust each other." I huff and try to remove my hand from his grasp, but he holds on tight.

"Ask me why I told Rex not to disclose the location of the scepter," Vlad says, his eyes locked on mine. I glare at him in silence, not willing to be the one to break first. But he's immortal, and clearly not in a hurry because he returns my stare for an uncomfortable amount of time.

"Fine. Why?"

"Because of you." I jerk back. "The most influential user of Mind Magic the world has seen in centuries. The Kingdom knows I'm the Vampire Count. How easy would it have been for them to capture me and have you probe my brain?

"And just because you're the most powerful, doesn't mean there haven't been others. This is why you, the leader of this movement, will never have all the information I have. But you can trust me with your life, as I trust you with mine."

I click my tongue at his explanation, but he does have a point. Lowell returns carrying a plate and three wine glasses, two filled with white and one such a dark red that I assume is blood. He sets them down on the table and slides the red glass to Vlad, before handing me mine. He then slides me the plate with a slice of cheesecake and a fork.

"So...dragons," Lowell says with a smirk over his wine glass and Vlad rolls his eyes.

"If I could justify killing a monarch, I would," Vlad says downing his glass, then grimacing. "Fucking bagged blood."

"Well, you have lots of leftovers, so get used to it," Lowell chastises and Vlad shudders.

"I'm guessing the dragon won't just give us the scepter?" I ask, already knowing the answer. "What if we offer a trade?"

"Dragons don't part from their treasure," Vlad tells me. "They'll never willingly give something like that up."

"And we don't have anything close to comparable," Lowell adds. "Unless you wanted to give them one of the other pieces of the blood oath."

"What if we promise to give it back?" I ask, hopefully, but they both shake their heads.

"They won't believe us," Lowell says.

"So, that means..."

"We need to steal from the dragons," Vlad says decisively.

Fuck.

AFTER THE SECOND PIECE of cheesecake, because a certain werewolf hogged my first piece, and a rough plan for stealing the scepter is devised, Lowell and I head upstairs to get a few hours of sleep before Adriana comes to teleport us in the morning. Vlad has a few things to do that he was incredibly vague about, so he'll join us in a couple of days.

I follow Lowell to his room, and he pauses outside the door.

"Are you..." his throat works as his eyes search mine.

"Oh," I breathe. "Right, I can go back to my room." The vampires have all gone. There's no reason for me to stay with him anymore. Lowell's mouth opens, but he must think better of what he was going to say because he closes it and just nods.

"I'll grab sheets from the hall," he says, turning from me.

He opens his door, stepping inside his room and grabbing my bag while I just stand watching him.

"Thanks," I murmur once my brain decides to work again. He nods curtly and motions for me to lead the way.

The room, mine until a few days ago, feels different now. Colder somehow, in comparison. The bed is stripped. I assume Aleksander had the wherewithal to clean up after himself. Lowell follows me with a fresh set of sheets and a comforter and tosses them into my arms before crossing back to the door.

"Goodnight," he says as he exits, closing the door behind him with a very final click. I release a breath and get ready for bed, painfully aware that the longing coming down the bond isn't just from Lowell.

Chapter Sixteen

ADRIANA ARRIVES IN A whirlwind, looking as chaotic as she did the first time I saw her. Her blonde curls are mussed, the bags under her eyes are much more pronounced than they were a few days ago, and her black cloak is haphazardly askew over her thin shoulders.

"What's wrong?" I ask immediately, but she just extends her arm, not even bothering to cross the boundary of the wards around Vlad's house.

"We need to go," she says. "Father convened a meeting with the other heads of the covens, like right now."

"I thought we were having the meeting tonight," Lowell says as we walk into the forest and take hold of her waiting hands.

"Yeah, that was the plan," she says warily, and then we disappear in a cloud of smoke.

Adriana and I both stumble during the landing, but Lowell somehow manages to keep us upright. We move quickly through the green hillside towards the moss-covered rock that marks the entrance of our underground headquarters. The clouds seem closer today like they've descended from the sky to rest along the hills, giving the valley an ominous vibe.

Adriana inhales sharply, coming to a complete stop and grabbing my hand to tug me to a halt beside her. Her gray eyes become cloudy as a vision overtakes her.

"There's someone to teach me clairvoyance," she says, her eyes darting left and right as she discerns what that means. "He'll come here but I have to go to him now." She shakes the vision clear and looks to me for permission.

"Go," I breathe, pulling her into a hug. "You need to go. This is important. I can handle Father."

She blinks as the future reveals itself to her again. "They're in the war room. You need to project strength. The tougher you are in there the more favorably they'll receive you. And don't bring up your magic."

"I won't be able to hide it forever, you know" I mutter.

"They're not ready. Talk battle strategies only."

She disappears in a cloud of gray smoke, leaving me and the werewolf standing in the exposed valley.

"Do you have a battle strategy?" he asks.

"Nope, totally gonna wing it." I press my hand onto the rock as it scans my magical signature. The rock swings aside, opening into the tunnels lit with the magical green light.

Lowell and I take off at a run, maneuvering through the labyrinth of underground pathways until we reach the war room. Loud voices float through the doorway, and I motion for Lowell to stop so we can listen in.

"You were the one who wanted her," someone bellows.

"For twenty years, all we've heard about is your child, our savior," someone else adds.

"And now you want us to start a coup?" a third voice asks.

"I'm simply saying," my father's voice intones, "that we should look into breaking the fealty vow. That way our hands are no longer tied."

"We deserve to know why," the third voice responds.

"I fear my daughter's upbringing left her soft," my father says. "She doesn't have that killer instinct that we'll need going forward. And she has no loyalty to our covens. We need someone to lead who knows better."

"And that's you Seth?" someone asks, at least they have the decency to sound pissed about it. Lowell growls next to me, but I hold up a hand to him to keep listening.

"I hoped we'd have more influence on her decisions. But then she went and made a werewolf her second in command and left the coven."

"It's a strategic move," another voice says. "We need the wolves. We don't have enough people to fight the entire Dragons army."

"She wants to restore the monarchs," my father hisses. "We haven't suffered this long to share the crown with our oppressors, healers, and dogs."

"And we're done," I say, and Lowell throws the door open so it clatters against the back wall. Everyone in the room simultaneously jumps as I stride into the room, glad I decided to wear my crown this morning.

"Morning everyone," I say cheerily. I charge the air around me to flicker with lightning, hiding my wand expertly beneath the sleeve of my sweater. Everyone in the room clambers to their feet as I round the table and come to a stop in front of my father.

"You're in my seat, Seth." I give him a false smile. Very slowly, his jaw grinding, he stands. He glares as he moves to the seat next to the head of the table, making the witches on that side slide down. "Ah ah ah," I tsk, and Lowell moves with his wolf speed to take the seat out from underneath my father.

Seth's eyes narrow to slits as everyone shifts down even further. "Kathryn," he says, pasting his smile on. "You're back early."

"Well naturally I heard the meeting was moved up, so I ran right over." I sit in the head chair, swiveling it slightly as I cross one leg over the other. "Thanks so much for waiting, I know we have a lot of important things to discuss."

The coven members all exchange glances.

"We can start with the treasonous things I heard from the hallway," I say, pulling my gaze from my father to the rest of the coven. "While my father has pointlessly spent his time developing ways to negate the fealty vow, I have been working to secure our allies. As mentioned on Christmas, the European Packs are on board with our plan. We've also secured the support of the vampires, and I'm currently amassing spies within the Dragons and should start receiving intel shortly."

"You did all that in a week?" the coven leader from Chicago, Cecelia, asks.

"Three days actually," I say with a shrug. "We had an incident with the mermaids that took up some time. We also have our ambassador to Faerie checking in within the week.

"Now," I say standing and leaning over the long boardroom-style table. "Does anyone else have a problem with sharing the crown with 'healers and dogs?'" No one moves a muscle. I turn my attention to my father. "Do not think for a minute that our shared blood grants you immunity. You have been a poison in my life since the beginning, and I have no issue cutting it out and naming a new head of the Highland Coven."

My father's teeth gnash together, and his silver hair is matted with sweat. He nods once before glaring at the other coven leaders who avoid his gaze. I smile before sitting back down in my chair.

"Now that you've heard my updates, what's been going on here?"

LOWELL SLAMS ME DOWN on the mat in the training room, which cleared out when we entered. Word of the threats I made against my father spread through the covens like wildfire, and now everyone is a little afraid of me. Which is fine. I can handle their fear.

"You're not supposed to use your extra speed," I grumble as he extends his hand to me and helps me up. I take it reluctantly and let Lowell pull me to my feet.

"I'm not," he says, bouncing on his feet and beckoning for me to attack. We've been sparring for about an hour, and I've pinned him twice. He's pinned me all the other times. And there have been a lot.

"You wouldn't guess, but I'm actually a decent fighter." I roll my neck and stretch my shoulders before putting my hands up to block my face.

"You're fighting without magic," Lowell says. "It's like having one hand tied behind your back. It's okay if it takes time to readjust."

He has a point. In the past, when I sparred against a bigger opponent, I was allowed to use both Battle Magic and physical strength. It's a lot easier to pin someone after you've mildly electrocuted them.

"We need to figure out a battle strategy," I say, launching a forward attack. "We got away without mentioning it in the meeting today but that won't last."

"What do you have in mind?" Lowell asks as he spins away from me, and I punch the air.

"I don't know," I say. "How hard will it be to get everyone to work together?" I land a couple of jabs to Lowell's ribs before he gets away from me.

"Hard, but not impossible."

"I'm back," Adriana's voice carries through the room, and pulls my attention long enough that Lowell gets the jump on me and wraps his arms around my waist. I scream in frustration as he hauls me over his shoulder, laughing the whole way as he carries me over to Adriana while I rain punches down over his back.

"How'd it go?" Lowell asks, not putting me down, but shifting so he's only holding me with one arm.

"How are you this strong?" I ask, struggling to free myself. He playfully swats at my ass and turns enough that I can see Adriana's confusion if I lift my head at an uncomfortable angle.

"It was...fine," she says tightly.

"Where's the teacher?" I ask, giving up my struggle and going limp. Only then does Lowell drop me back to my feet. I slap at his chest on the way down.

"Oh...he's..." Adriana trails off looking over her shoulder. "He's in a room. But listen, Katie—"

"Good," I say, grabbing her hand. "You can help me face off against Lowell."

"Two on one, little witch?" he says with a smirk, while Adriana's eyes widen in horror.

"Even if it were three on one, we'd be—"

Three on one.

Brow furrowing, an idea takes shape in my mind. Numbers run through my head too quickly for me to grasp them. I need paper.

"Katie?"

I push past Adriana into the hallway, smiling hastily as I pass by other witches who bustle around, making my way back to the war room. I'm vaguely aware that Lowell and Adriana are behind me as I skid inside the room and summon paper and a pen from the cabinet. I rip the pen cap off with my teeth and set to sketching out my idea.

"Use your words, little witch" Lowell says as I frantically draw diagrams.

"Right," I say around the cap before spitting it to the floor beside me. "Okay, so you know how I was a captain in the Dragons?"

"You've mentioned it," Lowell deadpans.

"So obviously I know their battle strategies, right? Which gives us a huge advantage."

"Yes," Adriana says again, her tone telling me to get on with it. I pass Lowell the drawing I've been working on before starting a new one.

"The generals argue about the best strategy for their soldiers, but in every large battle they've partaken in, the Dragons line up alternating Elements so they can cover each other. Every single soldier in the Dragons has Elemental Magic.

"Let's assume we have werewolves, Fae, vampires, and the Dark Witches on our side," I say extending my second paper. "That leaves us with only fifty percent working with magic."

Lowell shakes his head. "But the Magical Creatures have other strengths. Increased speed, heightened strength—" I shake the page at him, encouraging him to take it.

"I know. That's where my idea comes into play." He grabs the paper and studies as I continue explaining. "We need to combine into groups of three. One Witch or Fae, one vampire, and one werewolf per group. We teach them how to battle together, how to use their strengths to secure the team. That's something the Dragons won't see coming."

Lowell studies the two diagrams I've hastily drawn before passing them to my sister. "Even in the Four Kings War, the different forms of magic didn't fight together," Adriana says thoughtfully.

"Which is why this is so brilliant. When Vlad gets here, I'll work with the three of you to devise a concrete strategy, but I think that the witch is at the head of the triangle so they can shield, and the vampire and the werewolf flank them." I pause when Lowell's mouth pops open.

"What?" I ask. "Do you like it?"

"It's...Katie, it's amazing," Lowell whispers, and I feel his awe float down through our bond.

"Really?" I can't help the smile that springs to my lips.

"Really," Adriana confirms. "I'll be right back. I want to see if my teacher can help me see specifics about this plan." She takes the papers with her and disappears through the door, leaving me with Lowell, who hasn't stopped staring at me.

"People always view werewolves as expendable," Lowell says softly, "We're the muscle that goes in first. We're typically slaughtered. But this..." he moves forward and cups my cheeks in his large hands. "This puts us all on an even playing field."

"That's how it should be," I tell him. "We're fighting to restore the balance in the Kingdom. It would be hypocritical not to do that in our own army."

"I know you say that but—"

"Lowell," I rest my hands over his. "I'm not starting a war for one faction of magic. It's for all of them."

He continues staring, and my cheeks heat as his thumb brushes across my sensitive skin.

"Okay, what are you thinking?" I ask, when I can't take the silence anymore.

"I'm thinking," he starts carefully, "of all the ways I plan to worship my brilliant queen."

I try to cover the effect his words have on me with a roll of my eyes. "Anyone ever tell you you're a tease, pup?" I ask, echoing his question from a few nights ago.

"Nope," he pops his 'p' in a scarily accurate impression of me. His hands shift, falling down my neck, skimming the length of my arms until he reaches my waist and I can barely breathe. He pulls me closer, enveloping me in an embrace, which I return after my brain catches up.

"Thank you," he murmurs into my hair.

Adriana knocks on the door, and Lowell and I separate. He gives me a sheepish smile before we turn back to Adriana who looks guilty.

"What's wrong?" I ask. "Is it the plan? Did you see something?"

"What? Oh, no," she says softly. "I just...I have to introduce you to my teacher and—"

"And she's afraid of how you'll react," a male voice I recognize says from behind the door. Adriana steps aside, letting the man inside. My eyes scan his ripped jeans, faded band t-shirt, lip ring, and finally settle on his mud-brown eyes.

"Hey babe," Rodger, my ex-boyfriend sneers. "Miss me?"

Chapter Seventeen

"No. No FUCKING WAY," I fume as Rodger reaches a hand around Adriana, and she shrugs him off. "You're not clairvoyant."

"You sure about that?" he asks, flicking his tongue against his lip ring. Lowell snarls steps closer like he can shield me from this asshole. Rodger looks him over and scoffs. "Things didn't work out too well with the prince then?" he asks, his eyes dipping to my shoulder, even though it's covered in my long-sleeve top.

"Shouldn't a clairvoyant know that?" I deadpan and he smirks.

"I'm sorry," Adriana says. "If there was anyone else—"

"How did this even happen?" I demand.

"It started slow," Rodger says with a sudden vulnerability that catches me off guard. "And then it came on all at once right before..." His eyes connect to mine.

"Is that why you broke up with me?" I ask, the pieces coming together. When he broke it off, he looked spooked. I just assumed it was because he cheated or did something equally stupid.

"It was just easier dating a mortal," he shrugs. "Between your magic and your..."

"Impulsivity," Adriana offers.

"I was constantly seeing visions of you dying."

"So, the logical answer was to dump me?" I demand, but a little of the venom has drained from my words. I can't imagine seeing visions of someone I loved dying constantly. That would be torture.

"He trained with a master," Adriana continues. "And trust me, I tried to get his master to come here, but—"

"It's supposed to be me," Rodger says with surety. "I'll teach Adriana everything he taught me. How to control the visions and hone the power to see specific outcomes."

"He's going to be on his best behavior," Adriana assures me. I open my mouth to ask another question, but Rodger cuts me off.

"Yes, your strategy will work. Devise the plan privately and then roll it out to the entire army once the vampires and werewolves arrive. Have your witches start working on one-sided shields in the meantime."

"One-sided shields?" Lowell asks.

"They're exactly how they sound. They allow things to pass through one way," I explain. "So, a caster can throw up the shield and still use their Battle Magic to launch attacks. But they're hard to master."

"That's why you need to have them start working now," Rodger says. "Two months and they'll be ready by the time everyone else converges."

I know we've been heavily relying on Adriana's touch-of-clairvoyance, but there's something about having someone speak with such assurance about the future that's comforting. Even if I don't trust Rodger as far as I can throw him.

Rodger's eyes cloud over, and Adriana's cloud a half-second later. They exchange a glance and Rodger swears colorfully.

"Katie," Adriana says. "Father knows about your magic."

"How?" I demand.

"I can't see how, but he knows, and he will use it to rally people to his side." Adriana looks to Rodger who nods in confirmation. "He's in the throne room. You need to go now."

"Hang on, little witch," Lowell says, lifting me into his arms bridal style. I close my eyes tight as the wind blows around my face. I learned my lesson the last time Lowell carried me using his wolf speed never to keep my eyes open.

"We're right outside," he says a second later, and I open my eyes, staring at the door to the throne room. I haven't been back in here since I was burned. Since I was crowned.

I calm my breathing and pull my hair from my braid, shaking it loose so it doesn't look like I've been working out all morning. I release my breath and square my shoulders. Lowell's eyes flash in approval before his face hardens, becoming the Alpha leader I know he is.

"*Ma Reine*," he says, pulling the door open with a clang.

I stride with purpose into the throne room as an angry mob has assembled surrounding the dais with the glass throne. I arch an eyebrow as eyes turn towards me and Lowell takes a step closer. I can feel his aggression through our bond, and I let it quell some of the nerves I'm feeling. I might not have my magic, but I have a warrior at my back.

Take the throne, Adriana projects through our Mind Magic channel.

I take my time, sauntering through the giant cavern which is so quiet you can hear a pin drop. The hole Archer created when he tore into the mountain has been repaired, but other than that the room looks the same. The green light glows off the glass throne, which looks lackluster compared to the last time I was in here. Probably since I drained its power. By the time I reach the dais, Adriana has arrived, keeping to the back of the crowd.

I walk up the steps of the platform and pass my father without acknowledging him. Running my hand along the arm of the throne, I hope I'll feel even a sliver of the power it infused me with last time. I know it's pointless, but I can't help wishing my magic will be restored as I lower myself onto the glass. My diadem floats over the crowd, Adriana must have summoned it, and Lowell sinks to his knee in front of me as soon as it is lowered to my head.

"I hear you have more doubts," I call to the congregation as some of them also bow. The majority remain standing.

"Your majesty," one of the witches asks, approaching the dais before sinking to his knee. The boy can't be more than sixteen, he's all gangly limbs and messy brown hair, but his eyes are earnest and wide as he looks upon the throne. I recognize him from the memorial, he lost his younger sister in the attack. "Is it true?"

"Is what true?"

"Did you lose your magic?" he asks softly, his voice cracking.

"No," I whisper, smiling at him. "Not completely."

I remove the wand from my sleeve and several of the members gasp. They know I never needed a wand before. I perform a simple charm that guides the boy to his feet.

"While I was away, I saw a Fae healer," I tell the group. Swallowing thickly, I seek out Lowell, who nods for me to continue. There's strength in his golden gaze and I lean into it for a second longer before turning back to the people I plan to lead.

"He said," a lump rises in my throat, but I swallow it down, "he said my magic may never return to its full strength. The hellfire--" there are visible winces in the crowd, but I press on, "--is alive in my body and has a hold on my magic."

"Why not tell us?" the head of the Shanghai coven asks.

"I didn't know until recently how permanent it may be," I admit. "And I've had trouble coping with that. I needed time to mourn the loss of my power, to be able to say the words aloud." A tear falls down my cheek.

"How can we trust a leader who lies to us?" my father asks.

"As opposed to one who tries to usurp his daughter," Lowell hisses and there's chatter from the crowd. Mixed is the best way to describe the feelings pouring from the coven.

"Enough," Adriana says from the back of the room, and everyone turns to look at her. "We have come too far to start fighting amongst ourselves. Kathryn stepped in front of everyone in this room and took the brunt of an attack that should have killed her." She continues making her way to the front by the dais. "And in return, we reward her by questioning her loyalty and ability to lead us? Yes, she was known for her power, but she's also known for her military prowess. She can and will lead our army to victory."

She glares pointedly at my father. "Continuing on this path, dividing our forces will lead to our demise. We're stronger together."

I make a bold decision that I hope I don't regret. "I understand following me is a risk," I say carefully. "If anyone would like to renounce their fealty, I will offer you this one chance to leave, take your covens and return to your homes. All I ask is a magical vow that you'll stay out of our way and will not fight against us."

Adriana's pale gray eyes widen before glazing over. The mob has quieted, and my father smirks sinisterly.

How bad of an idea was that? I ask Adriana and she shrugs her shoulder.

Could go either way.

Lowell stands and takes a protective step closer to the throne as we wait in silence for the group to come to a decision.

No one steps forward.

"Cowards," my father swears.

"The offer extends to you, Seth," I say, the edge in my voice back. "If you believe me so unfit to lead, there's the door."

"This is my army, Kathryn."

"No, it's Adriana's army," I shoot back. "She's the one who set this up while you were in prison. She's the one with the plans, the one who built this sanctuary. You just showed up and started grabbing for power." He sneers at me but doesn't respond.

"This is the second time today that my authority has been questioned," I project to the crowd, standing in front of the throne. "Make no mistake, I've been kind and understanding to this point, but there's too much to do to prepare for this war. I will not waste another moment fighting against the nay-sayers of this coven. Any further *distractions* from our cause will be dealt with swiftly and permanently."

Lowell cracks his neck and several of the members gasp at the implication. My father glares at me before descending the dais and stalking out of the throne room. No one moves until I dismiss them with a wave of my hand. Lowell watches the dispersing crowd with rapt attention as Adriana jumps up on the dais and wraps me in a hug.

"I'm so sorry, my Katie," she murmurs.

"About Father or my magic?" She hugs me tighter, and I allow myself to sink into her embrace, burying my head in her blonde curls like I did when we were kids.

"Both will be fixed, I promise," she says as she pulls away.

"Five," Lowell says, tearing his gaze away from the now emptied-out throne room. "The Shanghai Coven leader, Sanderson, and three others followed your father."

"Do we have anyone we trust to keep tabs on them?" I ask Adriana and she points to the door. The sixteen-year-old somehow managed to blend into the shadows and is observing the dais. I beckon him closer, and he turns bright red before approaching and bowing.

"That's not necessary…" I say, searching for his name.

"Jeremy, Your Majesty," he tells me while rising.

"Did you see him back there?" I ask Lowell, who shakes his head.

"I didn't mean to eavesdrop—" Jeremy starts.

"How would you like to work directly for us?" I ask. "I need someone to keep tabs on my father and some other members and collect information. Is that something you can do?" He nods enthusiastically. "Do you know concealment charms? Silencing spells?" He nods again.

"You'll report to me," Adriana tells him. "I'll set up a Mind Magic channel, so you won't be seen with us. Infiltrate their group, hide in the shadows, do whatever you have to, but I need to know everything they plan, even if it seems unimportant."

"Yes, ma'am," he says as Adriana takes out her wand to create the channel. Without another word, he takes off in the direction my father went.

"What's next?" Lowell asks.

"Food," I say. The day is pressing down on my shoulders and making me exhausted. "And we need to solidify the plan for stealing the scepter. And I want to try to set up a meeting with the king."

"Why?" Lowell and Adriana ask in unison.

"If we can avoid an all-out war, I want to," I tell them.

"Why don't we try and talk to your mom instead?" Adriana suggests. "Maybe she can broach the subject, so we don't get killed on sight."

"She's got a point," Lowell agrees.

"Fine," I acquiesce. "Adriana, can you grab dinner and meet us in the war room?"

Adriana nods and runs off. I flop back on the throne, swiping my hand over my face as Lowell and I sit in a rare moment of silence. "I thought the throne might restore my magic," I admit.

"I know," Lowell murmurs, stepping to the side and petting my hair. I lean into the contact, letting my eyes drift closed.

"We could have died five times over today," I say, and Lowell grunts in agreement. "This is my life now, isn't it? Just waiting for someone to get balls big enough to try and kill me. Or overthrow me."

"Looks that way," Lowell says, continuing to stroke my hair.

"We could run," I muse. "I'm sure Vlad has a safe house somewhere we could crash in. Forget the war. Forget the Kingdom. We could live as mortals."

"You want to run away with me, little witch?"

"It'd be irresponsible to run away without my second," I say.

"Of course," Lowell smirks.

"And we'd have to take Adriana, so don't get any ideas about it being romantic."

"Never crossed my mind," Lowell says, and I meet his eyes. He patiently waits as I groan and stand up. We both know we're not going anywhere. We're in it now.

"Does Vlad even have a safe house?" I ask.

"It's fucking gorgeous."

"Damn it," I grumble as we descend the dais. "We'll call that plan b."

I TAKE A DEEP breath and roll my shoulders. Lowell is beside me, his hand on the small of my back, as we stand in the drafty hallway. I stare at the closed wooden door, hearing the muffled conversation behind the rock walls.

"You can do this," Lowell murmurs, and I feel a rush of pride flow down our bond as I lift my hand and knock on the door. The conversation stops and the sound of footsteps gets closer and closer.

"Katie?" An older woman opens the door, her hair stark white. She offers me a warm smile, her eyes bouncing between me and the werewolf for a moment before reaching out and wrapping me in a hug. "It's good to see you."

"You too, Mrs. Coleman," I gasp as she tugs me tighter.

"You're supposed to call her Your Majesty." Coleman's granddaughter, Chrissy, intones from inside the room. She's only a few years younger than me, and would always visit me in the barracks whenever she was visiting her grandparents.

"No, you don't," I smile as Mrs. Coleman ushers us inside.

Their room is a different setup than mine. While my room is a beautiful studio, this is a three-bedroom apartment. We enter into an all-purpose room with three adjoining rooms and a bathroom. Mrs. Coleman walks over to the little kitchen-like alcove, complete with a sink, cabinets, and a full-size pantry. The large kitchen table is positioned between the kitchen and a sitting area with two large sofas, where Chrissy sits thumbing through a tabloid with Archer on the cover.

"Chrissy, come boil this," Mrs. Coleman calls over her shoulder as she fills a tea kettle. Chrissy rolls her dark-lined eyes and calls a fireball to her hand as she crosses the sitting area. My body stiffens. Lowell is immediately there, his arm slung low around my waist.

"You're okay," he murmurs, as I struggle to breathe. I haven't been around an open flame since the attack. I had no idea the sight of flames would trigger me so strongly.

"Katie?" Coleman comes out of one of the rooms off the main space, his warm smile dropping when he sees me. "What's wrong?"

The healer gestures to the wooden table, and Lowell guides me into one of the five chairs. He stands behind me, placing his hands on my shoulders and simultaneously blocking my view of the kitchen. I reach up and squeeze the hand on my shoulder in silent thanks.

"How's everyone settling in?" I ask Coleman, who eyes me and the werewolf curiously.

"Fine, fine," he says. "It's nice having everyone in one space." Chrissy scoffs from the kitchen alcove.

"Chrissy, give us some privacy," Coleman orders. Chrissy opens her dark-painted mouth to retort, but the whistle of the tea kettle silences her. Coleman looks to her with authority I've never been on the receiving end of, and his granddaughter huffs a sigh and stomps off through the door, slamming it behind her. "I swear to magic, that girl. Were you that bad when you were sixteen?"

"I was worse," I laugh. "Next time you see my mother just ask her."

Coleman hums as his wife comes in a tray piled high with mugs of tea, honey, and cookies. She looks at Lowell and then back to the chair until he gets the hint and sits beside me. Satisfied, she kisses her husband on the cheek and he beams up at her. A feeling I can't identify floats down the bond between Lowell and me, but as Mrs. Coleman leaves the room, so does the feeling.

"They didn't have to go," I protest, but Coleman waves me off.

"You have something important to ask," he surmises, and I nod, swallowing hard. *Why is this so hard?*

"Adriana mentioned that you're running counseling for some of the coven members," I start slowly. Lowell's hand finds mine beneath the table and he laces our fingers together.

"I am," he says. His voice is soft and patient, not at all pressing.

"I was wondering..." I release a breath. "I've been having panic attacks," I confide, biting the inside of my cheek. I squeeze Lowell's hand so tightly I think I'd break his bones if he were human. "I think I might have PTSD."

Coleman waits as a tear trickles down my cheek. "And I need help," I admit. Lowell switches hands so he can slide his arm around my shoulders. "Do you think you could find time for private sessions with me?"

"Of course, Katie," Coleman says, and some of the weight crushing my chest eases. "As much time as you need."

I nod, the tears flowing from my eyes as I release Lowell's hand. He reaches out, adding a spoonful of honey to my tea before handing me the steaming mug. "Thank you," I murmur to them both.

"Can I ask a few questions?" Coleman asks, and I nod as I sip the tea.

Lowell and I stay in the healer's apartment for hours. Coleman asks gentle questions about my anxiety attacks and general mental state. He believes my self-diagnosis was correct, and that I might also be experiencing survivor's guilt. Coleman recommends a mood-stabilizing tonic for me to take daily that should help reduce anxiety attacks and depressive feelings.

I leave Coleman's feeling like a weight has been lifted off my chest. For the first time in a week, I can breathe.

Chapter Eighteen

I STEP INTO MY room, leaving Lowell in the hall to go to his setup next door. I'm not sure how he conned Adriana into giving him that room, but I'm glad because even the little distance has our bond pouting. That's literally what it feels like.

The familiarity of the room is like a warm blanket, and I move around in the dark, taking comfort in the familiar feel of the plush carpet beneath my feet. I flick my wand to turn the magical lights on so I can find my pajamas, and shriek when I come face to face with Rodger in all his naked glory, lying on my bed in what can only be described as a Burt Reynolds pose.

"What the hell are you doing?" I scream, scrubbing at my face like I can physically claw the image from my brain. I hear the bed creak and open my eyes a sliver, which is a horrible mistake because I get an eyeful of Rodger's very erect, very pierced cock. "Please put that away."

"You sure you want that?" he asks, his voice dipping to an octave that makes me want to vomit.

"Yes, that's exactly what I want," I say.

"I don't think you do," he says. "Whether you like it or not, I know you. And you hate being alone."

"I do not," I seethe, opening my eyes. Rodger is close enough that I can feel his derisive puff of air. "And so, what if I do? Everyone hates being alone."

"Not true," Rodger says, taking a step back and bending down to pull his jeans on. "Some people love it. But you can't handle it. Probably something to do with your asshole dad and emotionally distant mother."

I gape at him, my mouth opening and closing like a fish as he puts a shirt on over his tattooed chest.

"It's especially bad when you're stressed or feeling inadequate at work," he continues, sitting back on the bed to put on his shoes. "And with the attempted coup, I figured I'd help take the edge off." He stands and crosses back to me, arms open in offering.

"I appreciate the concern," I say through gritted teeth, "but you can fuck right off."

"No worries," he says, putting his hands in the air. "You know where to find me when you're ready. It's been what...a week or two since you and the prince went up in flames?" He laughs at his own joke and I swear if my lightning were working I would have electrocuted him by now. He brushes past me and heads for the door.

"Oh," Rodger pauses, turning back to me, "don't fuck the wolf if you're looking for a rebound. He's in love with you."

"Fuck off, no he's not."

"Okay, babe," Rodger says, laughing as he shuts the door behind him.

I pinch the bridge of my nose trying to reconcile everything Rodger just said. I continue stewing over his words as I strip the bed, balling up the sheets and tossing them so hard they knock over the hamper. I use my wand to summon a new set and guide them onto the bed while I rummage in my bag until my hand wraps around cold metal. I know it's wishful thinking that Edina will call tonight, but I've kept the mirror close by ever since Vlad gave it to me.

I flop down on the bed, resting the mirror on my chest and trying to banish Rodger's words. I hate that he got in my head and makes me question myself. He knows nothing about me. Maybe when I was eighteen and chasing after a rock star I couldn't be alone, but I'm not that girl anymore. I've changed a lot in the past few months.

Then why do his words hurt?

"As much as I've missed your tits, I'd much rather see your face." I scream as the melodic voice comes from my chest, and I yank the mirror away to find Edina's smirking face filling the frame.

"Are you trying to kill me?" I laugh, clutching my heart as it beats wildly. Her laugh floats through the mirror.

When I can breathe again, I notice that Edina's blonde hair is done in an elaborate up-do, short wisps of hair fluttering down around her slender face. To the casual observer, she would look fine, but I can see the emotion welling in her sapphire eyes, the subtle pallor to her usual tanned skin.

"What's wrong?" I demand, pushing the pillows behind me away so I can sit up straight.

"I miss you so fucking much," she squeaks. She looks over her shoulder and even with her head turned I can see her scowl. "Can I have the room please?"

Edina holds up a finger for me to wait as I hear the patter of feet across a rug and the click of a door. She waits, her pointed ears twitching as she listens. Finally, she breathes a sigh of relief and turns back to the mirror.

"I should be asking you what's wrong," she says, her eyes narrowing. "Some dude name Eirwen stormed in here and told me I need to call you immediately. And then he acted like I owed him a fucking favor for telling me." She rolls her eyes.

"My magic is fucked," I answer, honestly. "But I'm okay right now. Lowell and Vlad helped."

"Is that your way of telling me you had a threesome?" We laugh, but Edina's smile doesn't meet her eyes.

"Tell me about Faerie," I insist.

"I haven't seen much," she says. "It's all ice and snow and people to match. I asked about soldiers fighting with us, but they gave me the runaround. I'll try again today."

"You can come home if it's too much."

"No," she says resolutely. "I'll be fine. I grew up on the Upper East Side. I know how to handle ruthless people who smile in your face while trying to stab you in the back."

"Well fuck," I breathe. "Are you sure?"

"Yeah," she says, giving me a too-wide smile. "So, if the wolf and vampire daddy *helped* you—" she accents the statement with a wink, "—why do you look upset?"

"It's nothing..." I trail off as she fixes me with the rise of an eyebrow. "My father tried to overthrow me twice today. Oh, and Adriana's new clairvoyance teacher is Rodger...who apparently only broke up with me because he kept seeing all the ways I would die. But that didn't stop him from appearing naked on my bed tonight spouting some psychological bullshit about how I hate being alone."

"Huh," Edina says thoughtfully. "And that's bothering you because you're considering sleeping with the wolf."

"No," I sputter. "I'm not..."

"Mhmm," she intones, her mouth a flat line. "Okay, so two things. One...Rodger is a fuckwit."

"Accurate."

"Two," she sighs heavily. "How many times have you almost died in the past year? Hell, the last week."

"Where are you going with this?"

"My point is, if you don't want to be alone, don't be alone. Especially not when there's a hot as fuck werewolf who wants to be the one to keep you company."

"What about the necklace?" I ask softly.

"I would be honest with Lowell about it," Edina says. "And for all you know it's my heartbeat you're hearing."

"That would make things so much easier," I laugh. "Do Fae have true loves? Or mates or whatever?"

"Yes." Her tone is clipped and a shadow dances across her eyes. "I have to go soon babes, but can I ask a favor before I do?"

"Always."

"Can you call my parents? Tell them what's going on? It's the New Year there, right?" I nod. "They'll worry when I don't show up for my last semester."

"I'll take care of it," I assure her. "The second things get too hard there, you come straight home. I'll tell Vlad to leave the portal open for you."

"Okay," she murmurs. "Love you."

"Love you most."

The mirror goes dark, and I toss it into the drawer on my nightstand before turning off the light.

A WARM ARM BRUSHES across my stomach. My eyes blink open as I roll to my back, turning until I see a pair of golden eyes glowing softly in the darkness. Lowell is propped on his side, his free hand drawing fire along my midsection, gently lifting the fabric of my tank top with each pass. His gaze is intense, and I swallow under the heat of it.

"Miss me?" I ask lightly. His hand moves to my jaw, his knuckles running the length of it before his palm turns and his fingertips gently guide my face closer to his. "Lowell..." I whisper, unsure if I'm pleading for him to stop or keep going.

His lips brush against mine briefly before he pulls back, waiting for permission. I don't give myself a moment for guilt or worry as I close the distance between us, drawing his bottom lip between my teeth. It's all the permission he needs.

We crash together, the tension between us finally snapping as he positions his body over mine. His long hair cascades around us, creating a curtain blocking out the rest of the world. I moan as Lowell's tongue teases my lips as I open for him. Our kiss deepens, becoming frantic, our hands roving all over each other's bodies as my legs part so that he can seat himself between my thighs.

His hands slide down the strap of my tank top, and he moves his mouth over the exposed skin, groaning when my bare breast pops free into his waiting mouth. He draws my nipple between his teeth, and I whimper as he takes a long pull, gently scraping against my sensitive flesh before licking away the hurt.

Lowell moves to my other breast, showing it the same attention while his hand slips lower until he's toying with the waistband of my shorts. Instinctively, I raise my hips and he chuckles as his mouth follows the same trajectory, taking his time, drawing out the anticipation. His stubble is rough along the soft skin of my stomach, the sensation making goosebumps erupt all over my body. He slips my shorts down, following them down and then nibbling his way back up my legs before hovering over my sex.

He gazes into me as I lie bared before him. My breaths are fast and shallow, my chest rising and falling quickly as he slowly draws his tongue up my center. My resulting gasp ticks up the corners of his mouth and he flashes me a smile right before he returns his attention to my clit. I cry out, my eyes closing and my hands fisting in the sheets as his tongue teases, licking and sucking until I see stars. He slides a finger inside me, curling it deep within me and spiking my pleasure.

"Please," I whisper, my orgasm building. I reach forward, wrapping his short hair in my fingers to guide him even closer. *Wait.*

I jerk upright and find hazel eyes staring back into mine. Archer smirks, his finger still pumping in and out of me as he slowly licks me as I thrash to get away.

"Come for me, love," Archer says before his mouth collides with my clit again and white-hot fire erupts around us.

I JACK-KNIFE UP IN bed, my hand flying to my chest as I pant. My skin is dewy and every one of my nerve endings ignited from the mix of arousal and fear. I focus on the darkness surrounding me, letting the pitch-black room clear the images of my nightmare. I take a long deep breath, in through my nose and out through my mouth. Then another. Then another until my heart rate slows.

I lie back down, curling onto my side and wrapping my arms around a pillow. I'm wired. Wide awake. My instinct is to seek out company, to find Lowell or Adriana or even work out to expel some of the excess energy. But I'm okay. It was just a dream, I'm not in any danger. There's no panic rising in my chest.

I feel slight concern through the bond. It feels tentative, like an unasked question. Lowell probably felt everything I was feeling, so I can only imagine he must be ready to jump to the rescue. But somehow, the slight question, the small worry says so much more than if he burst down my door. He's always so attuned to what I need, and tonight I need to prove that I can handle this myself.

I send a wave of reassuring calm down the bond, promising I'm okay. A moment later, I feel the same comfort returned to me. It's like a warm hug that lights me up from the inside out. It eases the remaining pressure in my chest, and I can't help but smile. We pass this invisible comfort back and forth until I feel so warm and fuzzy that I drift into a dreamless sleep.

Chapter Nineteen

IT'S BEEN SIX WEEKS since we arrived at the Highland Coven. Six weeks of non-stop preparations and training. Every morning, I run physical endurance training for all members of the covens. The Dark Witches drill Battle Magic and one-sided shields all afternoon while Adriana works with me to increase my stamina and dexterity with a wand. My magic has gotten decent under Adriana's watchful eye. My individual spells are fine, not anywhere near the strength they used to be, but I can hang with the rest of the witches. I've learned how to set up Mind Magic channels with my wand, but shields are still proving difficult for me.

As much as I hate to say it, Adriana's clairvoyance has gotten much more specific under Rodger's tutelage, and he's been a real asset around the coven. Lowell has been gone for almost three weeks, traveling around Europe to get the other packs ready to come to the Highlands. Vlad comes and goes on his own accord, usually hanging around for long stretches when Lowell is away. We all agreed that the scepter would have to wait after my father's attempted coup. Rodger keeps assuring us he'll get a vision for when it's safe, but the fates have been quiet so far.

I walk into the training room in just my sports bra and leggings, my hair secured in a battle-ready braid. I try to sneak in some extra magical training on the nights I don't have therapy with Coleman. The room is cleared out as it usually is after dinner, save for one person and I can't stop the smile that springs to my lips.

"Hey, pup," I call and Lowell spins around from whatever he's doing at the far end of the training room, a wide smile that mirrors my own gracing his stubbled jaw. He's only in a pair of grey joggers, which just isn't fair. My eyes snag on his chest, a usual occurrence, but today there's a large pinking scar over the muscle.

I walk over and reach for it. He winces when I run my fingers along the line of skin that's well on its way to being healed.

"I didn't feel this," I murmur. I should have felt his pain through the bond. "What happened?"

"It's fine, little witch." I arch an eyebrow. "It was just a little disagreement with one of the packs. Nothing I can't handle."

"A little disagreement?" I repeat. "You heal fast, the fact that it's still there—"

"You're cute when you worry," Lowell says, grabbing my hand and pulling me into a hug. I nestle into his chest, carefully avoiding his injury, and the bond gives a sigh of relief. Whenever he's gone for long stretches it feels like the bond between us is desperate.

I reluctantly release him, pursing my lips because I'm sure there's more of a story, but I can tell he doesn't want to get into it. My eyes fall on the small table he has set up lined with guns. Everything from a machine gun to a pistol.

"What the hell are those?" I ask, and Lowell smiles conspiratorially.

"Since you don't have Battle Magic," he says, grabbing my shoulders and turning me to face a set of targets, "You need a weapon."

"And a gun was your answer? You know it's no match against magic. It'd be blown up before I even got a shot off."

"It'll make me feel better about leaving if you're armed," he says. "And if you know how to use it."

He lifts a little pistol with a silencer and starts showing me how to hold it, stand, and prattling on about other things about this weapon I am not interested in using. But I indulge him until he turns to the closest target, a cardboard cutout about twenty feet away.

"Why don't you give it a shot?" he asks, and I arch an eyebrow. "Two hands."

I flick off the safety in a practiced motion and lift the gun with one hand. I fire twice at the closest target, before firing off shots at the farther targets. Once I finish with the one on the back wall, I survey my marks. Two shots in each, one in the head and one over the heart.

"You could have just said you knew how to shoot," Lowell intones.

"I was in the fucking military," I remind him with a cheeky smile, putting down the pistol and picking up a shotgun.

I cock the gun and shoulder it, looking down the barrel and lining up my shot. I feel Lowell at my back one second before earmuffs are lowered onto my head and glasses are put in front of my eyes. His proximity unsettles me slightly, so I take an extra second to release the tension in my arms before shooting the farthest target again. Perfect bullseye.

I pull the earmuffs down and grimace. Guns have no finesse. I'm sure some will say there's an art to shooting, but I've never seen it. Even when you're using magic in a battle, there's something beautiful about it. There's nothing beautiful about a bullet.

"I had a feeling you wouldn't like the guns," Lowell says as he crosses to one end of the training room and grabs something tucked behind a stack of mats. He keeps his hands behind his back as he prowls back over to me. "I brought you a present."

I hold my hands out expectantly, but he shakes his head. "Close your eyes," he whispers, and I arch an eyebrow in defiance. "Close. Your. Eyes," he repeats, his voice dipping in a way that makes my mouth dry and my eyes close.

My breath hitches as Lowell's hand skims along my calf, and my tongue darts out to moisten my lips. "Lift this leg," he commands, tapping my thigh and I reach out to grip his shoulder to steady myself as I do as I'm told. "Good girl."

Fuck. He's playing dirty today. Something leathery slides up my leg, but I barely register it as Lowell's fingertips brush the material of my leggings. My core clenches as he tightens the strap so it fits snugly around my thigh. His fingers drift back down and away, trailing a line of fire before I lose the contact and have to fight the urge to pout.

"Open," he says, and my heart thrashes at the sight of him on his knees before me. I force myself to tear my gaze away from him and look at my thigh, at the empty holster.

"Umm..." I start as Lowell rises, his head dipping down low enough that I can feel his breath on my lips when I look up. His hands wrap around my waist, and I lean into his touch when I feel the weight of a belt slung along my hips.

"Did you..." My hands fall to the belt as he clips it in, and I find the smooth metal of a hilt. "Did you get me a sword?"

He smiles, stepping away and I pull the weapon from the scabbard. It's a long, perfectly balanced blade that ends in a silver hilt with a large crescent-shaped citrine gem in its center. I test it, slicing through the air with ease. The blade is light enough for maneuverability, but deathly sharp. *It's perfect.*

"How do you feel?" he asks as I swing again. The sword is like an extension of my arm, made for me.

"Like a badass," I breathe, and Lowell laughs deeply as I sheath the sword back in its scabbard. "I feel like a heroine from one of my books."

"Good." Lowell gives me a shy smile a second before I launch myself at him, and he catches me expertly, pulling me up so my legs dangle off the ground. I wrap my arms around his neck, burying my face in his hair and letting his scent wash over me.

"Thank you," I murmur into his skin, and he kisses my shoulder before setting me down.

"Happy Valentine's Day, little witch," he says with a smirk, handing me a dagger that matches the sword, and is the perfect size to fit in the thigh holster he secured.

"That was...you got me a dagger for the most romantic day of the year?" I stutter.

"And a sword," Lowell smirks. "Did I not do that right? Would you have wanted flowers or jewelry?"

"Fuck no," I laugh. "This is..." *Perfect. The most thoughtful gift someone's ever gotten me.* Because he didn't just get me a weapon. He got me security, power. Everything I've been missing. "I didn't get you anything."

"I'm sure you'll think of something," he murmurs, his eyes dipping to my mouth as I bite my lower lip. His hands skim against the bare skin at my waist and around to my back while I let mine fall back to the scar on his chest.

"Technically Valentine's Day is tomorrow," I remind him. "So, I still have a day."

Lowell hums as my hands move up to his collar bone and then slide back around his neck, toying with the hair at the nape of his neck. He inches closer. Each breath I take has my breasts brushing against his chest. It's a game of chicken now, both of us waiting to see who snaps first and breaks the tension. I've given up the illusion that I don't want him, I do. But it's not right. I'm being selfish letting Lowell get closer to me when I have a "true love."

"You gonna get me something too?" Vlad's voice drifts in from the entryway. He straightens his tie and buttons his navy suit jacket as I back away from Lowell, a blush rising in my cheeks. I'm silently grateful for Vlad's interruption because I don't think I'm strong enough to stop what was coming.

"The weapons came from my vault after all," Vlad smirks as he comes over and stops right in front of me, eyeing the sword in the belt. "Finley would be happy to see you wearing them."

"They were hers?" I ask, and he nods. "Thank you, Vlad." He pulls me close, turning his head at the last second so he can whisper in my ear.

"You need to put *all* of us out of our misery and fuck the wolf already," he murmurs, and I roll my eyes.

"Do you have this week in the pool?" I ask pointedly, pulling away, and the corners of his mouth quirk up. "That's what I thought."

"Where's Adriana?" Vlad asks.

"Here," she calls from the doorway. Her blonde hair is tied back and she's wearing a matching yoga pants and tank top, the corresponding jacket slung over the crook of her arm. She eyes my sword and nods in approval.

"Good, because we have a problem," Vlad points between my sister and me. "You two need to swap roles when we go to the dragons."

"We can't," Adriana squeaks, her grey eyes widening in panic. "We have to go tomorrow."

"What?" Lowell and I say in unison.

"I got a vision. I can't see much, but I can tell Lowell will leave the hoard with the scepter if we go tomorrow."

"Vlad, why do we need to change the plan?" I ask, turning my attention to the vampire. He runs his hand through his short blonde hair, his eyes drifting down my body.

"Because, and I mean this in the nicest way possible, there's no way in hell you'll be perceived as a virgin."

"Fuck," Lowell swears, swiping his hand down his face.

"Why is that important?"

"It is," both the werewolf and vampire say in unison, not elaborating.

"How would they even know?" I ask, and the two of them simply chuckle.

"You've been in two high profile relationships," Adriana reminds me, "And caught in some less than decent positions...."

"Fucking Rodger," I grumble. I forgot about those tabloid pictures.

"So, you need to swap with Adriana," Vlad says. "And we'll probably need to rethink that portion of the plan since your magic is faulty."

"Well," Adriana pipes up, "We can still proceed with the first part of the plan. I can still cast the locator spell from the front of the cave. Katie, can you still sense magical signatures?" I nod.

"I can too, especially if I'm used to the signature," Lowell says.

"We can practice tonight and go over any kinks in the plan," Adriana responds. "We should go to Vlad's house and spend the day there. It'll be easier for me to teleport us all from there."

"When do we need to leave?" I ask.

"Now," Lowell says, and the rest of the group nods.

"Okay then," I murmur. "Let's go rob some dragons."

CAN YOU HEAR ME? I ask Lowell through our newly created Mind Magic channel. He nods and drops his pants, shifting into a giant white wolf. *Now?* I ask and he barks.

I hear you, little witch. The statement floats right to the front of my brain and I give a little sigh of relief.

Lowell shifts back and pulls his sweatpants back on. He joins me on the swinging bench on Vlad's porch, not bothering to wait until I slow the movement before hopping on. Adriana is nervously pacing in front of us, wearing a pastel pink baby-doll dress that Vlad picked out for her. The three of us have our eye on the horizon, silently waiting for the sun to set so we can leave for the dragons' hoard.

We spent most of the night modifying our plan to steal the scepter so that Adriana and I swapped roles. Initially, we planned to have Vlad introduce me as the Queen of the Dark Magic Covens, but apparently a single woman's status is diminished if she isn't a virgin. So even though I'd be presented as a queen, I wouldn't be taken seriously. I rolled my eyes so hard when I heard that they almost popped out of my head.

So now Adriana is dressed up as a schoolgirl, which will hopefully distract the dragons long enough for me and Lowell to sneak inside and steal the scepter. She's less than pleased about the switch in plans, but when I asked if her wariness was related to a vision, she assured me she still saw the same outcome. Lowell will leave the cave with the scepter. And hopefully, the rest of us will leave with our lives.

Are you nervous? Lowell asks through our connection. His arm is stretched out on the back of the bench, his fingertips gently brushing my shoulder. I shake my head. I've mentally retreated into my military calm...focused and aware, not allowing myself to dwell on the fact that we can all die tonight.

We don't need to do this, Lowell offers. But we do, even if I don't quite understand why. I was told to retrieve the pieces of the blood oath, and at this point, I'll take any advantage we can get.

A memory surfaces. The words Lowell just said, I've said them before...to Archer. Right before he killed an entire coven of Dark Witches. Am I being just as stubborn? We've plotted for weeks and gone over contingencies. It's a good plan, but is it enough?

The sun dips below the hill and the stars poke through the last streaks of purple that color the sky. *No, we need to do this.*

Vlad emerges from the house, looking the part of Count in his full-length black cloak that's fastened at the neck by a ruby the size of my fist. His pointed leather boots click loudly on the wooden porch, and he pops his collar against the February chill.

"Ready?" he asks, flashing a fang-filled smile that somehow lessens the tension. Even Adriana stops her incessant pacing. Vlad's eyes scan down her body, taking in the high knee socks and pigtails, which is total overkill if you ask me.

"You look positively edible," he growls. Adriana gives him a small smile, her gray eyes dilating. He prowls over to her, entranced as he reaches out and gently brushes one of her pigtails behind her shoulder. His finger skims over her neck, and I hear her breath hitch.

"Adriana," he purrs, and she visibly swallows. "Are you going to open the mental channel for us?"

"Oh," she breathes and steps back, grabbing her wand. *Can everyone hear me?* Adriana's flustered voice asks in my mind. We each say yes, and she nods satisfied.

Let's get going, Vlad says and stalks towards the forest where the wards protecting his house end. Adriana follows in his footsteps eagerly. I chuckle and jump off the swing. I get to the first step of the porch when Lowell snags my hand.

"Give them a minute," he says with a wink. We meander slowly off the porch, but he doesn't take his hand back, our fingers intertwining like it's the most natural thing in the world.

"We should make a calendar pool for them." Lowell laughs and slings his arm around my shoulders. We walk silently until we reach the tree line when Lowell pulls me to stop alongside him.

"Katie," he says softly, grabbing both of my hands in his. "This mission is dangerous. There's a chance we won't make it out today."

"We'll be fine," I assure him, squeezing his hands. "We'll be in and out and back here with the scepter before anyone notices it's missing."

If we don't make it, his voice resounds in every inch of my mind, *I want you to know...*

I feel overwhelming emotion streaming through our bond, but it's so complex I can't name it. I reach up and cup Lowell's cheek, brushing my thumb against his stubble.

"No goodbyes," I tell him firmly. "We'll be back here in a few hours. You can tell me then."

"Now isn't the time for a quickie," Vlad calls, managing to sound bored even when he's yelling.

Lowell sighs and releases one of my hands so we can continue picking our way through the leaves and sticks cluttering the forest floor. When we reach Adriana and Vlad, the two are standing on opposite sides of a small clearing.

"Once I perform the cloaking spell, we won't be able to see, hear or smell you." She reiterates the first part of the plan. "Keep one hand on my shoulder as we teleport. As soon as we're in the mountains, I'll perform the locator spell."

"When we get to the cave," Vlad continues, as the four of us form a small circle, "stay behind us until we're positive they won't willingly hand over the scepter. We'll buy you as much time as we can after that."

I stick my finger out and jab Vlad in the chest. "Do not, under any circumstances, sell my sister to the dragons." Vlad laughs, but I hold true.

"I promise," he says, crossing his heart.

I nod to Adriana who takes a deep breath and mutters a spell. She waves her wand over Lowell who smiles at me before completely disappearing. If he wasn't still holding my hand, I'd think he was never there at all. Adriana repeats the process to me, and a wave of tingling magic spreads down my skin as I slowly fade into the background. I reach forward and put my invisible hand on Adriana's shoulder.

I feel you both, Adriana tells us, and extends her hand to Vlad. *Here we go,* she waves her wand over the group of us, and the now-familiar squeezing that comes with teleporting envelops us.

Chapter Twenty

WHEN THE SENSATION OF teleportation dissipates, I open my eyes. We're deep in the Carpathian Mountains, where the jagged grey rock is steep without many footholds. A thin layer of snow covers any flat surface, and the only color comes from the sporadic evergreens that managed to grow this high. Even the sky is bleak, the moon obstructed by a layer of thick clouds making it almost impossible to see.

Adriana's wand sparks, the locator spell streaking down the hill before becoming invisible. But all magic leaves a residue. Even though we can't see the evidence of her locator spell, I can feel it.

Vlad wraps an arm around Adriana as they begin to follow the magical signature down the slope. I spend a second trying to figure out how the hell I'm going to descend when I feel a wet nose bump against my hand.

Get on my back, Lowell says, inching forward along my hand until I feel his snout give way to his soft fur. Once I'm convinced he's far enough forward, I swing my invisible leg over an invisible wolf, hoping I don't kick him in the head. The whole thing is surreal, but I manage to mount him, and he starts picking his way after Vlad and Adriana.

It should be—Vlad starts, and then they disappear into the mountain.

Vlad? I call tentatively as Lowell halts.

Fuck that hurt, Vlad swears. *We're in. Drop into the fucking hole in the ground.*

I'm about to protest when Lowell does just that. He takes a running leap at the now visible hole in the mountain, and we tumble into the darkness as I grip his fur with all my strength. He lands on his feet a second later on a worn dirt path inside a cave. I can barely make out Vlad and Adriana, but I see them moving further into the cave, sticking to the pools of light created by ultraviolet flames that hang along the hewn walls.

Keep a few feet behind us Vlad says, as I slide off Lowell's back so he can shift back to his human form. I take a few steps before I feel his hand link through mine again and give me a tentative squeeze.

This seems like a tight fit for a dragon. The chamber is so small it's claustrophobic. Two of us walking across is almost the full length, and the ceiling is so low that Vlad is hunched over.

"State your business, vampire," a cold female voice rings out in the cavern, causing us all to halt in our tracks.

Holding a torch made of the same ultraviolet fire is a beautiful woman. She wears a dress that looks like liquid gold spilling over her ample curves. Her dark hair hangs in loose spirals around her shoulders but doesn't conceal the glittering earrings that are so heavy they drag her earlobes down towards her shoulders. Her neck is covered in necklaces that range from simple chains to a gem-encrusted choker. Bracelets snake up her arms.

I don't understand, I send to only Lowell, down our private channel.

She's a dragon shifter, little witch. Lowell squeezes my hand tighter. *Don't underestimate her, even in this form.*

"Ethelinda," Vlad says warmly, extending a hand toward the woman. "It's been too long."

She extends the hand not holding her torch and Vlad stoops to kiss her many rings. She looks down her nose at the vampire, not an easy feat with his height.

"No," she says simply, and Vlad huffs.

"Come now, Ethelinda," he purrs. The woman's eyes narrow and her pupils turn to slits.

"Your *associate*," she hisses the word in a purely reptilian way, "asked me to take the accursed blood trinket. Now, it's *mine*."

Get ready, Lowell murmurs.

Wait for the signal, Vlad replies.

"We could trade," Vlad offers, his hand falling to the egg-sized ruby holding his cloak together. "I have...several options."

The dragon shifter's eyes move to my sister, who is fiddling with the hem of her dress. She plays the part of innocent perfectly. It's not over the top, but it's enough to draw attention and mask the fact that she's a powerful Dark Witch.

"You think us still that primitive that we would trade for a virgin?" Ethelinda asks, her tongue darting out to run along her bottom lip.

Yes, Vlad says to all of us as he sweeps closer to Ethelinda, his black cloak swishing along the cavern floor.

"I think you know a good deal when it's presented." He takes her arm and leans in close enough to kiss her cheek. *That's the signal.* Lowell and I creep towards them. As we pass, I brush my hand against Adriana, and she releases a deep breath in response.

"How did you know I was here for the scepter?" Vlad asks as we approach.

"We hear things, even out here," Ethelinda says. "There's talk of a new Finley."

"Yes," he replies softly. I flatten myself along the cavern wall and inch past them, hoping she doesn't feel the magical signature surrounding us. "I've met her. She's everything we've been waiting for. You should join her cause."

"You have." Not a question.

"As have the wolves."

"I heard she pissed off Delmare," the dragon scoffs. *This lady is clued in.* I finally make it past her and pull away from the wall, waiting for Lowell to clear.

"That's not hard to do," Vlad says and the two chuckle.

"My answer is still no," Ethelinda says. "To both your requests."

Be quick, Vlad says. I swear down the channel as Lowell tugs on my arm to let me know he's made it past the dragon.

We start at a run, following the locator spell, barely able to take in our surroundings. We wind further and further until I can no longer make out Vlad's voice. The strange light makes it hard to tell how far we've gone, but I keep a count of the torches. When we pass number ten, the hall pitches uphill. We clamber up it, and when we get to the top, my mouth drops.

The narrow tunnel opens to a circular chamber that extends countless stories above us and another four or five to the base. We take a few steps onto a pathway that ends with a rickety railing. Doors are carved into the walls in both directions, and as

I approach the rail, I see that they snake up the other side of the chamber too. It reminds me of a hotel with internal balconies. The railing overlooks a little bazaar on the bottom floor. Colorful stands sell food, clothes, and toys. Children run around parents gathered in small groups chatting.

Lowell grabs my hand and pulls me back just as a swarm of small dragons with scales of every color imaginable sail by. Well, small is a relative term. They're about the size of ponies. One careens off into the space beside us, crashing into the stone wall. He shakes his little, green head and then jumps back over the railing to join the rest of the group as they follow a twenty-foot gold dragon as he ascends towards the top floors. *They're learning to fly.*

The distinct signature of the locator spell draws my attention to the center of the chamber, but I can't make anything out. Lowell pulls me along the railing until we find a staircase that leads us to the main floor. We weave around the unsuspecting dragons in their human forms, following the pulse of magic as it drags us further into the chamber.

It feels like it's right here, I say as the signature becomes overwhelming. I tentatively reach an invisible hand in front of me and gasp when I connect with something solid.

It's cloaked. I tell Lowell. I pull him alongside me as we circle the invisible wall. Finally, almost three-quarters of the way around, my hand disappears. *The door is here.*

What if it's warded? What if there's an alarm? Lowell asks.

Then it's a good thing you'll be keeping watch, I tell him and slip through the doorway, releasing his hand.

Fuck, Katie! Lowell calls, but his hand doesn't find me again.

I feel the slight tingle of magic as I pass through the doorway and hold my breath. No alarms. No swarms of angry dragon shifters descend on my location. My relief is immediately replaced by awe as I behold the hoard.

Gold coins are stacked in piles so high I can't see the top. There are treasures, from silver tea sets to chests full of gems. Then there's the current money; English pounds, American dollars, and Euros are wrapped and stacked in neat piles along the walkway. I pass cases with crowns, swords, jewelry and so many more baubles that I can't name them all.

I follow the signature to the back corner of the hoard. Haphazardly thrown in a pile of other silver trinkets, I see the flash of a ruby surrounded by Adriana's Dark Magic. The scepter.

Found it. Is the coast clear? I ask Lowell.

Yes, hurry. I bounce on the pads of my feet. This feels too easy. There's no way I can just reach out and—

The entire hoard begins shaking. The coins jangle as they clink together, sliding down their perspective piles. The ruby disappears into the pile of silver. *Fuck, no.* I jump in, tossing things over my shoulders until my fingers finally close around the scepter. Just like the necklace and the tiara, as soon as the scepter is in my grasp, it feels like it was always supposed to be there. Like it was made for my hand.

"KATIE!" Lowell bellows. *How the fuck can I hear him?*

I see his dark hair just as one of the piles of treasure tips over. They're going to block me in. One look at my body reveals that the concealment spell was shattered, and anyone will be able to see me as I flee this place. I swim through the other items, tossing things out of the way until my feet connect with solid ground.

Lowell, run! I send to him as I sprint towards the door, narrowly avoiding things being thrown in my path. I'm fifty feet from the door. I can totally make it. My feet pound against the hard-packed earth as my body flies through the cavern. Twenty feet. There's a growl behind me, but I refuse to turn. Ten feet, something hot licks at my feet. I start to serpentine, switching up my approach as the doorway gets closer.

A large roar draws my attention and I glance back over my shoulder, staring into the maw of a giant silver beast. He must be close to fifty feet tall, and his wide mouth is open, sending hot breath in my direction. The dragon's wings flap like he's about to head me off at the pass just as the largest pile of treasure beside the door starts to tip. I slide, narrowly making it through the open door and landing in a roll on the other side, the scepter still in hand. The door slams shut in the dragon's silver face.

"Ha!" I scream, jumping to my feet.

My victory is premature.

Lowell is next to me, back in his wolf form, snarling at the beasts before us. We're surrounded by at least ten dragons, each one bigger than the next. Their scales range from black and gold to the most vivid red and blue. All twenty giant eyes are staring at us.

Any ideas? I ask, as Lowell bares his teeth, which are toothpicks compared to the snarling fangs in front of us. I clear my throat, prepared to address the dragons when a really stupid idea comes to my mind.

Lowell, I need you to take the scepter to the others as soon as I cause a distraction. He growls in response. *That's an order from your queen, do you understand?* He dips his head slightly.

"My name is Kathryn Carmichael, Queen of the Dark Magic Covens," I tell the dragons. One huffs a ring of smoke in my face. *Douchebag.* "This was stolen from me."

"You accuse us?" A voice rumbles from one of the huge beasts in front of me. Huh, wasn't expecting him to be able to speak in this form. It seems unfair that he can, but my werewolf can't.

"No," I say, my voice nonchalant even though internally I'm rambling and panicked. "But I am taking it back." *Fuck this is going to hurt.* "If you'll excuse me."

I step towards the dragons, whose attention is now firmly on the treasure in my hand. I slide my wand out of my other sleeve.

Now, Lowell. I toss him the scepter, which he catches in his mouth. Lightning crackles in the air around me. I can't control it or send it at anyone, but it's enough to make the beasts balk. Lowell takes off through a gap created and I charge in the opposite direction, towards the biggest, meanest looking green dragon.

I whack him on the nose with my fist. He hesitates for one second, I think more from surprise than from being hurt by the electricity or the force of the blow, but that moment is all I need. I jump onto his foot and start scrambling up his back. He shakes, trying to dislodge me, but I release the lightning and cast a sticking spell so my shoes adhere to his scales.

I make it to his back by the time the rest of the dragons realize my position. They swipe at me, and I duck close to the dragon. When they miss me, they hit him, and he starts shooting them with fire out of his giant mouth.

The sight of flames has my heart rate increasing to an unnatural level. I didn't think this through. I've done so well in therapy; my panic attacks have practically disappeared. But I still can't control my body's visceral response to fire. I try to breathe, to focus on reality. The flames are purple, not white; this is dragon fire, not hellfire. My mantra doesn't work and I'm rooted to the dragon, unable to move for fear of being burned.

Suddenly, I'm free-falling as the dragon shifts back into his human form. I land hard on my side, and it jars me enough that I'm back in the room, thoughts of hellfire banished as I deal with the very real threat before me. Ignoring the pain, I stand, and the dragons surround me. I reach for my sword, unsheathing it from my belt and extending it as the beasts circle, penning me in with the shifted-green dragon.

He runs a hand through his greasy toffee-colored hair, not seeming to care that I can see every inch of his body in all its naked glory. He's a big fucker. He's easily seven feet tall and every inch of him is stacked in muscles. I won't win against him in hand-to-hand combat, but I have a weapon and he doesn't.

I can see the staircase, but I know I won't make it without being barbequed. *Get the scepter out of here.* I send down the channel.

Katie, where are you? I don't know who asks, but I can't dwell on it. They need to get out.

GO. I plead as the shifted dragon approaches me.

"We've heard stories about the great Kathryn Carmichael," he chuckles. "Tales of your lightning are legendary in the Kingdom of Magic." Several of the dragons huff in a way that can only be laughter.

"Tell me, Queen of the Dark Magic Covens," he hisses as he closes in on me. I hold my chin up high and square my shoulders. "Was *that* your best move?" He clicks his tongue.

"Well, I did steal your treasure," I say, cocking my head to the side.

"We'll need payment for that." He smiles sinisterly, and the rest of the dragons bare their teeth.

"Let me guess, that payment will be me?" I gasp in feign shock. "Will you ransom me to the prince, like the mermaids tried to? Or are you planning on perpetuating stereotypes and keeping me chained as some kind of sex slave?"

"We prefer our humans pure." He spits at my feet. "No, I think we'll add some more scars to your flesh. You burn beautifully."

"You can try," I seethe, and swipe my sword in the air as he jumps back, his eyes narrowing to reptilian slits.

"Release her," a cold female voice sounds from the balcony. The dragon shifter drops to his knee behind me, as do most of the ones still in their dragon form. When they lower, I can see Ethelinda's jaw ticking as her glowing green eyes focus on me.

"Your Majesty?" the shifted dragon asks.

"Release her immediately." Without another word of protest, the dragons separate, offering a clear path to the stairs. The shifted dragon bares his teeth at me as I skirt past him, keeping my steps even, despite my body begging to run.

I ascend the stairs, get to the level with Ethelinda, and approach her cautiously.

Act naturally, Adriana's voice flits down the channel. Up close I can see the tension in her body, the way her shoulders are up by her ears, the way her knuckles are white from her clenched fists.

"You may join your companion in the entryway," she says through gritted teeth. I get an overwhelming sensation of a magical signature that I recognize.

Adriana, are you doing this?

Just get the fuck out here. I already teleported Vlad and Lowell back with the scepter.

I bow my head to the queen before walking briskly into the tunnel.

Katie, hurry. She's fighting my control.

"SEIZE HER!" the queen bellows. I take off in a sprint. I fly through the tunnel, counting the torches. Five, six...almost there.

I feel the heat on my back before I hear Adriana screaming. I look over my shoulder and ultraviolet dragon fire is exploding down the tunnel. I round a corner to find Adriana jumping up and down under the entrance. She extends her arms toward me.

Sweat is pouring down my skin, the rubber of my sneakers starting to melt beneath my feet. *I will not be fucking burned one more time.* I summon extra speed and barrel into my sister, who flicks her wand and propels us out of the hole in the mountain. We sail up just as the wave of fire crashes beneath us. As soon as we see the icy rocks of the surface, I'm being squeezed by grey smoke as we teleport to safety.

Chapter Twenty-One

WE EMERGE IN THE clearing in the woods, the pale moonlight casting shadows amidst the bare trees. I kick off my destroyed sneakers, getting the burning rubber as far away from my feet as possible. My eyes immediately fall to Lowell, tethered to a tree trunk, wisps of Adriana's gray magic rooting him to the spot. He's thrashing wildly, his mouth opened in a magically silenced scream.

"Thank fuck," Vlad breathes and swoops over to me, his cloak billowing behind him, the scepter in one hand. He assesses me, his eyes lingering on my feet which hurt but aren't too badly injured. His fangs extend and he pricks a finger on his free hand and pushes it towards my lips.

"I'm—" He doesn't give me the chance to say *fine* before he slides his finger in my mouth. I swallow out of pure shock, the coppery blood flowing into my mouth. I feel it surge towards my feet and look down to find my feet healing. "What the hell did you just do?"

"Vampire blood has healing properties," Vlad says like it's obvious. "All Magical Creatures do, but only vampires can heal others. It's how we hid the bite marks on our victims for centuries."

"You didn't think to offer this when we met and I was charred?"

"You didn't ask." He shrugs. "Now what happened back there?"

"Why is Lowell tied to a tree?" I shoot back. Adriana waves her wand and I'm hit with a barrage of profanity as the silencing spell is lifted.

"Katie—" Lowell's voice breaks as Vlad steps back enough that I can see the werewolf. His eyes are glowing yellow, and his body shakes as he tries to shift but the Dark Magic keeps him from doing so.

"Adriana, let him go."

"He almost got us all killed," Adriana spits. "He wouldn't let go when I tried to teleport back for you."

"They left you," Lowell shouts.

"Katie told us to get the scepter out of there," Adriana states in an even, calm voice as she reiterates my orders. "I was going back for her."

"I should have—" Adriana waves her wand again, so Lowell's voice is silenced.

"No," she says, her quiet calm breaking. She gets right in his face, jabbing an extended finger into his chest. "You're too emotional when it comes to her."

Lowell opens his mouth to rebut Adriana, but no sound comes out.

"Do you know how hurt you could have been if I hadn't stopped the teleportation spell? Or where we could have wound up? Witches have ended up in pieces because of the bullshit you pulled. I know you feel the need to protect Katie, but if you can't handle her being in dangerous situations, then you need to step back as her second. Because this is the least of what we'll be up against."

Adriana spins around, her pink baby-doll dress fluttering out before it settles back down.

"And you," she points at me. "What the hell happened? Why would you tell us to leave if you didn't have an exit strategy?"

"We needed to get the scepter to safety," I say, squaring my shoulders as all three of my friends turn to me with outrage in their eyes.

"The scepter doesn't mean anything if you're not wielding it," Adriana says.

"We work together," Vlad continues. "You don't get to pull that self-sacrificing shit."

"The plan—" I start.

"I don't care if the plan went off the rails," Adriana screams, her voice shrill. "Do you really think I would go into a dragon hoard without a backup plan? Do you have that little faith in me?"

"Why wouldn't you tell me about a backup plan?" I counter, going toe to toe with my sister.

"Because you're impulsive," she sighs, exasperated. "And if I told you my plan to use Mind Control, it would have backfired, and you would have wound up dead."

"My job as your leader is to get *you* out alive," I stress.

"It's a war, baby queen," Vlad says sternly. "We knew what we were getting into when we signed up."

"This isn't the Dragons," Adriana says carefully.

"Capital D," Vlad adds. "Not the shifters who just tried to roast you."

"Yes, you're our leader," Adriana continues, ignoring him. "But you don't need to take that burden on alone anymore. Do you not trust us?"

"It's not that."

"Then what is it?"

"I won't be the reason you die again!" Silence spreads throughout the forest as if even the wildlife is afraid to disrupt this moment.

I meet Adriana's gray eyes, narrowed in confusion. "Katie—"

"I spent fifteen years thinking I killed you." My voice breaks. "You were my favorite person in the whole world, and then you were gone and it was my fault." Tears brim along Adriana's long lashes. "I know why you had to do it, I understand. But I can't lose you again."

I tear my gaze away from my sister, looking at Vlad and then Lowell. "I can't lose any of you."

There's a pulse down the bond that feels like a warm embrace. I try to latch onto that feeling instead of the lead ball of guilt settling in my stomach. I kick a clump of grass with my toe, keeping my head down.

"I knew how bad it was, and I needed to get all of you out so I could think. I can handle whatever they threw at me. Torture...death...whatever. But you're my family and—" The lump in my throat keeps me from finishing my thought.

Little witch, Lowell sends to my mind.

"I panicked," I choke out. "I'm sorry."

Vlad tilts my chin up until I can see a lone bead of blood in the corner of his eye. "Never again, do you understand me?" he says. "You talk to us, and we'll figure a way out together." I nod as my chin quivers in his hand.

Adriana pushes past Vlad, barreling into me and holding me so tightly I can barely breathe. "My Katie," she murmurs into my hair as I wrap my arms back around her. "I try to treat you like a queen, like a ruler. But—" she dissolves into tears, sobs shuddering her slender frame. "I love you and I'm so sorry."

"I know," I whisper. "I should have known you'd have a backup plan. It was such a badass move, Mind Controlling the Dragon Queen."

"As soon as I realized who she was I knew what I had to do." She pulls back, clearing her throat and wiping away the residual tears.

With a wave of her wand, Lowell is released from the spell, but he lingers by the tree. His emotions are so mixed I can't discern one from the next.

"We'll meet you back at the house," Vlad says, placing his hand on the small of Adriana's back, and escorting her back into the forest.

We listen to their receding footsteps, and even when I can't hear them anymore, Lowell waits. After what feels like an eternity, the werewolf prowls over, stopping right in front of me and making me crane my neck to meet his eyes.

"I know you're mad—"

He cuts me off with a kiss.

Lowell is usually so gentle with me. He's the man who holds me when I cry, who literally pieced me back together when I was broken.

There's nothing gentle about this kiss. It's *claiming*. Like he's trying to brand himself on my very soul. An Alpha reminding me exactly where I belong, and why I shouldn't take unnecessary risks. I should push away; I should be bothered by the frenetic way he thrusts his tongue into my mouth and tangles it with mine.

Instead, I melt.

We crash together in a flurry of movement. I match his fervor as six weeks of tension and wanting burst like a dam. His hands are everywhere, skimming down my throat, wrapping around my back, biting into my thighs as he hoists me higher. My legs wind around his waist as he walks us backward until the rough bark of a tree scrapes my back.

I can't get enough. Every stroke of his tongue against mine lights me up until my entire body feels like it's glowing with brilliant golden light. Heat pools in my core as he moves impossibly closer. I drag my nails down his back and his resounding growl sends shivers up my spine.

Lowell pulls away for a moment as we both pant, catching our breath. His eyes are hooded, his lips swollen, and I know I look the same.

"Little witch—"

I draw him back into me. This kiss is sweeter, coaxing. Like we're taking the time to savor every second. I love the way he tastes. The way his tongue playfully flicks against mine, the way his teeth gently nip my lower lip. I never want to stop.

My hands rove over his corded muscles. I've slept in his arms, lounged in his embrace, yet it feels like I'm touching him for the first time. His skin pimples in my wake, as I draw my hands from his chest to his shoulders and finally into his silken hair.

The bond between us is overloaded. Lowell's anger, fear, and ultimate desperation flow into me with something softer and delicate. It's too much to name and yet I understand it all because I feel it too. I'm stripped bare before him, every emotion on display for him to see. My heart soars. Tears slip down my cheeks. I've never felt so vulnerable, so open, so raw. Even so, I know I'm totally safe.

Nothing has ever compared.

Lowell's lips move along my jaw and I tilt my head back against the tree to give him further access. He pauses at the hollow of my neck, breathing me in, his chest heaving. I hold him close, and as one, we sigh, sinking further into each other's embrace.

"I'm sorry," I whisper as he kisses along my collar bone, hovering around the junction of my neck and shoulder. "I shouldn't have told you to leave."

His response is another kiss, just a gentle brush of his lips against mine. It still makes my heart skip a beat.

I lower my legs, and Lowell eases me back to the ground before pulling me back into him. I rest my cheek against his chest, listening to the thundering of his heart and soaking up the warmth from his skin. I don't know how long we stand there holding each other, it could have been minutes or hours, but I could have stayed there forever. Eventually, Lowell tips my chin up to meet his gaze.

"Never pull a stunt like that again," Lowell commands, his voice rumbling through me. I swallow thickly, and I know the minute he feels my arousal in our bond because his pupils dilate.

"That's it? Really?" I laugh. "No romantic confessions? No 'I can't live without you?'"

"That's a given," he whispers, taking my bottom lip between his teeth. His tongue flicks against the swollen flesh and he lingers just enough to stoke the flames of desire before he pulls away and leaves me wanting.

"Yes, Alpha," I pant and am treated with my own blast of desire from his end.

"You're going to be the death of me," Lowell groans and links his fingers through mine, pulling me back towards the house.

Chapter Twenty-Two

WE WALK INTO THE foyer, hands still intertwined as the lights in the iron chandelier spring to life and bathe the white marble in bright light. I feel a weight lift from my chest as we enter the space.

"Welcome home," Lowell murmurs, squeezing my hand.

Home. It's not something I've had since I moved to the Dragons' barracks four years ago. Nowhere I could simply be myself and not some persona. The captain, the powerhouse, the queen. I stepped into each role so fully that I couldn't let my guard down around the people I love. But here...

It's not about the house. It's about the people. My makeshift family.

We slowly make our way towards the dining room doubling as our war room. I know we need to debrief on this mission. At the very least we need to discuss where to store the scepter, but all I want to do is curl up in Lowell's bed and continue what we started in the woods.

"Are you hungry?" Lowell asks, his thumb brushing along my knuckles.

"Starved," I laugh. "I did a lot of running tonight." He glowers at me. "Too soon?"

"Entirely." I flash him a cheeky smile. Lowell stops and my hand falls from him as I approach the dining room. "Katie—" Lowell's head quirks to the side but I keep walking.

I open the door and my eyes pop out of my head. The maps of the Carpathian Mountains are haphazardly pushed to the side, and Adriana sits on the table with Vlad between her legs. His fangs are buried in her neck, and she moans in ecstasy, her head thrown back, and her blonde hair freed from the pigtails. Vlad's hands are gripping her ass, which is gyrating against his suit pants while he groans and starts matching her movements.

I slam the door shut, safely back in the foyer just as the sounds increase in volume.

"Holy shit," I breathe, my hand covering my mouth. Lowell crosses the space between us and lifts me into his arms.

"Permission to get us the fuck out of here?"

"God yes! Go faster," I laugh, and I close my eyes against his chest as he zooms through a door and down a flight of stairs.

When he slows, I reluctantly lower myself to the concrete floor and look around. We're in the basement stocked with state-of-the-art gym equipment, a boxing ring, and a freaking sauna.

"How did I not know this was down here?" I demand, and the werewolf laughs as he crosses to a hot tub and punches buttons until the jets come to life.

"Because I mentioned coffins in the basement, and you refused to come down here." *Right.* I shiver at the thought, not-so-sneakily looking around to see where they might be kept.

"Swimsuits are in there," Lowell says, gesturing to a white cabinet. "Get changed and get in. I'll be right back."

"You're going upstairs?" I grimace. "I mean they had clothes on, but it didn't look like they would for long..."

He zooms back over to me and kisses the tip of my nose. "I'll be quick, and I'll bring snacks."

"And wine?" I ask, and he chuckles before disappearing in a flash of his superior speed.

I cross to the cabinet and find it stocked with swimsuits in all sizes with tags on. I grab a little red bikini in my size and toss two towels on the weight bench closest to the hot tub. Changing quickly, I throw my hair in a bun on top of my head and my whole body sighs as I sink into the corner bucket seat, the deliciously warm water relaxing my tense muscles.

Lowell appears in his trunks, with a tray of assorted cheeses, fruit, crackers, and a bottle of wine tucked under his arm. He sets the tray down on the weight bench next to the towels, and slowly prowls over to me with the wine. I've seen this man naked more times than I can count, but I can't stop myself from drinking in his chiseled muscles, the deep-v just visible above his swimsuit, the dark smattering of hair trailing lower...

"My eyes are up here, little witch," he says, but his voice is gravelly, and I can feel the desire streaming between us as his eyes linger over the triangles that barely contain my breasts. I swallow as he climbs into the hot tub beside me, pulling my legs so my feet are resting in his lap.

Lowell extends the uncorked bottle to me, and I tip it back into my mouth, letting the warmth from the alcohol rush through my blood. I take another swig before handing it back to the werewolf, who does the same and then sets the bottle on the step, out of the way but still within reach.

"Vlad and Adriana," I laugh as Lowell's hands absently trace lines up my calves. "Never would have thought that."

"Maybe it was the school-girl outfit," he offers, his smile wide and easy.

"Or adrenaline."

"They could say the same about us."

"No," I say firmly, and his golden eyes meet mine. "No one would think that about us...this..."

"And what is this, little witch?" he asks, his hand sliding higher.

"What do you think?"

"I asked you first."

"Yeah, but I'm your queen, so..." He laughs and pinches my inner thigh, causing me to yelp and splash water at him. He snags my hand using it to tug me closer, so my thighs are now over his lap.

"I'll answer your question," he says, his arm winding around my waist while the other continues to caress my legs under the water, "if you answer one question first."

"Fine," I sigh, rolling my eyes.

"After we first met," he starts softly, "you and the prince were fighting."

"You heard?" I ask, and he nods. Of course he stayed close. I should have guessed that.

"Then we heard what happened in Sicily, and I felt your anger, your sense of betrayal." A stab of pain flows through our bond and I instinctively reach out and grab his hand. "After that, your emotions were muted. I guess you were back in London and our bond wasn't strong enough for me to feel you. The next thing I knew, Vlad showed me a picture of you and Archer at the Solstice Ball."

"Yes," I murmur, looking down at our hands. "But that wasn't a question."

"How?" he asks. "How did you go from hating him to being so in love that you declared to the Kingdom that you were a couple?"

"I wasn't in love with him," I assert. "Maybe I was falling, but..." I stop myself. It's not important.

"I was in a training class," I carefully continue. "And he came in and apologized, explained his side of the story. Archer said he heard the Dark Witches were planning on teleporting me to the Highlands, and he freaked out. I told him his reaction still wasn't okay...and he said that he'd burn the world to keep me safe."

Lowell's eyes narrow. "He said he'd...*burn the world for you?*" he reiterates. "And you fell for that line?" He laughs, and his amusement floods me even as I open my mouth in outrage.

"It was—" I sputter looking for the right word. In hindsight, *romantic* seems like the wrong choice. Lowell laughs harder. "You're such an ass."

I stand, aiming for the steps, but he wraps his arms around my waist and drags me onto his lap. My knees fall on either side of his thighs as I straddle him. "You're saying you wouldn't burn the world for me, pup?"

"No," he says, his laughter dying. "Why would I destroy something when I can help you conquer it and make it better?"

"That's a better line," I murmur as I push his hair back, my hands wetting the strands.

I don't know who initiates the kiss, but suddenly we're tangled together. It starts slow, like a low-burning flame that can't stop growing. My head tilts just as his tongue slips into my mouth. *Fuck this feels so right.* I know it shouldn't. I shouldn't be greedy and keep kissing this amazing man who wants to literally give me the world when someone else is destined for me.

Lowell wraps his large hand around the base of my hair and tugs gently, pulling me back so that I stare into his eyes. "Where did you go?" he asks softly, his other hand cupping my jaw.

"I'm literally in your lap," I smile, but he shakes his head.

"You think I don't know what it feels like when you're pulling away?" he asks, his golden eyes flashing with concern and hurt. He leans in, resting his forehead against mine. "Just talk to me. Was it too much? Too Fast?"

"No," I cup his jaw, my fingers brushing over his stubble. "God, no."

He waits, keeping his hold on me like I'll disappear if he lets go. "I just—" I force the words out. "You should be able to find your mate."

"What?"

"Archer is my—"

"Do *not* say another man's name while I can still taste you on my tongue," he growls, and my core clenches. The vibrations of his voice and his possessiveness rumble through me, making everything foggy except the throbbing need for him.

"The necklace I have," I continue slowly, "means he's my 'true love.' It only beats when you've found the person destined for you, and when he put it on me, it beat right away."

"Ah," Lowell says, but his face is unreadable. He's not upset or discouraged. It almost looks like he's figured out the missing piece to the puzzle.

"It's not fair of me to jump into something with you knowing that someone out there might be your mate and I'd be keeping you from her. Because, fuck, Lowell, you're—"

He pulls me closer and kisses me again, only breaking away when I whimper against him. "Ask me what this is, Katie."

"What?" I ask, slightly dazed.

"I told you if you answered my question, I'd tell you what this is," he smiles, brushing a stray strand of hair behind my ear. "Ask me again."

"Lowell—" he begins trailing kisses along my jaw, down the column of my neck. "What is this?"

"It's up to you to decide—"

"That's a terrible answer," I whine, pulling away and finding his eyes crinkled with laughter.

"Let me finish then, little witch." He flicks my nose before bringing both hands to cup my cheeks. His thumbs brush over my skin in a way that's both soothing and intimate. Then, he wets his lips before uttering two words that make my heart explode in my chest. "I'm yours."

Time stops as those little words sink into my skin, but he doesn't stop there. "You're all I want. I don't care about some hypothetical mate or the fact that you have a 'true love,' which I'm not sure is real. Because this," he places one hand right above my heart, "is real. I know you feel it too."

I nod emphatically. "I do. I just..." I fold myself into his arms, nestling into his chest. His arms instantly circle me, taking me to my safe place. "It's so fast."

"I know."

"It doesn't make sense."

"I know."

How did this happen so quickly? When I was fighting it with every ounce of energy I had. The bond between us gives a playful tug like it's mocking my efforts to stay away. But he's the person I want to see at the end of each day...hell, during each day too. He challenges, supports, and keeps me moving forward even when it's hard. And he's still the most attractive man I've ever seen.

"I'm tired of fighting this," I voice aloud, even though it's more to myself.

"So, stop," he murmurs.

"You're mine?" I ask, sitting up again to meet his gaze.

"Yours." He offers the words without expectation, without pressure for me to say them back. But it's not enough for him to just be mine. *I want to be his.* I want to belong to each other. Partners. Equals.

I've been in countless relationships, and no one has ever known me as completely as the man in front of me does. I always held back pieces of myself from my boyfriends. But Lowell knows it all and has never balked. What else could I ever ask for?

Fuck the necklace. This is what I want.

I tilt my head to the side, exposing the unscarred side of my neck. "Then claim me."

Lowell stills. I know what I'm offering, I've been reading up on werewolf culture, and Vlad helped me fill in a lot of the gaps. Fated mates are extremely rare amongst werewolves, but Alpha wolves will often claim a partner. It's temporary and needs to be renewed every couple of years, but it's a promise. A commitment. Something in the magic strengthens the connection between the partners, and it often leads to marriage.

In rare cases, it can override a mating bond.

And if Archer is my true love, being claimed by Lowell could break that bond.

"Is that too much?" I ask, suddenly nervous.

"No, it's not too much." Lowell leans forward, placing a kiss right above the pulse in my neck. "Are you sure?"

"If you're mine, then I'm yours."

Lowell kisses me frantically, his hand gripping my hair possessively, keeping me close. His tongue claims mine, and the friction from our wet bodies sends a spike of pleasure through me. I grind my hips into him, my body acting on its own accord. As my hips rotate, I feel him harden beneath me, the thin material barely a barrier between us as his cock rubs against my clit. My nipples harden beneath my bikini top as they brush against his sculpted chest.

He breaks the kiss, nipping his way back to my neck as I increase the pace. His desire and passion flood through the bond, doubling my own pleasure. We moan in unison as I shift in a way that has him hitting the perfect spot. I've never built to orgasm so fast, so intensely, but it's right there.

"Say it again," Lowell says against my skin, his teeth grazing the spot where my shoulder and neck meet.

"I'm yours," I pant, as the pleasure intensifies down our bond. "Please, Alpha, claim me."

His teeth sink into my soft skin and the pleasure mixed with the pain sends me careening over the edge. I scream Lowell's name, bucking wildly until I feel his cock twitch beneath me as he finds his own release. His ecstasy explodes down our bond, and a second orgasm barrels into me.

"Holy shit," I breathe in shock, slumped against him. Lowell barely touched me, and he made me come twice...harder than I've ever come before.

Lowell releases my neck and licks the hurt, making me shiver as aftershocks roll through my body. "*Mine*," he growls, his wolf instincts still at the forefront.

"Yours," I respond, smiling against his skin.

I don't know how long we sit there amidst the hot tub jets, but after a while, Lowell laughs, and I sit up enough to give him a questioning look.

"I don't think anyone has ever made me come in my pants before, little witch," he smirks. I laugh against his lips as he pulls me in for a kiss.

"Maybe you'll get a repeat performance when I claim you."

"You already have." He tilts his head, brushing his hair away from his neck, revealing a faint white bite mark. My mouth pops open.

"Was that..." I gasp as the realization washes over me. "I claimed you? That day by the lake?"

"You didn't know," he assures me, his hands rubbing up and down my spine.

"How could I do that without knowing?"

"I think it's because we might be—"

"I had a whole relationship since then," I squeal burying my face in my hands, and luckily, Lowell laughs. "Are you telling me you haven't been with anyone since we met?"

"I haven't," he says, and fuck if that doesn't make me feel all warm and fuzzy.

"Well, no wonder you came in your pants."

He snaps his teeth at me, and I laugh as he captures me. He deepens our kiss, my body pliant in his hands. I nip at his bottom lip, rocking my hips as his cock stiffens beneath me.

An irritated cough at my back has me pulling away. Vlad stands in the doorway, his blue eyes murderous, his cheeks flush, and his hair mussed. Oh, and he's also stark-fucking naked.

"Dude." I snap my eyes shut. "It's bad enough I have to see you dry humping my sister. Could you put some pants on?"

"Could you not fuck in my hot tub?" he snaps but zooms to a cabinet and pulls out a pair of joggers before hopping on a treadmill and turning it up to a speed I didn't know existed.

"What happened?" I ask, clambering off Lowell's lap and out of the hot tub.

"Nothing," he grumbles. I wrap myself in one of the towels and hold the other one over my shoulder just as Lowell comes up behind me. He takes it, drying off before slinging it along his waist.

"The scepter is in my vault," Vlad says, keeping up his insane pace on the treadmill. "It should stay there until we need it. I don't want your father getting any ideas about putting them all together."

"Okay," I agree. "Vlad—"

"Leave it, little witch," Lowell cuts me off, pulling me in and kissing me swiftly. "Go to bed and I'll be up in a minute."

I open my mouth to protest, but Lowell shakes his head. Reluctantly, I secure the towel around my chest and grab the untouched food tray before heading upstairs.

I'm trying to balance the tray and turn the doorknob to Lowell's room when I hear a strangled cry. I spin around, catching a glimpse of Adriana in her room across the hall through the crack in her door. She's curled in the fetal position, her shoulder shaking.

"What happened?" I ask, kicking her door fully open. She sits up, brushing away tears frantically.

"Nothing," she croaks, her voice raw. My eyes fall to the two puncture marks on her neck. *Vlad didn't heal her.* "I don't want to talk about it," she says, her gray eyes welling.

I open my mouth to protest but a new wave of tears overtakes my sister and I acquiesce. I set the tray at the foot of the bed, sitting beside her and wrapping my arm around her shoulders. "Is cheese enough to help or should I find wine?"

She laughs hollowly but takes a cube of cheese. "You made this for you and Lowell..." Her eyes fall to my neck where my own bite mark rests. "He claimed you. You should go be with him."

"One more night won't kill us."

Speak for yourself, Lowell's voice floats through my mind.

It's rude to eavesdrop...even with supernatural hearing.

Lowell's laughter rings in my ears. *I'm taking Vlad for a run. Take care of your sister.*

Thank you, I send down our channel.

I have four sisters, little witch. I've been in your shoes.

Your sister and Vlad?

Sisters, he corrects, and I can practically feel him shuddering. *Come to bed when you're done.*

I let Adriana eat most of the food on the tray, picking only at a few crackers so she can process her feelings. We talk for hours about our shared memories from childhood, about things we missed in our years apart, but I never get the story of what happened with her and Vlad.

I creep across the hall to Lowell's room when she finally falls asleep. He's already asleep, so I strip out of my now dry bathing suit and slide into one of his t-shirts before crawling into bed. I'm not even settled before he curls over to me, wrapping his arms around my waist and throwing his leg over my hip as he spoons me.

"Mine," he murmurs against my neck.

I fall asleep smiling.

Chapter Twenty-Three

THE DOOR CREAKS OPEN a moment before Adriana hisses my name. Lowell's arms tighten around me, cocooning me into his body.

"Katie," she whisper-shouts.

"Get rid of her and I'll make it worth your while," Lowell breathes in my ear, and I chuckle as I push my ass closer to him. He groans and the hand he has splayed on my stomach begins drifting lower as I grind into him.

"Come on, we have work to do," Adriana says, her voice directly in front of me. I open my eyes and glare at her as Lowell's hand pauses its descent.

"What work do we have to do that can't wait half an hour?" I ask.

Lowell chuckles, his fingers toying with the hem of my t-shirt. "It's cute you think it'll only last half an hour."

Fuck. Me. Sideways.

I really hate my sister right now.

"Just because you two are—" Adriana gestures wildly, "—doesn't mean everything stops. We're going back to the Highlands tonight and I want to teach you a new technique."

"Fine," I say through gritted teeth. "I'll meet you outside."

"Five minutes," Adriana says sternly before stalking around the bed and closing the door with a little too much force.

I roll over to Lowell who takes the opening to kiss me, his hands threading through my hair and tugging me closer. I sigh against his lips as his tongue teases me.

"I love that I get to do that now," he murmurs before stealing another kiss.

"Me too," I whisper. "So...five minutes?" I waggle my eyebrows at him.

"No, little witch." His hand tightens on the hair at the nape of my neck, using the grip to tilt my head back so he can access my neck. "I'll need at least an hour the first time I taste you."

A whimper leaves my lips as he releases me and stretches his muscular arm behind his head. He watches me hungrily as I get off the bed, my legs still slightly trembling with the promise he just dropped in my lap. I grab my overnight bag, which Lowell must have brought over from my former room, and take out a pair of leggings and a sports bra.

"This technique better be fucking brilliant," I grumble as I head into the bathroom to wash up and get changed. Lowell's laughter follows me, and I can't help the smile that tugs at my lips.

"THAT'S FUCKING BRILLIANT," I breathe as Adriana hands me my sword belt. We both stand on Vlad's lawn, squinting against the midday sun. It's weird being out this early. We've been either on a nocturnal schedule or underground, and I didn't realize how much I missed the way the noon sun warms my skin and burns off the winter chill.

"You really think it'll work?" I ask as I fasten the belt to my waist.

"Wand makers chose wood because of accessibility. That doesn't mean metal can't conduct magic," Adriana says, balancing her own sword in the palm of her hand. "We've been working to perfect it for a few weeks now. It's harder with spells than with Battle Magic, but it should work just fine."

I unsheathe my sword, my thumb brushing over the citrine gem in the hilt. Adriana murmurs a spell and a second later, the dummy from Vlad's gym soars onto the front lawn and lands standing on the plush grass. She takes out her cutlass and points it at the dummy's head.

"As you strike," she instructs, "say the spell you want to use. For today let's use something that will leave a visible mark so we can see if it works."

She swings the sword and magic bursts from the tip, hitting the dummy a moment before her sword connects with the rubbery neck. Purple welts decorate the chest in her wake. She murmurs another spell that removes them, and then motions for me to try.

I release a breath, trying to imagine the magic flowing down my arm and out the sword the way it would a wand. I land a perfect strike at the dummy's neck, but no magic. I swear under my breath, my shoulders creeping up to my ears.

"Maybe I should try a short sword?"

"Stop," Adriana says abruptly. "It's a new technique. It might take a minute to get used to. Warm up like you usually would with your sword, then add in the spell."

I purse my lips but do as I'm told. I work through my warm-up, moving until my muscles relax in the movement and my hips easily sink into my stance. A thin sheen of sweat coats my skin when I'm finally ready to attack the dummy again.

I slash forward, my sword skimming down the torso in a diagonal slice as I unleash my magic. I continue, following the momentum of my strike and spinning around to add an additional blow to the side of the dummy's head.

"Katie," Adriana squeaks as I pant, afraid to look back to the dummy to see if it worked. "Look."

I lift my eyes, finding two lines of purple welts across the dummy's torso, one on an area I didn't even touch with the metal. "It worked," I breathe.

"FUCK YES," a bellow from the porch turns my attention as Lowell barrels into me, scooping me into his arms. I have the foresight to drop the sword as he swings me in a circle. He somehow grabs Adriana in his other arm and swings her around too.

"Right," Adriana says sternly when he sets her down, but she's smiling widely. "Now do it again."

I do it seven more times, the spell growing progressively stronger each time. At the end of the last time, I sheath my sword and roll my shoulders. Lowell is beaming at me, his pride flowing down our bond.

"How do you feel?" Adriana asks.

"The best I've felt in a really long time," I murmur before wrapping her in a hug. "Thank you for this."

"Anytime, my Katie," she says, gripping me close.

"I HAVE A SURPRISE for you," Vlad says, swiveling slightly in his desk chair. Lowell, Vlad, and I are all holed up in his office, waiting for one of the Dark Witches to teleport and bring us back to the coven.

Adriana made some half-assed excuse about how she needed to go back early, conveniently leaving before sundown and having to see Vlad. Lowell couldn't get Vlad to admit what happened either, but the vampire looks haunted tonight.

We spent the latter half of the afternoon researching Baran's sword, the final piece of the blood oath. The only conclusion we came to was that it must have ended up in the palace after the Four Kings War. I phoned my mother, who promised to poke around discreetly, but she said no one's seen it for decades. She also informed me that Marcus asked the king if he would reinstate the four monarchs if it would avoid war. He predictably refused.

"Last time you said that you brought a Fae through the portal," I remind him, and he smiles sheepishly.

"Then it's not much of a surprise." He hops to his feet and swings the fireplace open. A small, squat man with elaborate brown horns that match his skin tone and hair steps from the swirling mist and into the office. Lowell sits up straighter, banishing the scroll propped on his lap and placing a protective hand on my knee.

"Relax, pup," I laugh, brushing him off and standing in front of the Fae. "Are you a healer too?"

He grumbles something in a language I don't understand. "He said he's better than a healer because he actually fixes things," Vlad translates.

"So why—" I start.

"I hired him to build us a portal." He flashes a toothy smile. "Thank you for your services, my friend," he says back to the Fae. "Give the Autumn King my best."

Another grumble in a strange language and then he's gone. "Specific breed of Fae directly related to the centaurs," Vlad explains. "It's lucky the Autumn King owed me a favor, or we would have never been able to afford him."

"You had him build a portal to the Highlands?" I ask, and Vlad nods eagerly. "Will this mess up the wards?"

"Baby queen, you wound me," Vlad dramatically clutches his chest. "I would never do something that would endanger the—" he breaks off when I arch an eyebrow. "Fine, I warned your sister and she made it work."

"Mhmm," I tsk, shaking my head. "Then, shall we?" I motion to the portal, but Vlad and Lowell exchange glances. "What?"

Lowell grabs my hand, turning me to face him and the knuckles of his other hand skim down my neck, slowing over the mark on my neck. "You need to cover this up," he says softly.

"Why?" I demand, my stomach dropping.

"Because your father is a sadistic fuck," Vlad drawls from near the portal.

"And if he sees the bite, he'll try to find some way to use it against you," Lowell murmurs.

"Or try to do something to Lowell to get you to fall in line," Vlad adds.

"Either way—"

"No one should know," I finish with a heavy sigh. "But—" Lowell wraps his hand around the hair at the nape of my neck as he lowers his forehead to rest against mine.

"Make no mistake, little witch," he murmurs. "You're still mine."

He kisses me quickly, but I'm having none of that. If this is the last time I can kiss him for a while, I'm sure as hell not making it a peck. I press up on my toes and grip his hair as he smiles against me. He circles his arms around my waist, molding my body to his in a seamless fit.

Vlad coughs loudly, and I flip him off before breaking away from Lowell, gently snagging his bottom lip between my teeth as I pull away. His resounding growl reverberates through me, and I shiver as his eyes meet mine, his pupils blown from desire.

"Let's use the portal every night and sleep here," I say, hooking my finger through the belt loop on Lowell's jeans. He chuckles darkly as I look up at him through my lashes, and he steals another kiss.

"This is actual hell," Vlad grumbles. "I really didn't think it could get worse than the flirting and tension-filled silences. I'll meet you at the coven." He practically dives headfirst into the portal.

Lowell chuckles as he zips into the hallway and returns with a scarf. He leans down and kisses the mark on my neck, pulling a moan from my lips.

"I'm not strong enough to resist if you keep making noises like that, little witch," he murmurs against my skin, his lips drifting higher, making my whole body come alive. I arch into him, my nipples pebbling.

Lowell groans and takes a very large step back. I step towards him, but he holds out a hand. "I need a minute or I'm going to throw you down on that desk and fuck you until you can't walk straight."

"I see no problem with that, Alpha," I purr.

"If you fuck on my desk, you're buying a new one," Vlad pops back in through the portal and I jump back, my hand flying to my chest as my heart races.

"Did you even leave?" I grumble.

"I did, and I decided I'm staying here," Vlad says, folding his arms over his chest.

"You could just apologize to Adriana."

"What makes you think I'm the one who should be apologizing?" Vlad demands, his face set in an absolutely terrifying scowl.

"If you just told us what happened, I wouldn't have to make assumptions."

Lowell's phone rings and he strides out of the line of fire as Vlad stares me down.

"You're the ones who said we're a team," I say softly. "I can't help if I don't know what's going on."

Vlad narrows and then a wistful look crosses his face. "You remind me of her so much sometimes."

"Adriana?"

"Finley," he amends, and a smile tugs at my lips. "She was my best friend for a bit there, the only one I've met in about six hundred years who would call me on my shit."

"Am I your best friend, Vlad?" I ask.

"Don't be ridiculous." He smirks. "You just have no self-preservation instincts."

"Because I want to know what happened with you and my sister?"

"Because you're pushing a thousand-year-old vampire," he amends. "Most people run screaming when I seem agitated."

"Yeah well, you haven't met my mother." He laughs, the sound warm and genuine.

"There are laws," Vlad whispers after a moment. "Laws I wrote. Laws I believe in."

"Okay…"

"I shouldn't have fed from Adriana," he admits, swiping his hand through his blonde hair. "Nothing can happen between us. I'm immortal. She's not. It's as simple as that. So, I stopped before anything could happen."

"You stopped," I repeat. "And Adriana was upset by that."

"You'll have to ask her."

"Did you want to stop?" I ask, and Vlad meets my gaze, regret swimming through his blue eyes.

Lowell comes back in looking positively murderous. "That was Lyra," he grumbles. "There's a problem with one of the packs."

"Provence?" Vlad asks.

"They've been bitching about the war since I visited. Now they decided to do something about it." My eyes scan down to the faint line across Lowell's chest, which is barely visible due to his quick healing.

"What?" I ask, and Lowell brushes my hair back behind my ears.

"Their Alpha challenged me." Vlad swears, but I'm still not understanding. "A challenge for Pack Master is a fight to the death."

Chapter Twenty-Four

A CHALLENGE FOR PACK Master is a fight to the death.

"When?" I demand, holding Lowell's unwavering gaze. He looks more agitated than nervous, but it feels like someone punched me in the stomach.

"Tonight," he says, glancing at Vlad. "They're here now."

I ball my fists to keep them from shaking and take a deep breath, raising my chin high. "Then let's go."

"Absolutely not," Lowell growls. "Vlad will take you back to the coven."

"Yeah, not happening." I reach up and brush my fingers over Lowell's neck where my bite mark resides, before wrapping my hand around the nape of his neck and tugging him down closer to me. "You're mine. I'm not letting you do this alone."

He sighs and scoops me into his arms, burying his face in my hair. "I don't want you to see who I have to become to do this."

"You've met me, right? You've seen me pull the evil-queen act," I chide, and he tightens his grip. "Nothing you can do will change what I think of you."

He kisses the bite mark on my shoulder, before straightening and looking at Vlad.

"Anything happens to me—"

"I've got them," Vlad solemnly promises before walking towards the front door.

"You stay with Vlad," Lowell says, cupping my face in his hands. "The wolves will be riled up from the fight, but they won't touch you unless..." He swallows.

"That won't happen," I say simply.

"Katie—"

"No." My lower lip trembles, but I bite down on it, hoping the pain distracts Lowell from the fear I'm feeling. "You don't get to die tonight. That's an order from your queen."

He kisses my forehead. "Okay, Ma Reine." I force myself to swallow hard as Lowell pulls me into his chest. "I'm not going anywhere." He tilts my chin and kisses me passionately, a thousand emotions and unsaid words swirling between our lips. It ends too soon. It always ends too soon. My need for him is bottomless.

"We have to go," Lowell murmurs. When my eyes drift open, he's wearing his hardened expression like armor. He seems taller, broader, his presence even more commanding. *My Alpha.*

He takes my hand, interlocking our fingers as I shake off the remaining dread and put on my own cold mask. We walk into the foyer, where Vlad is waiting, holding my necklace.

"Put this on," he instructs, and Lowell takes it from him to do it for me as I look at him questioningly. "A queen on the arm of the Pack Master wearing Aldonza's necklace makes a statement."

"Not to fuck with me?" I ask, and Vlad flashes me a cold smile.

"Exactly." Lowell finishes with the clasp and squeezes my shoulders before releasing me and heading towards the door.

"Let's go," Lowell says.

We trudge through the forest slowly, the crunching of our boots the only sound. Lowell holds my hand, squeezing tightly. When I look over at him, he keeps his gaze forward but brings my hand to his mouth and kisses my knuckles.

We enter a clearing, the pale sliver of the moon providing the only light. Vlad takes the lead, walking straight ahead before disappearing into thin air.

"It's shielded," Lowell says, gruffly. He tugs me forward and I feel the kiss of magic against my skin.

When we pass through the magical barrier, we're standing at the edge of a small village comprised of grey stone cabins that run in concentric circles surrounding an open patch of earth. A large pile of wood sits to one side, a bonfire waiting to be lit. People frantically move around the town square, pushing picnic tables to the side, roping off a large circle, and ushering small children into houses.

A woman breaks free of the crowd and right away I know she's one of Lowell's sisters...the eyes alone give her away. Her dark hair is cropped short, angled to accent her sharp chin and high cheekbones. She's long and lean, her legs practically come up to my chest, and she stands like she's completely comfortable being almost a head above everyone around her. The black tank top she wears reveals a tattoo depicting the phases of the moon down her arm.

She dips her head in respect to Lowell before turning to face me, her eyes immediately falling to the mark on my neck. She inhales through her nose as if she needs scent proof that Lowell has claimed me.

"You must be Lyra," I say, offering her a smile and dropping Lowell's hand to extend it to her. "I'm Katie."

"I know," she says, her smile making her seem more lethal. "He's been going on about you ever since he pulled you from the lake."

If Lowell hears her, he doesn't react, his eyes focused on a man standing in the center of town. He's tall, and even though he isn't a large man, I can see his muscle definition from here. His black hair is cut short and streaked with grey, showing his age. The man is surrounded by people rocking the leather biker look and is speaking with a short, plump woman whose face is set in a scowl.

Lyra says something to Lowell in French as more and more people start filling in the town square, forming a human barrier around the circle. A lot of them have plastic cups in their hands like they're here for a sporting event rather than a deathmatch that could decide the fate of the magical world.

Lowell hisses at Lyra, who bows her head in submission before stalking back towards the town square. Lowell squeezes my hand so tight I think the bones will break. Then he lets go, following his sister and leaving me trembling.

"Katie." Vlad appears beside me, a sinister smile plastered on his face. "Don't show them your fear." I nod and slide my mask into place as Vlad extends his arm and escorts me toward the makeshift ring.

Lowell stalks right into the center, turning around in a circle, greeting his pack with a cold smile. Calls of encouragement in multiple languages ripple through the crowd as Lowell bares his teeth. Vlad leads me right up to the side of the ring, next to Lyra who looks ready to murder a bitch.

The other Alpha shrugs off his leather vest...yeah seriously a leather vest... and enters the ring to a mix of jeering and applause from his wolves.

"Uncle," Lowell says coldly, and Vlad's hand tightens around my arm in warning to stay calm. Lowell's uncle growls something in French and Lowell rolls his eyes, looking bored. "English," he commands.

"You're no nephew of mine," he says in a heavily accented voice. "Any man who would lead his pack into a war for pussy doesn't deserve the title of Pack Master."

Lowell's body goes taut. "Do *not* speak of my partner in that tone," he grits out through a clenched jaw. His uncle laughs haughtily.

"Did she allow you to claim her back then?" he asks, searching for me. Vlad's fangs extend, but Lowell is faster. His hand snaps out, grabbing his uncle by the throat and keeping him from finding me in the crowd.

"Because you're blood," he whispers so low that if there had been any noise in the clearing it would be hidden, "I'll give you the option to surrender."

"Never," his uncle hisses. Then, he addresses the crowd. "You lead us into a battle to be led by a child—"

"I was her age when I was made Pack Master."

"How do we know this isn't some power grab between witches? And once they use us to fight their battle, we'll be discarded?"

"I've already told you it was Queen Kathryn's idea to use the witches on the front lines, to shield the wolves and vampires."

Heads turn to me, and I keep my chin held high.

"It's time for us to claim our place in the Kingdom of Magic," Lowell says, and the crowd erupts in applause, except for those from Lowell's uncle's coalition. "To have a say in how to grow and raise our packs. To leave fucking isolation for the first time in two hundred years."

Lowell glares at the man he's still holding, waiting to see if anything he said has been accepted, if he'll back down. His uncle sneers and spits at the ground before Lowell's feet.

"I challenge you, Lowell Dubois, for the role of Pack Master. I accuse you of treason against all the packs of Europe."

"So be it."

Lowell releases his uncle roughly just as the crowd around us roars. Lowell bends at the waist, and with a parting smirk, yanks off his jeans, shifting into his large, white wolf form. He bares his teeth at his uncle who does the same. The grey wolf isn't as big as Lowell, but he's still easily double the size of a regular wolf.

The uncle lunges first, tearing across the clearing in a burst of speed that Lowell meets head-on. The two wolves collide in a clash of teeth and claws. They move so fast that my human eyes can barely track what's happening. The grey wolf somehow winds up on Lowell's back, his teeth sinking into his flank as Lowell bucks, but can't dislodge him. Red blood blooms over white fur, but I feel no pain through our bond, only adrenaline.

Lowell dislodges his uncle, sending the wolf careening to the edge of the ring and landing with a thud. Lowell doesn't give him a moment of reprieve before launching forward and swiping his claws into the wolf's side. There's a terrible whine and a snarl and some of the other pack's members inhale sharply as their Alpha tries to swipe at Lowell with his claws. Lyra is screaming her head off in encouragement, her eyes glowing, nearly feral as she fights her nature to shift.

Lowell releases his uncle who attempts to stand and falters. His silver eyes look up as he whines in pain. Lowell barks once, and I can feel his intention through our bond. He's offering his uncle a final chance to submit. His uncle shakes his wolfish head and charges at Lowell.

They clash again, but this time Lowell never loses the upper hand. He fights viciously, and I can't help the flush spreading through my body as I watch.

"You're panting like a bitch in heat," Vlad murmurs.

"I shouldn't be turned on by this, right?" I respond.

"I'm the wrong person to ask, baby queen," Vlad laughs, and I note his fangs are fully extended. I wet my lips as Lowell slashes and bites until his uncle lies in a heap on the dirt floor, his breaths coming in shallow.

Lowell stalks towards his prey, who fixes him with a cold stare. There's a crunch as Lowell's teeth sink into his neck, and then a pop as bones break, and the grey wolf lies lifeless. Lowell tilts his head up and howls at the moon, the sound echoed by everyone around us.

Lowell shifts, every inch of his muscular body glistening with sweat. Blood drips down his chin as he lifts his arms in victory. His eyes connect to mine and my entire body tightens as I scan his body, my mouth drying when I see his very large cock is fully erect.

The pack surrounds him, someone handing him a towel to wipe his mouth, which he does without ever taking his eyes off me. The lust between our bond is enough to have a moan slip from my lips and his cock twitch in response.

"Definitely shouldn't be turned on by this," I murmur, and Vlad just chuckles.

Lowell shrugs off his pack members, zipping through the crowd until he's in front of me. His eyes hungrily scan down my body before he snaps out his hand, wrapping it around the nape of my neck and pulling me into a kiss. The crowd legitimately cheers as I jump into his arms and he grinds his erection against me, the thin barrier of my leggings the only thing separating us.

I vaguely register that we're moving, the sound of the crowd getting further away, the lights behind my closed lids growing dimmer, but all I can focus on is Lowell as his mouth crashes against mine. We're a tangle of teeth and tongues, stealing the very air from each other's lungs because we can't get enough. My nails rake down his back and he growls in approval before I'm suddenly thrust into darkness, a door slamming behind us.

Lowell pushes me back against a wall, uneven stone biting into my exposed skin. He pulls back only briefly, a rip cutting through the silence before my tunic and bra fall away. The scrape of a claw down my sternum tells me all I need to know as I feel his paw shifting back to a hand now that my top has been dispatched. He slides my leggings and panties down slowly, and I kick off my boots one at a time.

When I'm completely bare before him, he rises, his fingers drawing circles on my stomach, leaving a trail of goosebumps in their wake as he slides down my center agonizingly slow. "Did you enjoy that, little witch?" he murmurs between kisses along my jaw and down my neck.

"You know the answer." I gasp as his finger reaches my sex which is already drenched for him. He groans as he feels my arousal. He dips his head lower and captures my nipple between his teeth. The hand not between my legs palms my other breast, his fingers matching the movements of his tongue and driving me into a frenzy.

"Are you hurt?" I breathe, the haze around my mind clearing enough that I remember he was bleeding.

"Healing," he murmurs against my skin and the vibrations rumble against my nipple and shoot a line straight to my core, where his hand has stilled. He sinks lower, biting and kissing his way down my stomach, his stubble scraping against my skin. He falls to his knees in front of me, nudging my legs wider as he nibbles my inner thigh.

"We can wait until you're--" Lowell's tongue swipes a long, delicious line down my entire sex. "Fuck," I swear as he swirls the tip of his tongue around my clit and my hands fist in his hair.

"You were saying?" he asks smugly before sealing his lips around my clit. I buck against him. His fingers dig into my hips, keeping me close as he drives me closer and closer to orgasm. Every time a spike of pleasure rolls through me, he moans as it travels down our bond. The combination of his desire and mine plus the vibrations have me teetering at the edge in seconds.

Lowell pulls away and I cry out at the loss of contact. "Please." His fingers tease my entrance.

"Please what?" His eyes lock on mine as he hovers right above me. I thrust my hips forward, but he stays just out of reach.

"Make me come," I plead. He hums, slowly licking me again, keeping me hovering right at the edge. "Please, Alpha."

"I will," he smiles. "How many times has a man made you come in a row?"

The tip of his finger slides inside me, and my head falls back against the wall. It's hard to think of anything except his fingers, his warm breath against my sensitive flesh. "Umm.... I don't—" His finger slides inside me and curls. Just like that, I'm seconds away from exploding.

"Answer the question, little witch," he commands.

"Twice, I think," I murmur.

"Good girl," he praises. "Let's improve on that, shall we?"

My eyes pop open as his mouth surrounds my clit while his finger continues to stroke that perfect spot inside me, and I come hard and fast. I expect Lowell to pull back, but instead, he adds another finger, and I scream out as one orgasm merges into another. I scream his name, my hands tugging on his hair as I writhe against him, and he pumps and licks me until I come down from the incredible high.

A thin sheen of sweat is coating my skin when he pulls back. He pulls his fingers out of me and slowly rises to a stand as he sucks his fingers. His eyes are locked on mine as he licks them clean, and it's easily the most erotic thing I've ever witnessed.

"You taste so fucking good," he growls before kissing me, thrusting his tongue inside my mouth so I can taste myself on him. My hand skims down the hard planes of his stomach, reaching for his throbbing cock when he snatches my wrist and pins it above my head. "I'm not done with you yet," he says, grabbing my other hand and pinning it in the same way. My body arches towards him instinctively.

"So, fucking responsive," he murmurs into my ear, gathering both wrists with one hand and using the other to tilt my head to the side to access my neck.

"Do you like this?" he asks, his breath fanning across the shell of my ear a moment before his erection grinds against me, rubbing against my clit and making me whimper. One motion, one move, one inch of his hips or mine and he'll slide right inside me. Fuck I want that so badly I can't even form words.

"Do you like giving me control?" he asks, his grip shifting and holding my jaw in place. "Do you crave having someone you can submit to, someone who can take all that pressure away so you can just relax and enjoy? Is that what you want, Ma Reine?"

Fuck yes. I nod and Lowell's responding smile is feral.

"I need the words, Katie."

"Yes, Alpha," I moan. His eyes turn to liquid gold as he kisses me savagely and I go pliant in his arms, letting him dictate the pace and matching his intensity. He breaks the kiss and sinks into a crouch in front of me.

"Hang on," he whispers, before wrapping his hands around my thighs and lifting me until they're resting on his shoulders. Then he rises to his full height, taking me with him until I'm six feet in the air with nothing but the wall to hold onto.

"Fuck, Lowell—" I sputter as my hands splay against the wall, my legs trembling over his shoulders. Arousal and fear mix, overwhelming my senses.

"There's a beam above your head if you need to hold on, but I've got you."

I reach up just as Lowell's tongue plunges inside me, and instead, they fall to his hair as my head and shoulders tip back against the wall. I feel him smile against me as he fucks me with his tongue. His hand reaches up and over my thigh and squeezes my breast. When he pinches my nipple hard, I come again.

"More," he says against me, his other hand replacing his tongue as he pumps me to another orgasm. "That's my girl," he murmurs as he buries himself in my pussy again and I cry out as the waves of pleasure crest and break over and over so many times I can't even count.

His hands rove over my skin, igniting every nerve. My body is a live wire. My throat is hoarse from screaming his name, and even when I feel like I possibly can't come anymore, he strokes me to ecstasy again, devouring me like he can't get enough.

"Alpha," I plead, but I'm unsure what I'm asking for. I'm overly sensitive but I think I might die if he stops. Lowell pulls back enough to look at me as I convulse around his shoulders, riding out multiple aftershocks.

"You're so fucking beautiful," he murmurs, placing a chaste kiss on my clit and slowly kissing down my thigh. "What do you need, little witch?" he asks.

I mumble a string of non-words that he somehow interprets, and he slides me down his body until my legs latch around his waist. Lowell strokes my hair and peppers my shoulders with kisses as I bury my head in his chest, hearing his heartbeat steady beneath my ear. His calming scent, rain and earth, is mixed with sweat and something else. *Me.* Fuck, I love that. It's primal. Like I've marked him as mine for anyone to know.

When I can form thoughts, I pull back and he cups my cheek, tenderly brushing his thumb over my cheek and grounding me. "I'll never get enough of you," he whispers, sweetly kissing me. It's slower now that the adrenaline has burned off, but still makes my core tighten.

Do you want to lie down? he asks through our mental channel, not bothering to stop kissing me. He means it. He gave me immeasurable pleasure and he would be happy just falling asleep with me even though his cock is rock hard beneath my hips.

I pull back, drawing my lower lips between my teeth and giving him a sly smile.

"Nope."

I drop my legs to the ground, immediately sinking to my knees, my eyes remaining locked on Lowell's. His breaths come in pants as he watches in anticipation.

"Katie, you don't have to—" He hisses as my tongue runs along the underside of his head. My lips wrap around the sensitive tip, and I swirl my tongue, lapping up the bead of pre-cum that's gathered, the salty taste of him flooding my taste buds.

Lowell's body is vibrating with need as I pull back. Having him at my mercy like this is heady. It makes me feel sexy and powerful. I switch my attention to his balls, lightly sucking as my hand wraps around his thick shaft and pumps. His hands open and close, his knuckles turning white.

"There's something I haven't told you," I say, licking the underside of his cock until I'm hovering over his tip again. His forehead crinkles as he meets my eyes. "It's a long story, so remind me to tell you about it later."

"Okay..." It's a testament to how wonderful this man is that he doesn't try to shut me up. "What is it?"

I respond by taking him in my mouth with one swift motion.

Every. Single. Long. Inch.

I've seen Lowell naked a lot. I've long ago given up any illusion of modesty around him. But I don't think I processed his sheer size until he's hitting the back of my throat and my lips are pulled back to accommodate his girth. This man will break me in half when we finally have sex.

"Fuck," he swears, his head falling back. "You don't have a gag reflex?"

I hum in agreement, and he twitches in my mouth as I hollow out my cheeks and slide back up, releasing him with a satisfying pop. I'm done teasing though; I want him to fall apart. I pick up my pace, relishing as Lowell swears every time he bottoms out. I cup his balls, gently tugging as I run my thumb along the seam. He begins shaking with the need to move, and I grab his hand, bringing it to the back of my head.

"Katie—" he warns.

"I can take it," I moan around his cock. I keep my eyes on his as I slowly slide back up again. "Fuck my mouth, Alpha."

His control snaps.

His fingers thread into my hair and he uses the leverage to propel me up and down, faster and faster. His hips thrust wildly, so fast that it's all I can do to hold on as he uses my mouth. Saliva drips onto my chest and my eyes water as I keep them locked on my wolf.

"Such a good girl, taking my cock," Lowell moans as his movements become more erratic. "So. Fucking. Perfect." He punctuates each word with a thrust, his balls tighten in my hand, and his grip on my hair turns almost painful.

"You're gonna make me come, little witch," he grunts, releasing my hair and trying to pull out. "Where—"

In response, I grab his hips and bring him impossibly deeper as I feel his cock thicken and his release spill into the back of my throat. I swallow and he groans, panting as his body falls forward to lean against the wall behind me. I take every drop he has before slowly releasing him with a flick of my tongue against his head.

"Mine," I growl, my voice raw from the pounding I just took. A satiated smile spreads across Lowell's face as he hunches over me, trying to catch his breath.

"All fucking yours," he breathes.

Chapter Twenty-Five

I STAND AND LOWELL kisses me, backing me up against the wall. His tongue slowly strokes mine, turning my already weak knees to liquid. But he anticipates this and scoops me into his arms, nuzzling my hair before placing a kiss on my temple.

"Lowell?" I ask as he starts carrying me further into the room in the darkness. "Where the hell are we?"

He chuckles as he sets me on the edge of a mattress. His knuckles skim over my throat in a tender caress. "My house."

"You have a house?" I ask, trying to see through the darkness. All I can see is the wall of windows at the back of the large room, which let in the slightest sliver of moonlight.

"Give me two minutes," Lowell murmurs against my lips before kissing me and retreating across the room. He returns with a damp washcloth and cleans me up, his hands moving gently across my skin. He disappears again and I hear a kettle whistle before he returns with a steaming mug, extending it to me.

"You made me tea?" I ask, taking the mug from his hands and inhaling the earthy aroma. He shrugs and gives me a shy smile.

"I don't want your throat to hurt tomorrow."

"I—" my brain short circuits. "That's...so freaking adorable."

"I am *not* adorable," Lowell growls as he rounds the bed to the side.

"But you are," I drag out the word for ten syllables while I carefully crawl across the mattress and kneel on the bed in front of where he stands. "You're this big, scary, Alpha werewolf who kills people without even breaking a sweat, but you're really like a big marshmallow."

Lowell takes the mug from my hands and sets it on the nightstand. My pulse skyrockets as he turns around, a smirk playing across his lips. In a flash of wolf speed, he wraps his arms around me and throws me over his shoulders. My yelp of surprise turns to a breathy moan as he smacks my bare ass before setting me back on my knees but still holding me flush against his body.

"You wanna rethink that assessment, little witch?" he whispers in my ear before nipping at my lobe.

"If I say no, will you spank me again, pup?" I ask as he bites hard on my earlobe before licking away the hurt. I make a sound one can only describe as a mewl...but even though I want this man like nothing I've ever wanted in my life, my body is not ready for a second round. My legs are still trembling, and I think the only thing keeping me upright is Lowell's grip on my waist.

As if he knows exactly what I'm thinking, Lowell nudges me backward and lies down at the edge of the bed. I flop onto his chest, into the spot I've claimed as my own, and my whole body relaxes as I breathe in his earth and rain scent.

"Thank you," I whisper, the words all-encompassing.

"I like taking care of you," Lowell says as he kisses the top of my head.

"I'm not used to it," I admit, tracing his crescent moon tattoo. "I don't have the best track record with boyfriends."

His eyebrows quirk up, and my heart jumps into my throat as I realize what I said. "I don't mean—I know we haven't—" His lips press into a line like he's trying not to laugh. "I know we haven't discussed labels yet..."

"Do you want me to be your boyfriend, little witch?" he teases, his smile lighting up his entire face.

"Well, when *you* say it, it sounds stupid and juvenile," I pout, burying my head into his chest to hide my blush.

"Come here," he says softly, pulling my arm so that my body follows, and I wind up on top of him, my hips straddling his waist. "Are you mine?" he asks, pushing my hair back from where it's fallen in my face.

"Yes," I say, my fingers brushing against the near-invisible scar from when I claimed him.

"Then you can call me whatever you want, *Ma Reine*."

"Yeah?" I ask and he nods before pulling me into a sweet kiss. "Can I call you my consort?" He pinches my side and I laugh as I fold my body into him so I'm resting my cheek in the crook of his neck. "What did you call me before? When you were addressing your uncle."

"My partner," Lowell says. "When two Alphas get together, they usually opt for the word partner...cuts out on the patriarchal bullshit that comes along with boyfriend or girlfriend."

"Partner," I repeat. "I like it." Lowell kisses the top of my head and I snuggle further into his embrace.

"You have a story for me," he reminds me.

"Right," I chuckle, impressed he remembers anything I said from twenty minutes ago. "When Edina and I were sixteen—"

"No good can come from a story that starts this way."

"Hush," I chide, and I feel his amusement trickling down our bond. "We were dating brothers, and by that I mean I was dating one brother and Edina made out with the other at a party. Anyway, we got it into our heads that we would take the next step physically with them on the same night.

"Edina found a recipe for a tonic that takes away your gag reflex for an hour. I think witches used it in traveling circuses back in the day," I continue, and Lowell laughs like he knows where this is going. "She was always better at brewing tonics and potions than I was, so I told her to take care of it."

"And she made it too strong?"

I giggle. "We didn't realize until days later."

"I'll have to remember to thank her one day," Lowell murmurs and I laugh freely. We fall into a comfortable silence. The only sound in my ears is Lowell's heartbeat. Even the locket isn't bothering me. I've honestly forgotten it's on, which is rare. The thumping of the pendant is calm now, mirroring my little content bubble.

"I should have asked earlier—"

"You were busy," Lowell interrupts.

"--are you doing okay?" I ask, not moving from my little cocoon in Lowell's arms.

"Never been better." I don't stop the smile that blooms on my face.

"I meant with...everything else. You killed your uncle today."

Lowell sighs heavily and his arms tighten around me. "He was an ass," he says after a moment. "He's a lot older than my mother, and when their parents died, he took care of her...if you can call it that. She never spoke of it, but my father told me my uncle used to hit her. It's part of the reason they left that pack."

"Still."

"I've killed before," he says carefully. "And I'll have to do it again. It's not something I enjoy, but when it comes to the safety of my pack, of my people..."

"You do what needs to be done," I respond, and he kisses my forehead.

"Plus, my queen told me I wasn't allowed to die today."

"Aren't you glad you didn't?" I smirk, and Lowell hums in agreement. "Oh my god," I breathe, sitting up and almost clunking my head into Lowell's nose. "Your entire family saw you carry me off."

"Yes."

"They have to know what we were doing."

"Yes."

"I haven't even met most of them yet," I whine. "And their first impression is me climbing you like a tree while you were naked." His body shakes with his laughter, and I swat at his chest. "This is serious!"

"They know what this is," he says simply. "They won't get hung up on it. My sisters will probably tease you, but sex is nothing to be ashamed or uncomfortable about in our family."

"Is that a wolf thing?"

"It's a French thing," he smiles, and I roll my eyes as he guides my head back to his chest. "Don't worry, little witch. I'm sure they'll love you." I scoff but relax into his hold.

WE MUST BOTH FALL asleep, because the next thing I know, sunlight is streaming through the wall of windows. I reach for Lowell, but the scent of bacon frying tells me he's already in the kitchen.

I prop myself up, getting my first good look at Lowell's house. It's an open concept, one giant room with a ladder along the back wall that leads to a loft decorated with bookshelves, couches, and a giant flat screen. The floors are worn wooden floorboards, and the walls are comprised of natural grey stones, except for the back wall of full-length windows that overlook the forest. Lowell moves around a simple kitchen nook with white cabinets and a small island with stools instead of a table.

Keeping the sheets wrapped around me, I open the oak nightstand next to Lowell's massive bed, riffling around until I find an old t-shirt. I slip into the one door to find the bathroom impeccably neat, the gray and white tones giving it a simplistic feel. I steal his toothbrush and splash some water on my face before throwing on the t-shirt and heading into the kitchen.

Lowell is flipping bacon, attending to something in the oven, and brewing coffee in a seamless dance. I sneak up behind him and wrap my arms around his middle, my fingers brushing over his exposed abs because the man never wears a damn shirt. He hums and his hands fall to my forearms as I kiss his back between his shoulder blades.

"Morning, Alpha," I purr, and he turns in my hold and lifts me, carrying me over to the island and sitting me down on the countertop before kissing me.

"Morning, *Ma Reine*," he says against my lips. I sigh and he takes advantage of the opening to sweep his tongue inside my mouth, teasing the tip of mine as I surge forward to meet him. My legs fall open as he steps in closer, his large hands brushing back my hair.

"Fuck," he growls as he steps away, his eyes traveling the length of me in his shirt and nothing else. "You're always beautiful, but like this..." he cups my jaw. "You're a fucking goddess."

"Like this?"

"Just out of bed," he murmurs, his hands drifting down my side, leaving a line of fire in his wake. "Hair mussed from my hands. Covered in my scent, wearing my shirt."

"So possessive," I tsk.

"Pot. Kettle," he responds, kissing me on the neck before stepping away. I instantly miss his warmth.

"I have no idea what you're talking about," I snicker, and he shoots me a comical look over his shoulder as he pulls a muffin tin out of the oven.

"Might I remind you when you growled 'mine' while hovering over my cock a few hours ago?" His amusement trickles down our bond and I can't help but laugh even as I blush a little.

"Oh, that." Lowell brings over a plate filled with eggs, bacon, and blueberry muffins and hands it to me before opening a drawer and grabbing two forks. "How early did you wake up?"

"Early," he says, grabbing a stack of bacon strips and shoving them in his mouth. "I called Adriana—"

"Fuck," I breathe, realizing we never called her and told her we weren't coming back to the Highlands last night.

"Vlad called her apparently, explained the situation," he says. "He also told her we'd all be staying here one more night, which she said is fine."

"Why? Not that I'm complaining, obviously."

"There's a party tonight," Lowell responds, walking away and returning with two mugs of coffee. "And since I bailed early on the party last night—"

"Sorry." Lowell laughs.

"Never fucking apologizing for...what did you call it? Climbing me like a tree?" I laugh and roll my eyes, taking a bite of the eggs and moaning when the flavor bursts on my taste buds.

"I'm also going for a run with my sisters in a bit," Lowell continues, unease flashing through his eyes. "We have a special hill we go to that has a great view. I'd like you to come if you want..."

"I don't know that I'll be able to keep up," I laugh, and Lowell looks down at the plate.

"I was thinking...you could ride me," he says so vulnerably that I don't even point out the innuendo.

"Yeah." I set the plate on the counter and loop my arms around his neck. "I'd love that." He smiles broadly before kissing me.

The door bangs open, and Lowell very uncharacteristically rolls his eyes. I turn and find a short woman standing in the doorway, a pile of clothes in her arms. Her golden eyes flash between Lowell and me before she wipes her free hand through her black hair, tied in a messy bun.

"You must be Katie," she says, walking into the room and throwing the clothes down on the countertop. "I'm Luna, Lowell's eldest sister. These are for you since some alpha-asshole can't control himself and left you with nothing to wear." She clicks her tongue at Lowell, but even that motion can't conceal the amusement in her eyes or the laugh rising in her throat.

"You might want to put them on," she continues, walking straight to the oven and plucking a muffin from the tin. "The kids will be here in about thirty seconds."

Lowell's eyes widen. "I thought you told them I'd see them later," he says, and I quickly hop off the counter and throw on the pair of leggings Luna brought for me.

"Yeah, well..." she chokes out amidst a mouth full of muffin. "The inmates run the asylum."

"ALPHA!" The battle cry of small voices echoes through the open doorway. Lowell moves around the island and holds out his arms just as a toddler bursts through the door and launches herself toward him. Lowell deftly snatches her out of the air.

"Alpha! Alpha!" More voices call as they break through the threshold.

"We're under attack!" Lowell shouts as two more children around the same age as the young girl bull rush him, tackling him to the ground. "Save yourself!" He calls to me as the kids squeal in delight.

"All right, all right," Luna laughs, her voice like warm honey. "Off your uncle." The kids don't listen, all fighting for Lowell's attention as he pretends to struggle to get up.

"Look," Luna calls, pulling a muffin from the pan. "Muffins!" The two older kids hop up and run over to their mom and she tosses them each a muffin. "Go take one to your father."

They leave without the extra muffin, screaming for their dad. Lowell stands and approaches us, the youngest girl wrapped around his waist like a fashion accessory.

"Ava Marie, down," Luna commands. The little girl giggles but doesn't move. Luna gives Lowell a look like, *what can you do.*

"Uncle Alpha," Ava Marie says, and Lowell adjusts her so that he's holding her upright. "You said you were going to bring us home a princess..." her eyes look at me nervously.

"I brought you home a queen," he whispers, and her little mouth pops open in a perfect O.

"Wow," she breathes, but then frowns. "Where's your crown?"

"Oh. I left it at home," I tell the little girl. She gives me a stern face that looks a lot like disapproval.

"Is she a good or evil queen?" she whispers loudly.

"Oh, she's very good," Lowell says with a wink. The girl is satisfied and wriggles out of Lowell's grasp and comes over to hug my legs. Then she runs off in the direction of her siblings, leaving Lowell and Luna staring at me like I'm a mythical creature.

"I hope you like babysitting," Luna says with a melodic laugh. "She doesn't hug anyone." She claps Lowell on the shoulder and makes her way to the door. "One hour! Shower first. You smell like sex."

She shuts the door on her way out and Lowell laughs quickly before wrapping his arms around my waist and tugging me toward the bathroom. He pushes down my leggings before lifting my shirt and tossing it towards the bed.

"What are you doing?" I laugh as his sweats come off and he flips the shower on.

"You heard the woman," he says with a broad smile and then tugs me into the cold water. I shriek but he pushes me through the stream to the wall, trapping me against the tiles as his mouth descends on mine until the water is warm enough.

Chapter Twenty-Six

THE WIND WHIPS THROUGH my hair as I fist my hands into Lowell's silken white fur. The muscles in his back ripple as his paws connect with the earth beneath us at a sickening pace. My eyes are shut tight; my face is buried in his neck, clinging on for dear life as we run with his sisters at our heels.

I rode on Lowell's back at the dragons' lair, but we were picking our way down a mountain. It certainly wasn't Lowell's top speed, which if possible is even faster in his wolf form than in his human form. He puts on an extra burst of speed and his sisters' barks grow farther away.

Open your eyes, Lowell says through our mental channel. I shake my head against his fur wildly, keeping my eyes closed. *You'll like it, I promise.*

I hold him tighter, my knuckles turning white with the force of my terror. Slowly, I crack open my eyes a fraction of an inch.

The world passes in a blur of green and blue in the crisp winter daylight. I sit up a little straighter, still keeping my death grip as we ascend a hill, bounding up the steep incline with ease. Tall grass brushes against my bare feet hooked around Lowell's body. We reach the top and he pauses, looking over his shoulder at me, his wolfish face somehow smiling as he takes off at a run down the other side.

My screams turn to laughter as we fly down the side of the hill. That's what it feels like...like flying on a broom but connected to the earth. It's magical. Lowell leaps over a stream, not quite landing on the other side and splashing up freezing water, making me squeal and hold onto him tighter as it soaks the bottom of my leggings.

I bask in the sense of freedom as Lowell dives through an olive grove, the leaves still vibrant green even though no fruit graces their branches. His paws leave behind thick craters in the hard-packed earth as we bound through the grove and out the other side. We ascend another hill and Lowell's speed decreases. As we reach the top, he slows to a stop and I roll off him, lying in the grass and basking in the sun.

Lowell's wolf form hovers over me and he licks my face. I cringe and wipe it away as his bark turns to a laugh as he shifts back into his human form. The laughter dies as his glowing eyes face back to their usual golden hue and he drinks me in.

"What?" I ask softly.

"Every time I think you can't possibly be more beautiful, you prove me wrong," Lowell says before pulling me into a kiss.

"It's just because you like me," I murmur as he pulls away.

"Like is such a pussy word," he says.

"Then what would you say?"

He hums, thinking. "I need you," he says, kissing my neck. "I desire you." A kiss lower, along my collar bone. "I crave you."

"Fuck, Lowell," I hiss as his mouth surrounds my breast, gently nipping at me through the thin material of my shirt and bra.

My nipples harden as his hand trails down my stomach to the waistband of my leggings. "Your sisters are right behind us..."

"They're slow. We have at least four minutes," he says, descending further, his stubble scratching through the thin material of my t-shirt. His eyes glance up as he hovers over my core. "Countdown from a hundred."

"What?" I breathe.

"You have until zero to come."

"And if I don't?" I ask, propping myself up on my elbows.

"I'm not worried," he smirks, and his mouth closes around me over my leggings. I moan as his teeth scrape against my sensitive flesh. "Count, little witch."

This is crazy. So reckless. His sisters could get here any second and see us.

"One hundred. Ninety-nine."

Lowell's fingers hook around my leggings, and I lift my hips as he slides them down so tantalizingly slow. It takes ten seconds before they're off and lying in a heap with my boots in the grass beside us.

"Are you already wet for me, little witch?" he purrs as he kisses up my inner thigh.

"Eighty-five," I respond, nodding my head and continuing my count. I'm practically vibrating with need, knowing there's a very real possibility I won't get off in enough time.

"Fuck, Katie," he breathes as he reaches the damp fabric of my panties. He pushes them to the side and drags a finger through my arousal. I whimper and my head tilts back as he circles my clit lazily with his finger before dragging it back to my opening.

I lose track of the number as his finger slides inside me and my pussy clamps around him. I feel every single inch of the digit until he's fully inside me. He pauses, waiting for me to continue my count as my hips thrust wildly trying to get him to move.

"What number are you on, little witch?" he asks, a smirk on his lips.

I shake the fog from my brain and choke out, "Sixty-nine."

"Good girl," he murmurs and curls his finger, so it flicks against my g-spot. My count speeds up, the numbers flying from my lips as he slides out and adds another finger.

"Slow down," he murmurs right before his tongue flicks against my clit and I cry out the next number. He slows his ministrations, pulling me back from the edge and prolonging my pleasure.

I feel a brush lower, against my asshole as his pinkie circles the tight entrance.

"Keep counting. Just nod yes or no. Has anyone ever been back here?" he asks, teasing the nerves at my entrance.

A finger I respond mentally as I say "Fourty," aloud. *And a plug.*

"Fuck," Lowell swears and his desire flares through our bond making me pant. "Is that something you like?"

I nod.

His hand inside me stills and I feel him shift before his face is hovering over mine, his hair tickling my cheeks. He places his middle finger against my lips.

"Suck," he instructs, and then he continues my count. I take the reprieve to let the moan that's been building escape my lips as I draw his finger into the back of my throat. I swirl my tongue around it, watching Lowell's pupils dilate and he emits a deep guttural sound as the count dips into the twenties. He removes the finger from my mouth and lowers back between my thighs.

He adds a second finger inside me and resumes his pace. I writhe against him, fucking his hand as he brushes against my g-spot. In one motion, the finger slick with my saliva breaches my other hole, slipping past the tight ring of muscles to the first knuckle and his mouth closes around my clit, sucking on the sensitive bundle of nerves. My hand drifts to my breast and I roll my nipple between my fingers.

"Ten," I scream as I approach the end of my countdown. His fingers move faster, pumping in and out in a perfect rhythm.

"Eyes on mine," Lowell commands as the finger in my asshole slides in further to his second knuckles.

"One," I breathe as we lock eyes and I explode.

I come harder than I've ever come in my life, keeping my eyes on Lowell even when stars burst across my vision. My walls clamp down around his fingers as Lowell continues to wring out every ounce of pleasure he could possibly give me.

"That's right, milk my fingers," Lowell growls against me, the strokes of his tongue slowing as I spasm around him.

My heart rate slows as the post-orgasmic bliss settles in and Lowell slides up my body and kisses me passionately so I can taste myself on his lips.

"Fuck, little witch," he murmurs, pulling his hand from me and holding it out as evidence of my orgasm drips from his fingers. My mouth pops open.

"What the hell?" I ask, and a ridiculous grin spreads across his face.

"Have you never squirted before?" he asks, and I shake my head as I fumble around in the grass where I dropped my wand. He chuckles darkly as I quickly cast a drying and cleansing spell.

"He's going to be insufferable now you've told him that," a female voice says from the edge of the clearing. My eyes widen as Lyra crests the top of the hill, her short, dark hair waving slightly in the breeze. She's completely naked as she plops down on the grass not far from us, crossing one of her long legs over the other. Lowell also makes no move to get dressed but blocks me with his body as I toss away my soaked panties and slide my leggings back on.

"Oh, you don't have to put your pants back on," Lyra says, the glint in her eye almost feral.

"Fuck off, Lyra," Lowell says and she laughs, shaking her head.

"Four minutes my ass," I whisper under my breath as I sit, and Lowell laughs before sitting behind me, drawing me back into his chest and nuzzling into my neck.

"Seriously don't be embarrassed," Lyra says, draping her arms across her knees and giving me a view of the moon-phase tattoo down her arm. "We have pack orgies. Nothing's a secret."

"You have what now?" I ask, turning to Lowell who chuckles and just brushes a kiss along the bite mark on my neck.

"Why did you run so fast?" a high-pitched voice calls. A pair of identical girls emerge on the top of the hill, also completely naked. The only difference between the two is that one wears her hair tied back and the other wears it in loose waves. They move in tandem and have matching stern expressions.

Cocking their heads to the side in an animal way, they appraise me. Even though I'm the one fully clothed, I feel stripped bare before them as their golden eyes scan my body.

"I'm Laura," the twin with her hair tied up says.

"And I'm Leanne," the other responds.

"Lowell's twin sisters," they reply together.

"No shit," Lyra says, rolling her eyes dramatically.

"I'm—"

"What happened to your neck?" Laura cuts me off, eying the burn mark peeking out from my tunic. Lyra opens her mouth but both twins glare daggers at her until she closes it again.

"I think you might already know," I say carefully, and Lyra scoffs. "But I was burned."

"By the prince," Leanne states.

"Yes, by the prince," I say.

"Because you picked him over our brother," they speak in unison.

"That's not exactly—" I start.

"Seems like a downgrade," Laura says, clicking her tongue.

"Like a huge mistake," Leanne adds.

"Enough," Lowell barks, but the twins simply stare at their brother, challenging him.

"They didn't say anything wrong," I tell Lowell, and all eyes on the hilltop snap to me. "The prince—"

"You don't need to finish that," Luna's melodic voice drifts over the edge of the hill as she emerges, a tall dark-haired man following close behind her. I instinctively look down to avoid seeing another man's junk. I guess we're doing this first meeting naked; that's cool.

"I want to hear it," Leanne quips.

"Sit," Lowell barks in response and stares them down until the twins finally huff out frustrated breaths.

"Soon you won't be able to pull that Alpha shit on us," Laura says as she and her sister sit cross-legged between Lyra and Lowell. Luna has settled beside me, sitting in front of her husband like I sit with Lowell, her back pressed against his chest.

"But today's not that day," Lowell says, and I can hear his teeth grinding over my shoulder.

"They're baby Alphas," Lyra explained. "And sixteen so they're basically demons."

"Fuck off, Lyra," they both snap, and Lyra laughs.

"We just want to make sure she knows she fucked up, so she doesn't repeat her mistake," Leanne says with a shrug.

"I won't," I say sternly, glaring at them because I'm a fucking Alpha too and I won't be bulldozed by two teenagers. They assess me further and then both nod together. There's a tense silence and then Lyra clears her throat.

"I think you're wearing entirely too much clothing," Lyra says to me, and Luna reaches over to swat her on the arm.

"Lyra—" Lowell starts, but I'm already leaning forward, whipping off my tunic so I'm left in my red-lace bra.

"Holy shit," Lyra says, her eyes dipping down the length of my scar which is now on full display. "You have great tits." I don't fight the laugh that bubbles from my throat, and I feel Lowell relax behind me as he realizes I'm not offended by her joke.

"How do you get anything done?" she asks her brother, who laughs against me and pulls me closer.

"I've only recently been allowed access to them," he says, and I turn and snap my teeth at his jaw. "Productivity has dipped significantly." He kisses me quickly and I laugh into his lips.

When I pull away, I notice Luna and her husband sharing a conspiratorial look. Lowell notices too because he clicks his tongue and their attention snaps to us. "Have you had sex yet?" she asks like that's a normal question.

"You didn't hear them up here?" Lyra scoffs.

"Boundaries," Lowell responds.

"Humor me," his eldest sister responds.

"No," I finally say. She and her husband exchange another look and a smile. He leans in and gently kisses her lips as Lowell's arms tighten around me and unease flows down our bond. "Why?" I ask when no one seems inclined to give us a reason behind that question.

"Just a theory," she says with a shrug of her shoulder.

"You think?" Laura asks, and Leanne gasps.

"It makes sense," Lyra says.

"Stop," Lowell says with enough ire lacing his words that it makes me turn in his hold to face him. His jaw is clenched, every single one of his muscles is rigid and his eyes are glowing. I feel his sisters collectively inhale as Lowell starts to tremble like he's about to shift.

What is it? I ask, and he shakes his head almost imperceptibly. I turn fully and tilt my forehead to meet his. *One deep breath,* I send mentally down our channel, and he indulges me, his eyes drifting closed as he inhales. I pump calming energy down our bond. When he exhales, his muscles relax, and his hands unclench and fall to my hips.

Thank you, he says, leaning forward and pulling me into a hug. I wrap my arms around his back, drawing lines along his spine. *They just...hit a nerve.*

You don't need to explain, I say, even though I'm dying to know what Luna's theory is.

Later he responds, nuzzling into my neck, into the mark he's made. I've noticed he does that a lot, almost like he's assuring himself it's there. That I'm still his.

Okay, Alpha, I say, pulling back and kissing him before turning around. He wraps his arms around my middle, the heat from his body instantly warming me despite the freezing temperature and the fact that I'm half naked.

"Wow," the twins say at once. I look up and notice everyone is staring at us with a look of confusion and wonder.

"You calmed him down," Lyra says, her voice awed.

"I did..." I respond carefully, super confused. They all look at each other conspiratorially.

"I can be a bit..." Lowell searches for the right word.

"Broody?" Laura offers.

"Hot-headed?" Leanne suggests next.

"Of an asshole," Lyra says with a roll of her eyes.

"And when he's like that," Luna says softly, "it lasts for days."

"Weeks, sometimes," the twins say.

"Katie calms me," Lowell says simply, ending the conversation with three words.

"And you do the same for me," I respond. "When I can be a bit of an asshole."

Everyone chuckles and Lowell snags a quick kiss before we descend into a conversation about a hundred other topics. His sisters take turns asking me questions about my family, our relationship, our plans after the war is over...their words, not mine. I can't answer the last one, but they don't linger on it.

"Oh," Lyra says, looking up at the sky. "There's an elders' meeting soon, then the barbeque, the bonfire, the orgy--"

"That's a joke, right?" I ask, and all the wolves laugh.

"Sure," Lyra says, waving me off. "We should head back."

"Race you!" the twins yell, and instantly shift into matching grey wolves before bounding down the side of the hill. The rest of Lowell's sisters and Luna's husband, Cyril, shift, leaving the two of us alone. Lowell takes a step forward, but I grab his hand and hold him back.

"Yes, little witch?" he asks, a smile playing across his lips. I press up on my tiptoes and kiss him, running my tongue against his lips until he opens for me. He sucks my tongue into his mouth, and I grab his hair, pulling him closer.

"We have to—" I cut off his protests by drawing his bottom lip between my teeth. Once he's quieted, I drop to my knees in front of him. I wrap my hand around his already rock-hard cock. "Katie, we don't have much time."

"Then you should count down from one hundred, Alpha," I instruct, not giving him a second to hesitate before taking him to the back of my throat.

"Fuck," he swears and I still, my nose brushing against the coarse curls at the base of his cock. I look up at him expectantly, waiting.

"One hundred---"

He doesn't make it to zero.

Chapter Twenty-Seven

THE MEETING WITH THE elders goes off without a hitch, minus the fact that I don't actually get to meet Lowell's mom. Since there's a small gap of time between the meeting and the party at sundown, Lowell and I go back to his house to...nap. I can't get a straight answer from anyone about what to expect from tonight's party, but I know the whole pack will be there.

The sun sets, and not three seconds later, Lowell's door is flung open and Vlad walks in. He finds us lounging back on the bed. Luckily, it's one of the rare moments today where Lowell and I are clothed.

"You look happy," Vlad says by way of a greeting. I think I see a glimmer of sadness in his eyes, but it's gone before I can question it. "I have news."

Lowell and I both sit up straight, and I adjust the strap of my black tank top as Vlad comes over and sits at the edge of the bed. He gives me a slow smile.

"While you two were fucking the night away last night," Vlad says, neither Lowell nor I bother to correct him, "I spoke with your mother."

"*My* mother?" I ask as he nods.

"She called your phone, which was at my house. We had a lovely conversation, by the way. She's a treat," he deadpans. "And through our conversation..." he draws out the last word and leaves it hanging in the air like a bad smell.

"Some of us aren't immortal," I deadpan.

"I think I figured out the answer to your magic problem," Vlad finishes calmly like it's not a big fucking deal.

"What?" I breathe, and Lowell grabs my hand and squeezes.

"The method your father used to give you your Dark Magic is the same as the Fae used to give humans magic. Your mother has been reviewing his notes since you told her your magic hasn't been behaving."

"I don't understand," I look between the men, both smiling.

"If someone does another infusion...?" Lowell starts.

"It could give you added magic that's not being held hostage by the hellfire," Vlad finishes. "It might not work, because we don't know much about hellfire. But there's a chance—"

He doesn't finish as I launch across the bed and throw my arms around his neck.

"I think our best bet is to find a Fae to perform the infusion. I've already contacted the royals from the Day and Night Courts who owe me favors, but if you'd rather, Adriana said she would try."

"Vlad, I—" I start to pull away to thank him, but he holds me tighter, so I pour my thanks into the embrace.

"You smell like dog," he says after a minute, and I swat him across the back of the head.

"Come on," Lowell calls from the doorway. "They're about to start the bonfire."

"Yes, the orgy waits for no wolf," Vlad chides as I tug on my boots.

"Okay seriously, someone has to warn me if I'm about to walk into an orgy," I huff. "I mean, I'm gonna go either way. But a heads up would be nice."

The boys laugh loudly and Lowell comes over to me, his hands resting on my hips. "We'll start with dinner. Then there is drinking and dancing, which can turn quite—"

"Carnal," Vlad offers with a very uncharacteristic eyebrow waggle.

"But," Lowell draws my attention back to him with a firm grip on my chin, "I'm not sharing you. So, we'll leave before things get too wild."

"Wow, a werewolf orgy..." I breathe. "Edina is gonna be so fucking jealous."

I push past the boys snagging a leather jacket to wear over my tank and leggings. It's entirely too big, but it smells like Lowell so I'm claiming it. Their laughter follows me out of Lowell's cabin as I start down the path towards the center of the village. Lowell catches me and wraps his hand in mine as we cross into the open clearing, the picnic tables that had been removed for the fight last night are back and crammed full of eager werewolves. As we make our way to the front of the pack, Lowell explains that the Alpha is always served first, a gesture that is an honor as much as it is to make sure the meat isn't poisoned.

"Alphas are the protectors of the pack first and foremost," Lowell explains. "Not some figurehead."

"Is that why you want to be on the front lines?" I ask softly.

"I'll be wherever you are," Lowell says seriously and jerks his head ahead of us to where Lyra walks. "As my Beta, Lyra will be in charge of the pack while I help command your armies."

He brings me to the front, where I know he'll be addressing the pack and where two men stand in stained aprons in front of giant smokers.

Would you like the first bite of food? Lowell asks through our mental channel. *It would be my honor as Alpha to serve you.*

Is that appropriate? I ask.

It would go a long way to prove you're willing to protect our people. But you don't have to.

I smile and give him a nod. He doesn't say that it's important for me to be accepted by his pack, his family, but I know it is. His smile widens and his hold on my hand tightens before he turns to the wolves in charge of the cooking.

"Welcome home, Alpha." The men dip their heads to Lowell, and he shakes each one of their hands. They turn towards me and sink to one knee. "Queen Kathryn. Welcome to our pack."

"Oh," I start, turning to Lowell who gives me a nod of encouragement. "Thank you so much for having me. But you really don't need to bow."

They stand hastily and I extend my hand as Lowell did. They enthusiastically shake my hand and I feel pride surge down the bond from Lowell.

"My brothers and sisters," he calls, and instantly the din of the crowd falls silent. "It has been a trying few days." There are a few chuckles, but most are silent and somber.

"After the full moon, we will relocate our soldiers and their families to the Highland Coven. The elders will remain with those unable to train for battle. This may be the last moon where we run as a pack for some time." An uneasy silence falls over the crowd. "But when we run together again, it will be in a Kingdom that accepts us and values our opinions."

A chef hands him a plate with a giant hunk of steak. Lowell holds the plate aloft to the crowd like he's toasting. "Tonight, we celebrate in our human forms to remember that no matter our appearance, we are pack."

"To pack," the group reiterates.

"And tonight," Lowell smiles widely at me, "we welcome a new member of our pack, my chosen partner and the Alpha who will lead us to victory. Queen Kathryn, welcome."

"Welcome," everyone echoes.

"I present you the first bite," Lowell picks the meat up with his hands and arches an eyebrow at me expectantly.

Do I take it from you? I ask, suddenly very aware that people are watching me.

Open your mouth.

You really do get off on feeding me, I tease as I open my mouth as daintily as I can. Lowell barely contains his laughter as he extends the steak to my lips. I take a bite and don't hold back the groan as the rich spices explode around my taste buds. I was afraid the meat would be tough, but it melts like butter in my mouth.

"Holy shit, that's delicious," I say, and the crowd stills for one moment before they explode in laughter and applause. The chefs beside me are beaming with pride as Lowell takes the rest of my piece and shoves it in his mouth, the sign for everyone else to start eating.

Wolves move about delivering large platters to the tables. Others have pitchers of a rum drink that Lowell hands me a glass of. We spend the next hour or so talking to everyone, and they all welcome me warmly. The warriors ask about my military training, and some of the younger girls ask what it was like to date a rock star and a prince. Lowell stands at my side the entire time, a hand on my lower back as a reminder he's with me even when we're having separate conversations. He sends names down our mental channel when he can tell I've forgotten them and steers me away when people start asking probing questions about our relationship.

Finally, we reach the table with Lowell's family, and Lowell motions for me to sit so we can eat more than a bite...which is good because the rum drink is strong and I'm already tipsy. His four sisters are joined by Vlad, Lyra's girlfriend, Alaina, and Cyril who spends more time chasing down his and Luna's children than sitting with the family. The only one not there is Lowell's mother, who is visiting with some of the elders.

After we've eaten, everyone disperses, leaving Vlad and me hanging at the table as the pack gets the bonfire started. Musicians drag chairs to one area and begin tuning various instruments. I watch as Luna yells at Lyra for help as the twins run in a flash of their teenage speed to avoid being sent away before the fun can begin. In the end, I think Luna gives up and goes to put her children to bed.

"Vladimir." I look up at the heavily accented voice that calls to Vlad. He hops up and embraces the older woman, stooping low to accommodate her short stature.

"Mama," he croons, and she chuckles and rolls her golden eyes at the nickname. She clucks something at him in French, her voice melodic and filled with cadence despite its lower timbre. Vlad responds in French in return, and I suddenly feel lacking.

Vlad pats Lowell's mom on the shoulder and disappears in a burst of speed, leaving her staring at me. "May I?" she asks, gesturing to the seat next to me. I smile warmly, ignoring the fact that I can hear my pulse in my ears.

You need me? Lowell asks through our bond, and I follow the tether to find him chatting and laughing with a group of pack members over by the musicians. I shake my head as our eyes connect and he winks playfully as I turn my attention to the woman beside me. Her eyes are knowing as she appraises me.

"We haven't been officially introduced," I say softly. "I'm Katie."

"Lorraine," she responds. Her face is set in a serious expression, but there's mirth dancing across her eyes. "You don't need to be nervous, Katie."

"I've been told I don't make a great first impression," I tell her honestly.

"I have an impression already," she chuckles, and my cheeks warm, remembering she saw me practically mount her son last night. "Don't be embarrassed. It's endearing to see you so taken with my Lowell."

"I don't know what I would have done without him these past few weeks," I tell her honestly. "He's...it feels wrong to say amazing. Like it's not enough." She smiles knowingly and her eyes widen as they fall on the locket around my neck.

"Vladimir told me you had that," she murmurs, her hand reaching instinctively towards the pendant, but then she halts. "Does it beat?"

I sigh heavily. "Yes."

Her hand flies to her mouth and tears brim around thick black eyelashes. "My daughters suspected, but..." This time when she reaches, she connects with the pendent, feeling the soft thudding. "You're his mate."

The background fades away as her words echo in my mind. "What?" I squeak out.

"You didn't know." It's not a question. She laughs, the melodic notes carrying across the clearing, but somehow no one hears this life-altering conversation. "Vladimir didn't tell you?"

"No."

She clicks her tongue as both of our eyes find the vampire, who smirks and then returns to his conversation with two female wolves.

"Queen Aldonza was a werewolf," Lorraine says, drawing my attention away from Vlad. "Her locket was imbued with magic to beat when the wearer met their mate. Wolves don't know if someone is truly their mate until intercourse. You can see how that's problematic, especially if one is dealing with warring packs."

"I thought mates needed to both be wolves," I breathe, my hand floating to the pendant.

"One partner is always a wolf," Lorraine says. "But wolves have mated with witches before. The most notable example of this was—"

"Finley," I finish her thought, and I laugh. I had already met Lowell when I put the necklace on for the first time. I had already met my mate.

Lowell is my mate.

It was never supposed to be Archer. It was always Lowell.

"Can you sense each other's emotions?" Lorraine asks me. "Does it feel like a tether leads you to each other? Drawing you closer, urging you to stay close?"

"Yes," I breathe, tears springing to my eyes. "All this time, I was trying to stay away from him because I thought it meant..." Lorraine chuckles. "Does he know?" I ask.

"He hasn't said anything to me," she answers, her face softer now.

"I need to tell him." I stand abruptly. My heart is hammering against my chest, a million beats a minute. Lorraine grabs onto my forearm and uses me to pull herself up. She holds on tight for a moment before pulling me into a hug that I melt into.

"Welcome to the family, Katie," she whispers before letting me go and pushing me toward her son.

Chapter Twenty-Eight

THE MUSIC STARTS JUST as I start moving like a bullet to my singular focus...my mate. Holy shit, *my mate.* I can't even wrap my head around that word. I was just getting used to hearing Lowell call me his partner, which is just as significant. But mate...it's rare and special and I need to tell him about it right the fuck now.

The wolves start gathering around the bonfire, blocking my path as they call me, trying to snag my attention. They fling their bodies around with such abandon it makes it hard to walk in a straight line. I offer small smiles, but my eyes are locked on Lowell.

"Katie!" Lyra's arm loops around my waist and, with extraordinary strength, she tugs me closer to the bonfire. My body seizes as we approach the flames, and she knowingly halts. "Stay right here. I'll get the others."

"Lyra, I need to talk to—" she thrusts a drink in my hand and disappears, returning with the rest of her sisters in the blink of an eye.

"We've decided you need to be officially welcomed into the family," Luna says, taking a long drag from her plastic cup.

"Which we do with a dance!" The twins say, their cheeks pink and splotchy and gesturing to the crowd that has amassed. The wolves surround the fire in concentric circles, moving in pairs or in small groups in a pattern so quickly that I can hardly follow.

"I really need to find Lowell—"

"This is a sacred dance of our people," Lyra says seriously. "As our future leader—"

"I don't know the steps," I call as the drums intensify and a fiddle gets added to the mix.

"She's fucking with you," Luna says, shaking her head. "There are no rules. Just follow the beat."

Lyra motions for me to down the contents of my cup...and I do, sputtering as the harsh alcohol burns on the way down. It's strong...strong enough that my tongue instantly feels fuzzy. Someone dances by and refills the cups of the group. Everyone holds their refilled cups up, and I mimic their motion.

"What are we toasting?" I ask.

"To victory," Lyra says.

"To family," Luna adds.

"To PACK!" the twins call, and the entire pack lifts their cups, saluting us as we drink deeply.

Without warning, both twins take a hold of an arm and pull me into the throng. I look around at the group surrounding us, still seeking out Lowell when the music picks up and so does the dancing. The drum beat invades my senses, and my hips begin to sway. *One dance...then I'll tell him.*

I'M WASTED. SERIOUSLY THE drunkest I've ever been in my entire life, including when Edina and I went to an all-inclusive resort and each drank our weight in rum. My eyes are closed, the firelight flickering behind my closed lids as I sway to the music. I can't help but compare how different this dance is to the waltzes of the palace, how free I feel under the sky around a fire in the middle of a forest. I'm completely at ease here, with these people. My people.

The music stops and the crowd applauds loudly as the drummer stands and takes a bow, replaced by a man with a giant accordion. He joins the fiddlers, and they play a light, lilting melody. The circles around the fire start dissipating as people break into couples and Lyra grabs me around the waist.

"We do this dance in pairs," she says, spinning me around in her arms. "We change partners, so just follow whoever you dance with." We twirl in small, tight spirals as we cover the ground. Lyra keeps us far enough from the bonfire that I don't feel any panic, but close enough that I'm not freezing my ass off since I discarded Lowell's jacket at some point. I barely keep up as Lyra moves with abandon. With a giant shove, she pushes me away and I get scooped up by an older were.

I change partners several times, dancing with each of Lowell's sisters, Vlad, Cyril, and countless others I can't remember. They all take the lead when they realize I'm their partner, guiding me through the steps. Thankfully I've had enough training that I can follow a lead, even completely trashed.

I'm spinning around a final time, and I land in a pair of familiar arms, the scent of rain and earth mixing with the scent of the bonfire. Lowell's golden eyes smile down at me and he lifts me and twirls me around. I'm still in the air when the drums pick back up and the music slows ever so slightly. It's a deep, throbbing beat that thuds through my blood.

"Ahh," I whisper as my hips sway on their own accord. "Is this the carnal portion of the night?" I start laughing hysterically.

"Are you drunk, little witch?" Lowell smirks and I scoff, hiding my empty cup behind my back, which someone takes from me. I turn in Lowell's hold, and his hand splays across my stomach as I roll my hips in a wide circle.

Lowell releases me and I dance a little way away from him. He drinks in my movements as I toss my head back, my hair falling to the small of my back. My hands slide up and down my sides before I tangle them in my hair, watching Lowell's reaction as I roll my body, drawing his attention to my chest. His jaw works and I draw my bottom lip between my teeth as lust pours down our bond hotter than the fire at my back.

"Dance with me, Alpha," I command, holding out my hand. He smiles slowly and stalks toward me as my entire body tightens in anticipation. Taking a firm hold of my hand, he spins me around and then ensnares me in his arms, my back pressed against his chest. His mouth ghosts along my neck and my movements become localized to my hips.

Lowell's hands skim down my ribcage as I press my ass into the growing bulge in his pants. My eyes drift closed as we grind against each other, the music and the heat of Lowell's body the only things in my world.

"Are you ready to go?" he asks, his voice deep and rough as he tugs me impossibly closer, and I feel exactly why he wants to leave.

A moan in the distance has my eyes popping open and I see Lyra on the other side of the fire, sandwiched between Alaina and a man I don't recognize. The three of them are moving in a way that suggests clothes will be optional fairly soon. Lowell's hands inch forward on my hips so they're dangerously close to sliding beneath my waistband.

"How much did you have to drink?" he asks, and I spin around, throwing my arms around his neck as our bodies still roll together.

"Are you worried about taking advantage, Alpha?" I ask, my hands drifting down his biceps.

"No," he leans closer, his breath hot in my ear. "I just want to ensure you won't forget a second of tonight."

"And what's happening tonight?" I ask, biting my lips at the growl that rumbles through his chest. He doesn't answer but instead rolls his hips in a way that has him rubbing against me and I can't help the sound that escapes my lips. "Please tell me you're finally going to fuck me," I breathe, and he chuckles darkly.

"Is that what you want, little witch? For me to be buried so deep inside you, that you won't be able to walk straight tomorrow?"

Yes. Yes. *Yes.*

Fuck that's all I want.

But we need to talk first. Because as soon as we have sex, Lowell will know we're mates, and I don't want to spring that on him. I want him to know first, so he has time to process...

Lowell's lips find mine and I'm groaning into his mouth as he kisses me savagely. Fuck I really had too much to drink, I'm not going to be able to hold back at all. His hand finds the hair at the nape of my neck, and he tugs hard enough to have my head snapping back. It's like a string connected straight to my clit, and if I wasn't already, now I'm fucking soaked for him.

"We need to talk—" I start but the words die in my mouth as Lowell's tongue skims down my neck, lapping up a bead of sweat that's collected. He hums as he tastes me, and all sane thoughts leave my brain.

"Your Majesty?"

Lowell snaps his teeth at the man who called me, and I shake off the cloud of lust enough to open my eyes. The world blurs and I blink several times to get it back into focus.

"Jeremy?" I ask. The gangly teenager from the Highland Coven runs his hands through his mussed brown hair and keeps his eyes on the ground. "What's wrong?"

"Adriana sent me," he says softly, keeping his eyes down. Vlad is at my side in a second.

"What happened?" he demands as I sway at the sudden shift in the ground he must have caused. Lowell's hands wrap around my middle, keeping me still.

"They..." Jeremy's eyes widen as he gets distracted by the sound of skin slapping together behind me, and Vlad rolls his eyes so hard I can hear them.

He grabs Jeremy around the waist, eliciting a shriek as they take off toward the woods. I ask Lowell if we're following when he lifts me and runs without warning. As soon as he stops, I take three steps away and puke my guts up, ridding my body of the alcohol. Lowell dutifully stands behind me, scooping my hair back and out of the splash zone.

"Fuck, how drunk is she?" Vlad asks.

"She was with Lyra," Lowell grumbles in return, which apparently serves as an answer. I stand and swipe the back of my hand against my mouth.

"Katie," Vlad says and thrusts a bleeding finger in front of my face. "Drink."

"Ew, Vlad," I say, gagging but he jabs the finger into my mouth and my tongue subconsciously laps at the bead of blood that's gathered. My head clears, and my stomach settles as the coppery flavor invades my mouth. "Thanks."

Vlad turns back to Jeremy who is shaking. "What happened? Is Adriana okay?"

"No," Jeremy says. "Seth...he figured out a way to hide from her visions. And then he broke the fealty vow so he could..."

"What did he do?" I demand, standing upright.

"He killed the king."

The words echo off the trees in the darkened forest, their impact the only thing heard despite the party raging feet away from us. The breath whooshes from my lungs and I stumble only to be caught by Lowell and Vlad, who flank me on either side.

"What else?" I ask, my voice devoid of emotion.

"He's removing the fealty vow by force from all the coven leaders. As soon as Adriana realized what was happening, she shoved me through the portal. She tried to get Coleman out too, but they already barricaded him in his room to keep him from getting you."

"Fuck," I breathe, and turn to Lowell. "Tell me wolves digest alcohol quickly."

"They do," he says. "I'll get Lyra. She'll ready everyone and call the pack stationed closest to the Highlands."

"I'll call some of the vamps in the area as well," Vlad says.

"Good. Jeremy—"

"I'm ready to fight with you, your majesty," he says, puffing out his chest.

"You've put yourself in enough danger," I respond. "I need you to stay with Lowell's sisters...they're about your age and will probably try and sneak off to join the fight if we leave them unattended."

"Accurate," Vlad scoffs, and Jeremy follows Lowell as they walk back towards the party, leaving me in the woods with Vlad.

"He killed the king," I breathe, still not believing it. "They'll think all of us are behind this."

"Probably," Vlad agrees.

"This is going to hurt our cause."

"That's tomorrow's problem. Katie," Vlad says, ensnaring me in his ice-blue gaze. "You know what needs to be done."

"I know."

"I can do this for you," he says softly.

"No," I shake my head. "It needs to be me."

"But your magic..."

"Isn't any less effective than a sword," I shoot back. "I need you to get Coleman and Adriana out of there. If I know Seth, he'll have her tied up somewhere close so she can witness him undo her magic. But she will probably be hurt, so get Coleman from his room first, and then come get Adriana."

Lowell appears next to me in a flash of speed. "They'll be five minutes behind us."

"Let's go," I say, holding my hand out to my mate. I'll tell him when this is all over. "I need to get my sword."

Lowell scoops me into his arms and kisses me sweetly before taking off at top speed towards Vlad's house and the portal that will lead us to the Highlands.

Chapter Twenty-Nine

I'VE ONLY USED A portal once before in my life, and it's not something I'm eager to repeat. It's akin to a moving walkway going thousands of miles per hour. Each portal entrance is marked by a door. Some require authentication with a magical signature, some are locked outright, and some, like the one in the palace, are wide open but monitored on the opposite side. The Elemental Witches think most portal entrances are permanently locked, but that's clearly not the case.

Lowell holds onto my waist as we speed past door after door, the purple mist swirling around us making it hard to read the plaques that mark the locations.

"Ready?" Vlad calls from ahead of us. He bends his knees and I follow suit. Without warning, he jumps into the mist...where there's no door.

"Where—" I don't finish the question as Lowell pulls me along with him as we leap off the walkway. I scream as we hurtle through the mist, only seeing the door opening as we're crashing into it.

Lowell keeps hold of me as my legs buckle once we're on solid ground, my head still feeling like it's moving even though we've stopped. We're in the war room in the Highland Coven.

Considering the room is centrally located to most common spaces, it's deadly quiet.

"What the fuck was that?" I sputter as the world stops spinning and I can stand on my own. I straighten my sword belt and glare at Vlad, who is casually leaning against the doorway.

"Oh right," Vlad says. "I meant to tell you. I had them create a hidden door. You can only see it if you know exactly where it is."

"Thanks," I breathe, and Vlad salutes me before taking off. He's going to free Coleman from his chambers. He'll bring the healer and his family back to the mansion, where Lyra will hopefully be waiting with the wolves. Coleman can use his healing magic to sober anyone who needs it, and he'll wait there for any injured we can send his way. Or until we're forced to flee.

My eyes snag on the enchanted mirror, broadcasting a feed of the palace, where hundreds of Dragons soldiers are running around in full armor. It's chaos. I frantically look for my mother and Marcus, hoping to God they survived my father's ambush.

"Katie, we need to go," Lowell says, his voice strained. I nod and he scoops me into his arms, making a beeline for the throne room. We're there in seconds.

I steal an extra moment in Lowell's arms, nuzzling into the crook in his neck. "This is so fucked," I breathe against him, and he kisses the top of my head.

"I know, little witch," he says into my hair. His calloused fingers brush my chin, tilting it up so I'm staring into his golden eyes. "Katie, I—"

I cut him off with a swift kiss. "No goodbyes," I say firmly. He kisses me again, longer, sweeter.

I steel my spine when I drop out of his arms, watching as Lowell does the same. With one hand on the hilt of my sword, I enter the throne room.

I was prepared for destruction, for signs of a struggle. I expected my father to be sneering at me from the throne. But I was not prepared for the line of witches, the heads of the covens, magically tied together and kneeling in a row as he stands over them like some twisted priest performing an exorcism. The Shanghai leader and Sanderson are at his side, the latter licking his lips, getting some perverse pleasure from this display. The remaining witches stand in lines, most of them shaking in fear.

The witch at the front of the line is released from the rest of the group, and they force her to her knees in front of the dais. My father walks to the edge before throwing magic at her in a powerful blast. The entire cavern inhales sharply as her back bows with the force of it. When he stops, she slumps to the floor, her legs too weak to support her.

"Your fealty vow has been removed," my father says, his voice cold. "You are no longer pledged to Kathryn." Two witches drag her off to the side of the room, and a group of coven members rushes over to check on her.

No one noticed we came in, so we sneak along the carved rock wall, blending into the shadows between the orbs of magical green light. I search for Adriana, knowing in my gut she's close by, but I don't see her face amongst the crowd or in the two gatherings of witches conversing in hushed whispers on the opposite side of the dais. One of the groups looks distinctly excited while the other looks nauseated. Those must be the coven members whose leaders were released from the vow. I note members from

Sanderson's coven in the excited group. Those are the ones we need to keep an eye on once the wolves get here. I jerk my head in their direction and Lowell acknowledges my warning.

We're inching forward when Lowell grips my arm, pulling me to a halt. He tilts his head to the ceiling, and I follow his gaze. A gasp falls from my lips, echoing in the silent cavern. Adriana is hogtied, dark ropes of magic keeping her immobile as she hangs suspended over the crowd. Her eyes are closed, tears seeping from her light lashes. My feet move on their own accord towards my sister, reaching for her even though I'm miles away.

"Ahh, Kathryn," my father coos as I leave the shadows. "So glad you could make it."

"Let her go," I command, and my father just clicks his tongue.

"Can't do that, I'm afraid," he says, his tone cavalier. "She went a bit feral when I killed her boyfriend...or was he your boyfriend? I never could keep track."

He extends a bony finger to the back of the room, where Rodger's head is mounted on a pike next to the head of the king.

"I'm not loving the new decoration," I chide, motioning to the two pairs of open but sightless eyes surrounded by bloated, graying skin. "Nor the direction you're leading our cause. Care to enlighten me on what you were thinking when you went to kill the king?"

"You weren't getting results," he hisses, and there is enough agreement from the group that my grip on my sword tightens. "You're not fit to be queen."

"Then, and I mean this with zero respect...why the fuck did you drag me into this?"

"Because of the prophecy," he bellows. "If you had any sense, you would have died from the hellfire like you were supposed to."

The only sound in the cavern is a tear falling from Adriana's cheek onto the stone floor.

"The prophecy didn't say I would die," I say, choosing my words carefully.

"It didn't say you'd live either," he says with a sinister smile. "When I learned how little control the prince had over his emotions, I knew he was our best option. Create a villain and a martyr in one strike of hellfire."

It feels like I'm getting punched in the gut over and over. I search for the mental channel with Adriana, but my father must have destroyed it. When I glance up, she looks just as shocked as I am, her mouth open in a perfect O. Beside me, Lowell is snarling.

"You told Archer I was here," I confirm, and my father smirks. "*Children* died in that attack. I've been blaming myself for months, and it was *you*."

"That wasn't my intention, but we will avenge them," Seth continues. "I knew he wouldn't be able to get past Adriana's wards without an invitation, so I told him we kidnapped you and issued the challenge to get you back. I didn't think he'd come through the top of the mountain, but beggars can't be choosers."

He descends the steps of the dais. "Then you had to go and recover, even weaker than before."

Wolves are one minute out, Vlad's voice trickles through our open channel.

Hurry the fuck up, Lowell says. I can tell he's seconds from shifting and tearing my father's head off.

I'll stall as long as I can, I respond, and then send him a mental picture of where Adriana is suspended, knowing I can trust the vampire to save her.

"You were never supposed to survive that night," my father hisses, now mere steps away.

Stay, I tell Lowell who is coiled so tight it's only a matter of time before he snaps.

"But it's no matter now," my father continues. "The vow of fealty will be broken tonight, and we'll no longer be forced to follow your ridiculous plan. The Dark Witches will rise, and I will become king."

"There's one problem with that plan," I say coolly, catching Lowell's eye. He gives me a slow smile, revealing his extending canines. "My army is bigger than yours."

The wolves burst into the throne room just as I unsheathe my sword. I blast my father with a spell as it leaves my scabbard and charge after him. Lowell is at my heels, completing his shift into his wolf form. Several witches charge forward to aid my father, but they don't make it before wolves descend upon them, tearing into muscles with their large teeth.

"Go for the hands," I call. Witches can't cast without the use of their hands. Take a witch's ability to use Battle Magic and our casualty count will be significantly lower.

I vaguely register Vlad's cloaked figure flying in like the grim reaper, a group of similarly dressed vampires behind him as they dive into the fray. He jumps with extraordinary strength and somehow shreds the magic that holds Adriana captive. I lose track of them once he descends into the crowd but I trust he'll take her to safety.

My father throws his magic at me, which I dodge by dipping into a roll and slashing at his ankles with my sword. He launches attack after attack, and I'm forced on the defensive, struggling to maintain my shield and unable to parry his attacks. I need another fucking witch.

As if she hears me, the head witch of the Chicago Coven, Cecelia, appears at my side and throws up a flawless one-sided shield. I nod my thanks before charging my father.

"Hiding behind another witch," he tsks. "I taught you better than that."

I free my dagger from its holster on my thigh and throw it, casting a spell in its wake so that the aim is true. My father's eyes widen as the dagger streaks toward his heart. It pierces his shield, but before it can connect with flesh, it's blasted away by the Shanghai coven leader.

Lowell takes off after the witch as I approach my father, getting closer and closer, my sword meeting every strike of magic he throws at me and releasing its own. I slash diagonally and score a line of fire across my father's resurrected shield, which he holds up seamlessly while he casts his raw magic.

"You're not going to win this one, Kathryn," he taunts. "You're weak. Broken. *Damaged.*"

His words slide off my skin like water off a duck's back. He's trying to make me lose concentration, but I've never been more focused in my entire life. I know my worth, and it's nothing to do with magic. I'm resilient and strong, and in the eyes of my mate, I'm perfect. The rest is just noise.

He continues with a barrage of insults until Cecelia blasts his shield with a silencing spell. We press forward, more witches falling in behind us to attack my father. Somehow he keeps up, his shield doesn't waver. It's really fucking annoying.

How do we know who's on our side? Vlad asks. His blonde hair streaks around the room, blood exploding in his wake.

If they attack you, they're bad.

Brilliant strategy, baby queen.

Dark Magic collides with the shield protecting me and it shatters. My father snarls as he throws an attack at the witch at my side. Without thinking I shove her out of the way, prepared to take the blast head-on when a blur of white leaps in front of me. The spell connects with his side and Lowell crashes to the ground and skids towards the cavern wall.

"NO," I shriek.

His body shifts back into its human form, the color slowly leeching from his face as I stare at the gray splotch on his chest, waiting for the tell-tale rise. *He can't be dead. I won't believe it.* I tug on the golden tether between us, the mating bond, holding onto it as I feel a spiderweb crack splintering the connection.

A blast of Dark Magic narrowly misses my face, and I'm forced to turn my attention back to my father. Dark Magic pools in his hands, but he waits, baiting me to make the first strike.

He hurt my mate. My partner.

I will end him. And I'll make it fucking hurt.

Golden magic explodes from my outstretched hand, illuminating the green cavern with bright light. It spreads along the rock floor like a wave of lava, shattering shields and absorbing spells before they can reach our allies. Somehow, the magic knows who is on our side and protects them.

While the witches scramble to cast, the magic sneaks up on them, starting at their feet and rooting them to the ground. It looks like thick honey as it coats their bodies, trapping their hands, cutting off their screams as they're completely encased.

The vampires, wolves, and witches on our side act fast, corralling the enemy into a pack and binding them in ropes of Dark Magic. Once they're subdued, I drop the magic surrounding them and turn to my father, who breaks free of my hold with a blast of black smoke.

He charges, but this time I swat away his magic like it's no more than an annoying insect. This new power sings in my blood and I let it guide me, let it call the shots. This is different than any raw magic I've ever felt. It's not healing or aggressive. *It's protective.*

The magic seeps from my sword, spreading up my father's legs, anchoring him to one spot. He thrashes, shouting for help that will never come. Panic sets in when the magic binds his hands and he's unable to cast. It drifts up to his neck, immobilizing him as I stalk forward until my sword is pressed against his jugular.

"Princess..." Seth squeaks out, his auburn eyes pleading.

"I'm not a princess," I sneer. "You made me a queen."

I slash out, using a heating spell so my sword cuts through tendons and bone like it's moving through warm butter. His head, silver ponytail and all, separates from his shoulders and lands with a thud before rolling back onto the dais. I pull the magic back inside me and the entire cavern goes silent as my father's lifeless form crumples and falls at my feet.

Metal clatters against the stone as my sword falls and I run to my werewolf.

"Katie—" Vlad appears in front of me before I can reach Lowell, his black cloak billowing around him on a non-existent wind. He braces me with both hands on my shoulders, his imposing frame blocking me from seeing my mate.

"Back off," I growl.

"It's bad. You need to prepare yourself," Vlad says as he steps aside. He walks behind me, keeping one hand on my back as I sink to my knees at Lowell's side.

"I need Adriana," I bark, brushing the hair away from his face. He's always so warm, but his skin is cool as I cup his stubbled cheek.

I'm vaguely aware of movement in the cavern, of Vlad repeating my orders to get Adriana and Coleman, of two wolves whining as they kneel by Lowell's head. I pay them no attention as I feel for his pulse, but my hand shakes too much to find it. I can't feel my necklace beating at all, which means it's faint. I refuse to believe anything else.

Alpha, I say through our mental channel. *If you can hear this... you don't get to leave me. Do you understand? That's an order from your queen.* I clutch his hand, squeezing his calloused fingers until my knuckles turn white.

"I'm here," Adriana's voice squeaks behind me. She's weak on her legs and her color is still off, but she's alive. Coleman escorts her over, keeping a firm hand around her waist.

"I can try and heal him," Coleman offers.

"No," I snap. "We need to remove the spell. Adriana, use your Dark Magic to draw it out. That's what I had to do for Deavers when he was hit with Dark Magic."

"The soldier from your mission? He was hit with a stasis spell," Adriana says softly as she kneels beside me. "Katie, I don't know what spell this is. If he's alive—"

"He's alive."

"Katie—"

"He's my fucking mate," I scream. "I would know if he was dead." Tears are streaming down my face, but I keep my eyes locked on my sister. Inside I'm holding onto the fractured mating bond like I can keep Lowell here with the sheer force of my will.

"Show me how," Adriana says, calling her Dark Magic to her hands. I guide them, hovering over Lowell's injury. His entire body bows as she begins to suck the magic from his body. The inky dark smoke wraps around Adriana's arms, snaking closer and closer to her chest as she shakes with exertion to remove the spell.

"It's out," Adriana whispers as she withdraws the last string of magic and flings it to the ground with a shudder.

I hold my breath, clamping down on my lower lip to keep it from trembling. One second passes. Then another. Then another.

"Should he be waking up?" Adriana asks, but I can't draw the breath to answer. Yes, he should be breathing. He should be waking up. The wolves tilt their heads to the cavern's ceiling, releasing a mournful howl.

Please.... Lowell, please, I send down our mental channel. My whole body is trembling. *We--I wasted so much time. We didn't have enough time. Please don't leave me.*

His chest rises. My breath catches and I hold it, waiting. Slowly, his golden eyes blink open and find mine.

"I'm not going anywhere, little witch," Lowell says, his deep baritone rough around the edges. I flop forward, my forehead falling right over his heart.

I can't control my sobbing as Lowell floods our bond with reassuring, calming energy. When I can breathe again, I lift my head off Lowell's chest and kiss him like I can't get enough. He follows me as I sit up, chasing my lips, and threading his fingers through my hair.

When we finally break apart, the two wolves stationed by Lowell's head jump into his lap, licking his face as he chuckles heartily. The rest of the pack yips in celebration, and even the witches look relieved to see my Alpha alive.

I turn back to find Adriana, her gray eyes rimmed in red.

"Thank you," I whisper, my voice still breaking. I put my blood-covered hand on Vlad's, which is still gripping my shoulder.

The reality of what happened here tonight settles over me. I expect to feel regret, sadness...something about killing my father. All I find is relief and the desperate need to wash off the blood coating my skin, clothes, and hair.

I turn back to look at my mate as his knuckles gently brush against my cheek. "You did it." Not a question, but I still nod. Lowell leans forward and kisses me, despite the blood.

"Go shower," Adriana orders, clearing her throat to rid it of emotion. She stands, her legs faltering, but Vlad is there, wrapping an arm around her waist, and she offers him a small smile as a thank you. "We'll deal with this mess."

"What are you going to do with them all?" I ask, gesturing to the people now surrounded by snapping wolves and vampires.

"That's up to you," she says. "But I built a magic-suppressing dungeon. I figured we might need it. We could put everyone in there or we could execute them."

"Lock them up for now," I decide. "We'll meet in the war room in an hour to discuss it further. Someone should get Jeremy, we left him in the pack—"

"I'll send someone to bring him and the twins here," Vlad offers. "We might as well start moving everyone in. The rest of the vampires will be here in the next few weeks."

"The packs too," Lowell says, pushing himself to his feet.

"We have a lot to figure out," Adriana says. "But it'll still be here in an hour. Go, shower."

Lowell motions for me to wait and walks over to where my father's head is lying on the dais. He grabs the ponytail, swinging it around and splattering blood on the nearby stones as he crosses the cavern and the stakes in the ground. He removes Rodger's head and replaces it with my father's.

"Let this be a lesson," he calls to the traitors being held by the wolves. "The only reason you haven't been torn into pieces is at the request of your queen. Keep that in mind."

In a burst of his speed, he's back at my side, wincing from the exertion before we walk out of the throne room.

Chapter Thirty

WE WALK INTO THE war room and a cup of coffee is thrust into my hand. I nod my thanks to Adriana as she falls in behind Lowell, who won't remove his arm from around my waist. Not that I'm complaining, I'm very content feeling his warmth after everything. We didn't talk as we showered; I don't think either of us knew where to start. So, we just held onto each other under the scalding water as it washed away the remnants of the day.

Vlad is already seated at the boardroom table, his eyes fixed on the enchanted mirror that shows the footage of the palace. His skin is ashen and the bags under his eyes tell me he's running on empty. He probably hasn't fed since... was it only two days ago when I walked in on him and Adriana? I flop in the seat at the head of the table and wordlessly extend my wrist. He opens his mouth to protest but thinks the better of it and sinks his fangs into my skin. The familiar rush of pleasure spikes through me and Lowell wheels his chair so he's directly next to me, his arm dropping around me as I lean into him.

Vlad extracts his fangs and thanks me. The exhaustion is still there but his color looks much better.

"I don't even know where to start," I say, looking around at the small group gathered. I take a long gulp from my coffee, willing the caffeine to kick in faster.

"I have an idea," a melodic voice speaks from the portal door. I gasp and look up to find Edina's sapphire eyes staring back at me. Her blonde hair is tied up in an elaborate twist and piled into a crown on the top of her head. Her ballgown—yeah she's in a ballgown with a poofy skirt and everything—is made of a pale blue velvet.

A strangled cry leaves my lips. Edina takes two steps out of the portal entrance before I vault over the table and barrel into her. She squeals as we tip backward, the weight of her dress causing us to capsize. We laugh as I manage to roll off and pull her to her feet, so she's not stuck like an upside-down turtle.

"Hang on," she says, and with one graceful move, her monstrosity of a dress is shredded to ribbons by icicles that sprout from her fingertips. She steps out of the discarded yards of fabric in a white slip. Adriana summons a black robe and sends it to Edina, who makes two strategic slashes down the back for her wings.

Once she's situated, we waste no time hugging again, sighing in tandem as we sink into each other's hold.

"You smell different," she says, burying her head in my neck, as I do the same. She still smells of rosewater, but there's a hint of magic that wasn't there before.

"Is everything okay?" I ask, finally pulling back. There's an undercurrent of pain in her expression, and I worry that sending her to Faerie was the wrong call.

"Yeah," she says so softly I almost don't hear her. "I just...I needed to get out of there. But the Fae agreed to help. I'm not sure when they'll send reinforcements since they have no sense of urgency but they're coming."

"What did you have to promise?" Vlad asks, and I lead Edina towards the front of the table, rolling a spare chair with me so she can sit at my side.

"It's not important," she says with a wave of her hand. The gesture would look unaffected to anyone who didn't know her, but I can hear the weight behind those words.

"E—"

I'm interrupted by a Fae male stepping through the portal door. He looks like he could be Edina's brother. He has the same skin tone and pin-straight, blonde hair. The only thing different is his wings, which are slightly less rounded, and his eyes are more of a dark navy. He straightens the lapels of his white tuxedo, which would look ridiculous on most people, but he pulls it off in his tall, lean frame.

"This is Astor," Edina says as she flops into her chair. "My babysitter."

"That's an incorrect description, Princess," Astor says, eying everyone in the room. His eyes settle on Vlad, and he tips his head in respect.

"The Winter Court Fae also have no sense of irony," Edina says, leaning her head against my shoulder the second I'm in my seat. "I was super well received."

"Actually, her entrance was quite controversial. Her Majesty—"

"Sarcasm, Astor, we've been over this," Edina groans.

"Can we find Astor a room?" I say to Adriana and Vlad. "Astor, Edina is safe with this group so you're free to retire for the morning. Maybe change into some more comfortable clothes." Adriana stands, but Astor is rooted in place.

"My queen instructed me—"

"The queen will be fine if Edina is in my care," Vlad steps in, standing. "Go, follow the pretty witch." Adriana's cheeks flush and she exits with Astor following close behind her, casting looks over his shoulder at Edina.

Edina arches an eyebrow at Vlad once they are out of earshot. "Not a word, Tinkerbell," he grumbles, and Edina purses her lips in laughter.

"So," my best friend says, some of her pep returning to her voice. She swipes the coffee from my hands but passes it back when she sees it's black. "What have you all been up to?"

Vlad, Lowell, and I exchange glances before we dissolve into hysterical laughter fueled by exhaustion. Once we get it together, we catch Edina up on everything that's happened in the past two months. By the time we reach the evening events, Adriana is back, bearing some kind of coffee drink for Edina that's covered in whipped cream.

"Well fuck," Edina says succinctly when we finish. "And I thought I had a rough time." My eyes widen but Edina holds up a hand. "Nothing that affects us here, I promise. I'm not ready to talk about it."

"What's next?" Lowell asks before I can protest.

"The wolves and vampires arrive in a few weeks," I say, unable to hide the exhaustion in my voice. "We need to have the situation with the traitors sorted out by then. Does anyone know if the leaders speak for their entire covens or if they were acting alone?"

"I'll find out," Adriana says. "If they acted alone, I say we wipe their memories and send them back to their home cities."

"And if they didn't?" Vlad asks, and Adriana gulps.

"We can bond them," Lowell answers for me. "We use a surveillance type of bond to keep tabs on problematic packs. The wolves will know how to set it up and we can keep tabs on the covens while they're still here."

"I like it," I respond. "I also think we force them to take a vow that prohibits them from acting against us or betraying our secrets."

Everyone nods in agreement, so I turn back to Adriana. "Can we talk about Rodger?" Her head drops, finding something in her lap very interesting.

"He was with me when Father stormed in," she says softly. "He tried to protect me, and they killed him. It was quick."

"Why was he in your room?" Vlad asks, and Adriana's responding glare is murderous.

"None of your business."

"Intrigue," Edina murmurs, propping a hand under her chin, the black robe sliding down to her elbows. Vlad snarls at her but my best friend just takes a long sip of her coffee, holding his gaze.

"Adriana, was your clairvoyance training complete?" I ask quickly.

"For the most part," Adriana grits out, refusing to meet anyone's eyes.

"I'll call Rodger's family in the morning. We can cremate the body and send them the ashes."

"That just leaves the situation with the Kingdom," Lowell says, his hand resting on my thigh.

"How bad is it?" I ask, looking at the mirror while Vlad and Adriana simultaneously take out their phones to see what the media is reporting.

"Bad," Adriana responds. "They were sloppy. Walked in, killed a bunch of guards, slaughtered the king, and teleported out with his head. I don't know if something went wrong or this was the plan, but they didn't even try and look for Archer."

"Seems shortsighted," Vlad comments, flipping through an article before passing it to Lowell to read.

"The Dragons will have everything locked down for a while," Lowell says, his fingers brushing my inner thigh in a calming motion. "We should wait to hear from your mom. We're not ready to attack yet, and it isn't the time to broker peace."

"I agree."

"Then," Lowell continues, his hand squeezing gently, "it's almost dawn. Let's get some sleep and go over the finer details tomorrow." Everyone murmurs their agreement and stands except for Vlad and Edina

"Katie, can I have a word?" he asks, and I sit back in my swivel chair. Lowell pauses.

"I'm five minutes behind you," I reassure him, and Lowell looks between Vlad and me before exiting the room. Once he's gone Vlad turns to Edina, who simply cocks her head to the side, daring him to question her presence.

"E—" he says, exhausted, and my brows arch at the familiarity.

"I need to talk to my best friend," she says simply. "And I bet our conversations overlap so I'm not going anywhere."

Vlad rolls his eyes but turns to me. "The golden magic--" he starts.

"Was were-magic, right?" I ask, and Vlad's eyebrows shoot up to his hairline. "It was the same color as Lowell's eyes."

"It usually manifests after.... everything is solidified."

"Can it be brought on by trauma?"

"Your guess is as good as mine. When two wolves solidify the...thing," he says with a sideways glance at my best friend, "their strength, speed, and other aspects of their shifting magic are enhanced. But when it's a wolf and a witch, that witch can utilize the magic the way you would utilize raw magic. Finley had were-magic too."

"Does Lowell know you're mates?" Edina asks, and Vlad rolls his eyes. "Just another one of the many perks of being Fae...scenting mates." She mimes gagging.

"Did you know before you left?" I ask.

"No, babes," she reassures me. "I got better at understanding my powers in Faerie. When did you find out?"

"Earlier tonight. Lowell doesn't know yet."

"You should tell him. If I can scent it on you, the other Magical Creatures probably can too."

"Plus, she screamed *he's my fucking mate* in front of Lowell's entire pack," Vlad adds.

"I'll tell him, just not tonight," I respond, and both parties narrow their eyes. "I just... is it so bad that I want the moment to be special?"

"No," Edina says, squeezing my hand "That's not bad."

"I'll tell him tomorrow," I tell them, and they both give me reassuring smiles as I stand and head for the door.

"Oh, E," I stop in the doorframe, turning over my shoulder. "When we got the news that the king died...we were at a werewolf orgy."

I run out of the room, my laughter mixing with Vlad's, as Edina screams, "Fuck all the way off!"

Chapter Thirty-One

THE WHOLE WAY TO my room my mind spins with ideas of how to tell Lowell we're mates. I go back and forth between taking him to Vlad's, outside in the hills, or simply in my room over breakfast. You'd think with all the fantasy romance books I read I'd be good at grand gestures. I get to the room with no progress.

I close the door softly behind me. I can tell by the gambit of emotions Lowell is feeling that he's awake, but he's stretched out on top of my comforter, one hand behind his head with his eyes closed. I kick off my shoes and tread over to the bed, climbing on top of him, my legs on either side of his hips as I settle my head on his chest. I feel him chuckle beneath me before kissing the top of my head and encircling me in his arms.

"Hey, little witch," he murmurs against my hair.

"You're my mate."

Fuck.

Fuck fuck fuckity fuck.

Lowell's body goes rigid around me before I push out of his hold, not meeting his eyes as I sit at the foot of the bed. I drop my head in my hands, pressing the heels into my eye sockets and cursing myself for screwing this up.

The bed shifts, the mattress dipping as Lowell sits beside me, his thigh brushing against mine. The bond is atypically silent. Of course, now when I want to know what he's feeling it decides to shut the hell up.

"Say it again," he murmurs, his large hands wrapping around mine and slowly guiding them away from my face. I take a deep breath and look at him. He has the biggest smile, and his eyes are brimming with tears.

"Okay," I breathe. "But first—" Lowell arches an eyebrow. "I don't think we should...solidify the bond or whatever you call it. Not right now, I mean. I still want to take things slow, to get to know each other without that pressure. I've jumped into relationships fast before, and the last time, it went up in flames. I don't want that for us. I want it to be special because we fucking deserve that. This is rare and *magical*, and we deserve more than this room in a freaking bunker while we're hiding out from the Kingdom on a day when I killed my father and he almost killed you."

"Breathe," Lowell says, his eyes crinkled in laughter. He's still holding my hands and runs his thumb over my knuckles in a soothing motion.

"Are you okay with that? With waiting?"

"Yes, of course," Lowell says. "Come here." He tugs gently on my arm and I crawl into his lap so he's cradling me in his arms. I rest my head on his shoulder, letting his rain and fresh earth scent wash over me and calm me down. I stroke his jaw, the coarse feeling of his stubble contrasting with the soft hair that brushes against my cheek.

"Say it again," he whispers, pushing the hair that's fallen in front of my face behind my ear.

"Aldonza's locket is imbued with were-magic," I say softly, and his eyes widen. "Your mom told me earlier, but apparently Vlad has known this whole time."

"That doesn't surprise me."

"It beats when the wearer has met their mate, not their true love. I think you're right and that's not actually a thing. When I put it on the first time, you were the only werewolf I'd ever met. Which means…" Lowell's smile is infectious as he leans close enough that the tips of our noses touch. "You're my mate."

He kisses me and the bond erupts in light, sending pure happiness flowing straight to my center. The kiss is soft and sweet, and I don't even know if it counts as a kiss because our lips are both pulled thin by our smiles. Lowell flips us, gently laying me back on the bed as he hovers over me, kissing every inch of my face like an excited puppy.

"My mate," he repeats over and over between kisses.

"Did you know?" I ask.

"I hoped," he says, resting his head on my chest. "Fuck, I wished so hard. My sisters suspected, but I was afraid to believe it."

"That's why you got angry with them?" I ask, running my fingers through his hair.

"I didn't want them getting your hopes up. I figured we'd know soon enough." He lifts his head, the tears shining in his golden eyes making them brighter. "It wouldn't have mattered. You're mine. But—"

"But fuck does it feel good," I finish for him, and he pulls me back into a kiss. I sigh, completely content as Lowell's tongue slides into my mouth. My hands skim down the rippling muscles in his back, settling by his hips and pulling him closer so he's grinding his hard length into me.

"Little witch," he laughs as I wrap my legs around him and flip us, so I'm straddling him. "If you want to take things slow, we can't..."

He doesn't finish the thought as I trail kisses down his chest, sliding my body down his. I follow the smattering of dark hair, hooking my fingers around the waistband of his sweats and tugging them off. I need to feel him inside me in any way I can get. Our eyes connect as I smile and take him in my mouth.

Lowell groans as I bury his length in my throat. He props himself up and gathers the hair that's fallen in front of my face into a ponytail that he uses to guide my pace.

"You're so fucking beautiful with my cock in your mouth," Lowell grunts as I continue to swallow him down. "My mate. Made for me in every fucking way."

I continue to work him, hollowing out my cheeks until he's panting. His hands shift and he grips my jaw, guiding me off him as he sits up. I crawl back up to his lap as his mouth crashes against mine, devouring my lips and tongue.

"Off," he growls, shoving my leggings down as far as he can. "Before I rip them off you." In the interest of not losing any more clothing, I slide back down Lowell's body, pausing only to lap up the bead of precum from the head of his cock before hopping off the bed. I make quick work of my clothes. I probably should have teased him a bit, maybe put on a show in removing them, but I'm too needy to be that far away from him for that long.

I climb back on the bed, hovering over him.

"Turn around," he murmurs. He circles his finger in command, and I tentatively start shifting, straddling him backward.

"I don't know what you want me to—" Lowell yanks my hips back so they hover over his face, and I fall forward, my hands bracing on his powerful thighs. "Oh shit."

I groan as he starts feasting on me. His tongue sinks inside me, tasting my desire for him before he rises back up to my clit, alternating between sucking and teasing me with the tip of his tongue.

I lean forward, trying to reach his cock, but he's so damn tall that there's no way I can get to it with my mouth. I shimmy forward, intent on my mission, but Lowell grips my hips hard enough to bruise and yanks me back, so I'm flush against his face.

"But I can't—" Lowell growls, and uses one hand to keep me in place while a finger on his other hand slides inside me, hooking and brushing against my g-spot. I swear, my head falling forward onto his abs while my hands fist the sheets.

When I can half focus, I push myself up, leaning on one arm as I spit in the other hand. I wrap it around the base of his cock, the smooth skin already slick from my earlier ministrations. I work him with my hand, twisting my hand as I pump his length up and down. Lowell's moans send vibrations that rattle my bones and have me crying out in pleasure.

Think I can make you squirt again? Lowell asks through our mental channel. I try to lift my hips, so I won't drown him because I'm so fucking close already, and he pulls me back down. *Let it go, little witch. I want it all.*

He adds a second finger, fucking me faster as he continues to devour my pussy. My hands tighten around his shaft and Lowell bends his knees, lifting enough that I can get part of him in my mouth. What I can't reach with my mouth I keep working with my hand. Lowell thrusts his hips as my own rock back of their own volition.

That's right, fuck my face. Take what you need. The filthy words have me ready to combust, and when his pinkie brushes against my other opening I explode, crying out around him.

Lowell doesn't let me come down from my orgasm, he keeps going, silently urging me to give him more. His finger is now slowly pushing inside my back entrance and stars explode in front of my eyes at the taboo intrusion that feels so fucking good.

Come with me, he commands. And I oblige...hard. As I cry out his name, my lips still wrapped around his hard cock, I feel him thicken as his own release hits the back of my throat and I swallow everything he has to give me.

Lowell's legs relax and I clumsily maneuver off his face and the bed. Evidence of my orgasm is dripping down my thighs, and I can't help but laugh in my euphoric haze. "I think we need another shower."

Lowell stands, his smile still out in full force. "I'll run the bath," he says, and I watch as my mate disappears into the bathroom.

I'm so glad I told him.

"Absolutely not," Lowell says, pacing back and forth along the length of the war room. The feed of the castle is playing, the chaos in the halls mimicking that in the coven.

We got in touch with my mother this afternoon. She said they're rushing to get Archer coronated. Everyone is panicked that my father will come back and attempt to seize the throne, and there's only so much the Dragons can do until Archer is officially the King. She spouted some bureaucratic bullshit that basically means they're having the ceremony tomorrow.

"This is the only option," I say into my hands, swiping them down my face and pressing my heels into my eyes. "I should already be leaving—"

"You're not going to the palace alone," Lowell growls.

"I agree," Adriana says.

"If Lowell comes with me, Archer is going to lose his shit," I say for the eight-hundredth time. "And we won't survive an attack from his hellfire. The only chance we have at talking to him calmly is if I go in alone."

"I should be the one to go with you," Edina says.

"Walking into the palace as a Fae is still suicide," I remind her. Everyone falls silent again, the only sound in the war room is Lowell's bare feet against the stones as he paces. "Archer won't hurt me if I go in alone."

Lowell scoffs. "Forgive me if I don't believe that."

"I know how it sounds," I sigh. "But I don't think he would maliciously hurt me. He wasn't in his right mind the day of the attack. So, I'll go in, play up the scar, get some sympathy, and convince him to restore the four monarchs."

"What if—"

"I can't imagine Archer is thrilled about the idea of taking over so quickly," I tell them again. "He expected to have decades of further training. And when we tell him it'll be me and my mom representing Light and Dark Magic, I think he'll agree."

"What about Lowell?" Vlad asks.

"I'll tell him the Pack Master of the European packs will be the monarch for the Magical Creatures and let him draw his conclusions. Once he makes a vow with me to enact this plan, then we'll bring Lowell in."

"And if he says no?" Lowell asks.

"Then I'll get the fuck out of there, and we go to war."

"What if we send someone who can teleport?" Vlad offers. "That way you have an escape plan."

"Anyone who can teleport past the castle wards is wanted," I say with a pointed look at Adriana. "My mother will be close. She can get me to the portal if things go south."

"She never said what kind of force she has on our side," Edina says.

"But she has something," I counter. "I won't be completely defenseless. And I'll have you all linked to my mental channel, so I'll be able to warn you if anything seems wrong."

"Can we have the room?" Lowell growls, and the other three leave so fast they're gone before I can blink. Lowell comes over to where I'm sitting and swivels my chair to face him as he kneels before me.

"What are you planning on offering him?" he asks softly. "What if he agrees to the plan, but only if you marry him?"

"No," I say sternly, and Lowell chuckles.

"I know you, Katie," he says, his jaw ticking. "You'll do anything to keep everyone safe. It's your best and worst quality."

"I won't let it be an option," I say resolutely. "You're my mate. And even if you weren't, I claimed you."

Lowell nods as I grip his hair, bringing his lips to mine. "I'll be home in an hour," I murmur against him. "Hopefully with an agreement that makes us official royalty."

"No longer your consort?" he teases, and I snap my teeth and bite down a little too hard on his bottom lip.

"Partners, always," I whisper, and he tugs me to the floor. I straddle his waist where he kneels, and we kiss passionately.

"Katie, I—" he starts, and I silence him by pressing my finger to his lips.

"No goodbyes," I say firmly. "I'll be home in an hour. You can tell me then." He pulls me into a hug anyway, wordlessly pouring emotion into our bond that I try not to dwell on, not when I have to go and deal with this.

"I'll open the channels," I say, pulling myself away and whipping off the sweater I'm wearing so that I'm only in my tank and leggings. Lowell scowls and I roll my eyes. "Going for the sympathy vote here," I say gesturing to my scar on display.

I don't look back as I step into the portal to head back to the palace.

Chapter Thirty-Two

"DROP YOUR WAND!"

With my hands raised, I step out of the portal onto the plush red carpet in the palace. It looks the same in its over-the-top opulence, the cream walls studded with the same golden accents.

I left my sword and dagger in the Highlands, but my wand is wedged in the waistband of my leggings. I drop it to the ground as soldiers in their familiar black tunics embossed with the crest of the Kingdom surround me.

"My name is Kathryn Carmichael," I announce, keeping my voice light and unthreatening. "And I'm here to see the prince."

"Katie?" A booming voice calls from behind the pack. The circle surrounding me opens and I'm met with a pair of warm brown eyes.

"Marcus." My stepfather scoops me into his broad arms, his thick beard brushing my bare shoulder. I can't help the tear that trickles out of my eye. "I've missed you so much."

"I've missed you too kid," he says. "Your father made a fucking mess here recently."

"He paid for it."

Marcus sighs as he sets me down; there are a million unsaid things in that exhale. He once offered to be the one who took care of my father for me, back when I was arrogant enough to claim his death like it was a trophy to display on my shelf. I'm sure he's worried about the fallout for me, both mentally and within the coven. But I'm...weirdly okay. Maybe it's because I stopped viewing Seth as my father the day Marcus started training me.

"Good," he says finally. He assesses me, his jaw tightening as his eyes trail down my scar.

"I need to see him," I say softly, drawing Marcus's attention back to my face.

"Stand down," he orders the other officers, and they lower their wands. "You two," Marcus points to the O'Malley twins, their red hair sticking out in the throng of faceless officers. "Take her to the throne room."

"Yes, General," they say in unison, motioning for me to follow. I start, but Marcus grabs my arm.

"I'll check on you in one hour," he says sternly, and I nod, not bothering to bow in respect. It's a motion that doesn't go unnoticed by the other men, but Marcus only gives me a warm smile as he shoos me down the hallway.

I fall into step with the O'Malley twins, who keep sneaking glances over their shoulders at me like I'm a ghost that will disappear again. I want to talk to them. We developed a sort-of friendship after our mission for Archer's Moment of Valor, but now the silence between us is tense. I wonder if they're secretly working for my mother, and that's why Marcus selected them to bring me to the throne room. Of course, there's no way I could ask that. We'll have to think of a code word for the future.

We reach the entryway and the doors that lead to the throne room all too soon. It seems like a lifetime ago that Archer and I stood here waiting to tell his father of our relationship. It was the first time I ever heard him say he loved me. The time he stood up to my mother.

Those memories are sour now...tainted with the scent of ash and burning flesh. But despite all that, I think Archer and I will rule well together. I still believe he's a good man, one who's been raised for the throne. We'll need that as we restructure the Kingdom into a place that accepts and welcomes all forms of magic.

The twins pull open the doors, standing to the side as I enter.

The room is the same, filled with rows of empty chairs that cover the white and black marble floor. The black pendants with the Kingdom's crest hang from the arched rafters. A red carpet runs to the flame-shaped, opal throne with the dragon armrests.

My throat catches when I see him hunched over, the palms of his hands pressing into his eyes. His skin is paler, the edge of his jaw sharper beneath his hands. I step forward, my boots clicking on the gold-flecked marble, echoing off the walls of the giant chamber and announcing my presence. Archer looks up, his hazel eyes latching to mine, and I freeze. How many times have I dreamed about those eyes, filled with malice and hate? Now...they just look empty. Broken. Exactly how I felt six weeks ago.

I steady my breath, trying to calm the panic rising in my chest.

"Your Highness," barely a whisper, but the room's acoustics carry my greeting.

Archer moves slowly, standing and descending the small dais. I can't move as he comes closer. My legs feel like jelly. He stops inches from me and extends a hand toward my neck. I flinch as he brushes my hair from my shoulder so he can see the extent of my scar.

"Katie..." a tear slides down his cheek as his fingertips skim the jagged skin.

"I'm sorry about your father," I manage. "I swear, I had nothing to do—"

He pulls me into his arms, a sob shuddering through his body. I go stiff as a board, not returning the affection, but he doesn't seem to notice as he clings to me.

"I thought...oh god," he breathes. "I thought I lost you." I tentatively pat him on the back, and he latches onto that comfort, using it to somehow bring me closer.

"I'm so sorry," he murmurs against my skin, as he places a kiss on my scarred skin. I freeze again, as he kisses me again, higher this time. "I love you so much." He threads his fingers through my hair and pulls me closer, aiming to kiss me in earnest.

"Archer," I place my hand firmly on his chest, putting just enough pressure that he backs away. "We need to talk."

"Later," he whispers, moving in again. This time I duck out of his arms and walk away.

"Damnit Archer, this is important." I put a foot of space between us, and Archer just gives me a pitying look.

"I know," he hangs his head. "I know it'll take time." *Time for what?*

"I need you to listen to me," I say slowly. "We need to reinstate the four monarchs."

"What?" Archer looks at me like I have eight heads. "Where is this coming from?"

"It's why I'm here. The balance of the Kingdom is so out of whack. I've seen it firsthand. But if we reestablish the monarchs, we can prevent any other violence. We can rule together."

"We're going to rule together," he says with a smile.

"Really?" I breathe as relief floods through me.

"Of course, love. You're going to be my queen." He crosses the space between us as my mouth drops open. "I'm so sorry for the way everything happened. But I've found a way to get you the help you need."

"The what?" I ask.

"Katie," he brushes his knuckles against my cheek. "I know you don't see it now, but your father and the Dark Witches... they've brainwashed you."

"Excuse me?"

"I'm just sorry I was too late that day. I left as soon as your father contacted me, but I had to fly—"

"He doesn't matter, Archer," I say. "I killed him."

"Oh," Archer's forehead furrows, but then he nods. "Good then."

"You think he brainwashed me."

"I know it seems crazy," he says soothingly. "But you have to have recognized it. Why else would you be here?"

"To make a deal with you," I'm seeing red and practically vibrating with pent-up energy. "Archer, I'm not brainwashed. I was chosen to restore the balance of power in our Kingdom."

"Okay, love," he says placatingly.

"Fuck, Archer, I'm serious. I need your help with this."

"I know," he says, and suddenly I'm surrounded by Dragons officers. I don't even know where they all came from. "And we've found a way to help you. We don't want to hurt you."

The men start closing in on me, and I raise my hands defensively, very aware of the fact that I have no wand. "Archer, just listen—"

One of the men lunges for me and the heel of my hand connects with his nose. The next few minutes are a whirl of avoiding magical binds and physical blows. I drop low, sweeping someone's legs out from beneath him and at the same time punching another in the groin. When I pop up, I deliver a sharp jab in the stomach to the man whose nose I broke.

I pant as the men fall around me, knocked out or unable to stand. I step out of the circle of their bodies and run to the door. It's locked

I turn back, and Archer is advancing slowly like I'm a wild animal he doesn't want to spook. "Archer, please don't do this."

A wall of fire springs up around me. Red and orange flames dance so close to my skin that I'm screaming in panic. I curl onto myself, huddling in a ball on the floor as the heat becomes overwhelming. The flames seem to be getting closer, closing in. They're stealing the oxygen from the air, stealing my magic from my body. I'm shaking uncontrollably, unable to move and look past the fire.

There's a brief reprieve from the heat before everything goes black.

THE FIRST THING I notice when I wake is the pain in my shoulders. The kind of pain when you sleep wrong but intensified by ten. I roll the offending muscle, and pain lances through me when I can't move my arm. I hesitantly try the other and get the same results. I yank harshly on my wrists and feel the sharp sting of metal digging into my flesh. They must have magic-suppressing cuffs suspending my arms above my head. But I don't feel like I'm lying down on a bed.

I open my eyes, but there's no light. Squinting against the darkness, I search for anything that might clue me into where I am. I don't think they would have left the palace with the coronation tomorrow, so I must be in the dungeon. As my eyes adjust, I can see the outline of bars that hum with magic suppressant. I can faintly make out the floor and ceiling, which means I'm suspended upright. I flip my palm and swat behind me, connecting with thick, cold metal.

I spare a peek down at my body. My tank and leggings are on, my legs spread wide, and my feet, sans boots, are also secured with magical suppressant cuffs. I wasn't burned further, which means someone knocked me out...magically or with a blow to the head based on the pounding in my skull.

I curse myself for not thinking about my were-magic. I haven't practiced with it so I'm not sure it would have worked again, but it didn't even cross my mind in the heat of the moment. I take a steadying breath. Marcus told me I had an hour, which means it couldn't have been longer. I'm sure he and my mom will be here any minute.

The clanging of the cell door has me focusing back on the present. Archer and two Dragons officers walk in, shutting the door behind them. The officers remain in the shadows as Archer approaches me, so I can't see their faces.

"Good, you're awake," Archer says with a smile that's so at odds with the situation.

"Bondage isn't my kink, Your Highness," I rasp, my throat raw from the smoke inhalation. An officer scoffs and clears his throat to cover the sound, but Archer's eyes are glued to me.

"I'm glad they didn't take your sense of humor," he murmurs, brushing a piece of hair behind my ear. He reaches out to the side and someone hands him a notebook. He reads for a moment and then nods, returning the object.

"It will all be back to normal soon, love," he smiles, approaching me and placing his hands on either side of my head.

"What are you doing?" I ask, ignoring the memory of my father holding me like this, a similar excited glint in his eyes as the prince.

"Ten minutes," Archer directs to the officers. "Katie, this might hurt."

"Your Highness," a third officer runs to the cell doors and Archer pauses. "Generals Carmichael and Weatherbeak just arrived looking for the captain." My body sags. *They're here. They've come to save me.*

"What did you tell them?" Archer asks coolly.

"That she left." The officer says simply. *Fuck fuck fuck.*

Mom? I shout down mental channel between my mother and me. *If you can hear me, Archer has me in the dungeon.* There's no answer. The magic suppressant must be blocking it.

"Good. No need to get their hopes up if this doesn't work." Archer turns to me and puts his hands back up as the officer bows and leaves again.

"Archer, what are you doing?" I ask, my eyes meeting his.

"Removing your Dark Magic," he says, and my mouth falls open. "Begin."

EPILOGUE

Edina

"FUCK, I'M CLOSE," I moan, as a cold hand slides down along my stomach and finds my clit.

"That's right. Come for me," Vlad's voice rumbles as he relentlessly lifts my body with his superior strength and slams me down on his cock. His hand starts moving in fast circles and I scream as my orgasm crashes over me. Vlad grunts as my walls squeeze around him and I feel his length thicken as it spills inside me.

We pant, and I lower my legs from around his waist, landing in a mop bucket that thankfully isn't full of water. "Fucking hell," I swear, kicking the thing across the cramped broom closet. "Next time, let's just go to my room."

Vlad shakes his head as he pulls up his suit pants. "It's too close—"

"To Adriana's room?" I roll my eyes emphatically, pulling on my leggings. My thong is torn and discarded somewhere in here, and I'm not in the mood to search for it. "Isn't that the point of this? To make her jealous?"

His hand whips out and grabs my arm, his ice-blue eyes piercing into me. "That's not what this is, E. I'd never use you like that."

I nod, stepping into him. Vlad is tall enough that I can rest my head underneath his chin. He wraps his arms low, avoiding my wings and the sadness collectively settles back into our bodies.

Vlad and I realized during our trip to Faerie that we both like to avoid emotion with sex. And the sex was good enough that when he grabbed my hand last night and dragged me to his room, I let him. I didn't mention that Adriana probably slept with Rodger, and he ignored that I was crying during most of our fuck-session.

At least I didn't cry today. So...progress?

"You don't have to talk about it with me," Vlad says against my hair. "But you should tell Katie...about whatever it is."

"Are you gonna tell Lowell about what's going on with you?" I clap back.

"No, but—"

"No," I say firmly. "I know Katie. She'd use this to keep Lowell at arm's length, and I'm not going to be the one that keeps her from being happy."

"Then it's something to do with your mate," Vlad guesses, and I shoot daggers at him. He nods knowingly and pulls me back closer. "He's a fucking idiot."

Tears brim in my eyes, but I pointedly ignore them, clearing my throat. "You should talk to Adriana," I say, stepping out of his embrace.

"She's mortal," he sighs. "And there are rules."

"And ways around them if that's what you decide. You have a way to be with the person who..." I swallow and shake my head to ward off the rising emotion. "You should talk to her."

"But then who would you have to distract you?" he asks with a smirk. "A wolf?"

"Maybe. But Katie told me you have a hot brother." Vlad laughs loudly, some light returning to his eyes, and he pulls me back close and pecks me on the lips.

The door opens, and eerie green light floods the broom closet. Vlad and I spring apart, but it doesn't matter. If Adriana knew exactly where to find us, it means she saw everything.

"Adriana—" I start, walking towards her.

"Something's wrong," she says, her voice clipped. She turns on her heel and I follow her down the hall towards the war room.

"Adriana, I swear it didn't mean anything." My wings flutter, trying to help my legs move faster.

"I'm not mad," she says in a tone that begs to differ.

"We're just friends." A loud crash sounds at the end of the hall and it has the two of us sprinting. The breeze that ruffles my hair is the only sign that Vlad passes us with his vampire speed.

We reach the war room and find Vlad and two women I don't recognize holding Lowell against the wall as he thrashes against them. The chairs are overturned, and some have definitely been tossed across the room.

"What the fuck happened?" I ask. Katie opened our mental channels to tell us she was leaving for the palace, but I still look for her. That's when I notice the enchanted mirror is reflecting the room, not the palace.

"The feed cut," one of the women calls over her shoulder. Adriana flicks her fingers and her grey magic wraps around Lowell, lifting him and forcing him to sit in the only chair left upright. It binds him quickly. The women relax before greeting

Vlad, and I realize now that they're not turned away that they must be Lowell's sisters. They all have similar coloring and the same eyes.

"Calm down, Lowell," Adriana says calmly. "It's done this before. It doesn't mean anything."

"Has she said anything?" one of the sisters asks, and we all shake our heads. "Okay, so no need for all this." She gestures wildly to the mess in the war room, which Adriana promptly starts cleaning with her magic.

"Have you felt any pain?" I ask Lowell.

"I felt something earlier, but it ended abruptly."

The portal door swings open, blueish purple mist pouring in through the opening as two people stumble inside. At first, I think it's Katie, but as she straightens and tugs down her tunic, I realize it's her mom. Marcus is behind her, his brown eyes wild.

"Where is she?" Misty demands, her eyes skimming over everyone in the room. "They said they sent her back here."

"Who did?" Vlad asks, and Misty levels him with a glare that would make a lesser being cower.

"The Dragons officers," Marcus answers. "They said she and Archer argued and she came back here."

"She's not here," Adriana whispers.

"Adriana, get the feed up," Lowell grits through his teeth. Adriana looks at me like I'll know how to magically fix whatever contraption she set up in the palace. I'm still sputtering when the mirror comes to life. Adriana waves her wand, zooming in on one of the feeds showcasing the dungeon.

Katie is hanging from a giant x-shaped cross in a cell, her arms and legs wrapped with thick metal cuffs. Archer is standing in front of her, his hands on her head as she thrashes wildly. Her mouth is closed so tight that I know she's not giving him the satisfaction of hearing her scream. Lowell is growling, his eyes glowing as he watches her. The cuffs must be suppressing her magic and the mating bond, which is why he's not feeling her pain.

"No," Adriana breathes.

"What is it?" I demand. "Did you see something in the future?"

Archer removes his hands, and we all watch as Katie slumps down, her head lolling to the side. Someone hidden in the shadows hands him a notebook and Misty inhales sharply.

"How did he get that?" she hisses.

"What the fuck is happening?" I demand, looking at the room. Even Vlad looks paler.

"He's using the same technique that Father used to give her Dark Magic," Adriana answers finally.

"Why would he do that?"

"A few weeks ago," Marcus says softly, "he asked me about removing a person's magic. I told him it couldn't be done without killing the person."

"And he's doing it anyway?" I breathe.

"He must think because Katie's magic was given, it can be taken away."

The room dissolves into chaos as people start talking over each other, trying to figure out what to do to get Katie out. Misty and Marcus are shell-shocked, while Vlad and Adriana are talking over each other, both on the verge of leaving to go rescue her.

"Enough," Lowell bellows, and everyone falls silent. "Adriana, untie me. *Now*." Adriana complies and Lowell stands. He looks murderous and formidable, but he's clearly calmed down.

"Lyra, tell the packs we're moving up the timeline and to meet us in London," he dictates to one of his sisters. "How soon can we have them here?"

"Three days if everyone leaves now."

"Fine. Misty...and Marcus I assume?" Marcus nods. "I need you to return to the palace before anyone realizes you're gone. Get whatever soldiers you've recruited on guard duty for Katie. Make sure they're assigned to her and ready to go."

Misty opens her mouth, but Marcus tugs her back through the portal.

"Vlad, I need to know everything you remember about Carman's experiments," Lowell continues and then turns to me. "Go get your trainer and start mastering your magic. You have three days."

"We can't leave her there for three days," I insist, looking to Adriana for backup. Her gray eyes are glazed over as she searches for possibilities. She inhales sharply, shaking clear the vision and looking at Lowell.

"He's right," she says. "I can't say what will happen, but Katie will be okay for three days. Edina, focus on sealing portals."

"What is the plan?"

"We're laying siege to the palace," Lowell says, turning his golden gaze back on me. "And while we do that, you'll sneak through the portal to save our queen."

Author Note

Heyyyy. How you holding up? Are you raging at me? Would it help if I told you originally the cliffhanger was worse? I mean, really, you should be thanking me for that minor, baby cliffhanger where only Katie is in mortal danger. It could have been worse...

Okay but real talk. Thank you so much for reading. My dream of being an author has been a long time in the making and I'm so honored and humbled to make that dream a reality. And that's because of you.

Reviews are SO important to Indie Authors, and I'd greatly appreciate it if you could take a few minutes to leave a review on

Goodreadsor Amazon

Need to actually rage at me? Join our Readers' Group or follow me on TikTok.

ONE LAST THING: Check out this deleted scene from Made to Conquer.

All links can be found on www.marianneascott.com

ABOUT THE AUTHOR

Marianne A. Scott is a Sagittarius and a Ravenclaw...which should tell you all you need to know.

She enjoys writing fantastical stories adjacent to our world because she's secretly hoping that one day a rift will open between realms and magic will be real.

Also by Marianne A. Scott
The Made from Magic Series

Made from Magic

Made to Conquer

Made to Rule (coming spring 2023)

Need to know what happened while Edina was in Faerie? Coming November 26, 2022: A Court Where I'm Freezing My A** Off (A Made from Magic Novella).

ACKNOWLEDGMENTS

First and foremost, I'd like to thank all of you who have made it this far. Thank you for helping me realize this dream.

To the best husband in the entire universe of the world, thank you for always supporting me, and for always comforting me when the imposter syndrome hits. Thank you for being a sounding board when I need to talk through plot points, even when I don't listen and just need to talk at you. And thank you for taking care of all the behind-the-scenes things I wasn't prepared for when I went into self-publishing.

To my amazing parents, thank you for being excited every time I tell you page read numbers and Amazon rankings. You're my biggest cheerleaders and I thank you so much for your never-ending support. And for John, thank you for reading and providing me with up-to-date texts to let me know what you think. PS: I hope you all collectively skipped some sections.

To my writing partner/sounding board/plot-hole cannon Rachel, thanks for listening when I talk about this series every single week during our chats. Thank you for every note, every hour spent listening to me dissect the magic system only to scream "there's a spell for that" when I couldn't answer your question, and every creativity check-in.

Thank you to my first beta reader and future audiobook narrator, Rosemary Adler. I am so excited to hear you bring these characters to life.

To all those who have helped me along the way, including my amazing editor Paige Lawson who made me sound way smarter than I am, and Cassidy Townsend for listening to my ramblings about the cover and turning it into something truly stunning.

Thank you Luke for providing your mental health expertise and helping me make Katie's anxiety and depression authentic and real.

Thank you Danielle for proofreading and catching the typos that everyone missed! You're a lifesaver.

And last but not least, thank you to my family who are literally the most supportive people in the entire universe. I'm seriously so lucky to have not only my parents and brother, but my entire extended family and the wonderful family I married into rooting for me. I hope you know how invaluable your support has been.